FADED DIAMONDS

Camille Burke | Stacey Pacouloute | Mellissa Thomas

Cover design by Mellissa Thomas.

ISBN-10: 0991140702

ISBN-13: 978-0-9911407-0-1

All scripture quotations taken from the Authorized King James Version of the Bible.

FADED DIAMONDS

The .45 shot cracks the air so loudly, my ears ring. But before that pain even registers, me and the white dude in front of me, my friend, fly backwards, and a sudden white-hot pain strikes my chest. The hole in his back sends a big splash of blood my way; some of it even hits my face. The psycho that fired the shot is still standing there for some reason, though I can't see what she's doing now, my counselor's off to the side screaming in horror, and my enemy's standing outside the cafeteria doors, watching all of us drown in darkness. My body temperature drops faster than an anvil off the side of the Empire State Building, and my lungs feel like an elephant's sitting on them, applying more of its weight by the second. I can taste blood in my breath and mouth.

"Leila!" I hear a voice cry. "Leilaaaaaaaa!"

All this drama is unfolding, and all I came in here to do is find my cell phone.

In my half-death my brain manages to squeak out just one question, probably the same one you're asking.

How did I get here?

GENESIS

1

It's been a month now. I've been giving these people every lie in the book to extend my stay and keep them from kicking me out to make room for other girls that come in off the streets. They've had to turn some away. Makes me feel bad. But I gotta eat too.

And so does this baby.

I only want to stay here as long as it takes to get a job and save up some money to rent my own place, but for now, this is my crib.

I'm looking down at my left hand, staring at the faded line where a ring should be. I still got it, but for my own sake, I just took it off. It's not like the dude loves me anyway. Crazy bastard tried to kill me. And if you're expecting some sob story out of me, forget it. My tears dried up after day two in this place. I done met girls worse off than me in here.

I feel a poke in the middle of my back.

Oh, right. Forgot where I was for a second. I take my plate and cup forward to get the breakfast. I offer a nice smile for the lady, and she piles on some homemade scrambled eggs -- not the ugly, processed, government kind, some link sausages, a slice of toast with jelly already spread on it, and she puts a separate small bowl filled with oatmeal on the only part of my plate with any space left. The next lady fills my cup with hot tea.

I make my way to the dining area and sit in my usual spot by the window. And as usual, my shadow comes. She don't say much, though. She's like me that way, I guess. We exchange nods and dive into our food.

She looks like she could be my little sister, but it turns out she's actually older than me. Short skinny thing just turned 21. And pregnant too. Her roots are starting to show through all that blonde...like mine; but my hair color isn't as drastic as hers -- mine's more auburn, hers is straight blonde. Although technically, she could get away with wearing it that light. She's mad light herself -- barely black at all.

She catches my look and frowns away. "Sorry," I offer. She just shakes her head. She waits for me to finish my meal before she says anything. Once I'm done, she looks around, scared someone will snoop on us. "You're up today."

She'd taken it on herself to announce my counseling sessions ahead of time. Ever since she saw me storm out of my first one on day three, she realized I hated them. That little explosion was what drew her to me in the first place. I guess she figured I needed a friend, and announces the sessions to get me mentally prepared.

I guess my tantrum was that bad.

I give her my usual nod. "Thanks." Somehow this time, my usual response isn't enough to get the sad look off her face. She lowers her eyes like she gave away some deep secret she wasn't supposed to.

"What's wrong?" The words come out annoyed, which I technically was, but I didn't want her to know that.

"This one's different," she confesses.

"How?"

She looks up and all around. "Remember where we are. Remember what this place is called."

The Godhand Women's Home is what this place is called. So?

She sees my clueless look and shrugs. "You've been warned," she sighs as she finally gets up with her tray. "You start in fifteen."

I kick the name around in my head a few more times before I finally get up. I still don't get it, but a warning is a warning, so I'm on my toes.

I wash my hands and face in the restroom before making my way to the counseling room. The office is white and cold with a high ceiling, like a doctor's office. The only wood in the space is the counselor's desk, where a small plant sits, leaning its leaves and branches toward the window to suck up the morning sun.

As usual, they send me in here first and have me wait for the counselor to show up. It's a crappy feeling, not knowing who will walk in through the door behind me and what they'll do or say once inside.

And I guess that's part of why I hate these things. The whole suspense bit is stupid, like they want your thoughts to crowd your mind so that by the time the counselor comes in, you're an emotional mess, and they can just label you, shove a medical prescription at you, and send you out the door.

Someone knocks. I turn around to see a tall black woman with short, straight, shiny, deep black hair -- probably a wig -- leaning in the doorway. She's thick, looks like she's broken a few noses before. She gives me this bright smile. "May I?"

"I don't know, can you?" I reply. "You the counselor, ain't it?"

She chuckles and finally comes in, closing the door behind her and making her way to the seat. Baby girl was right. I've never seen this lady before. My counselors are always white.

"So how are you doin', Leila?"

"Decent, Miss," I barely say.

"Diana." She holds her hand out for me to shake. I almost don't, but something in me tells me to be polite, so I finally do after a second or two.

"Where's my file? Don't you need it?"

She rests her elbows on the table and lifts her hands to her face. "I'd rather hear it all from you, Leila."

My face frowns on its own. Is this chick playing? I have to tell my story from the beginning again?

She answers my look with a smile, like she's been digging around in my head from before she came in here. "You don't have to start from the beginning if you don't want to."

"Where else would I start from?"

She shrugs. "You can start with how you ended up here."

I shrug back. "Chance, I guess."

She lowers her arms and leans in with a "come on now" look. "You and I both know better, don't we?"

Excuse me?

"There's no such thing in this life as chance, Leila. Everything happens for a reason."

My grandmother used to say that garbage. And I believed her -- until she kicked me out for something I wasn't responsible for.

Diana's eyebrows jump, and a curious smile spreads. "I suppose we can start there."

Dag. I didn't realize I'd said all of that out loud. My teeth lock together as I glare at her. I want to call her something ugly for so easily digging that memory out of me, but I know better. I brought that on myself. So I shake my head. "If we're goin' there, we might as well start from the beginning. If I start from there, the story won't make sense."

She gives me a questioning look, as if she really cares where I start. I don't take the bait though. Not that I can -- my stomach's already starting to turn and burn in expectation of the memory. I nearly puked the first time, too. My eyes find the trashcan, which is thankfully close enough to me, sitting next to the desk on its right side, my left.

I look back at her, suddenly remembering something. "You timin' this too?"

She shook her head. "Take your time."

At least she was nice enough to do that. In the first session, the counselor wouldn't stop looking at his watch. I wanted to reach across the desk and slam his head into it, rude bastard.

"You probably hear stories like mine all the time," I say, still disgusted that I have to relive all this.

She gives me that same digging-in-your-head smile. "No story is like yours, Leila. Every girl's experience is different."

She's playing her nice card hard. Maybe too hard. I just nod it off, ready to finally start.

LEILA'S STORY

Melanie stumbled into the sloppy apartment room and fell right on the carpet. The noise startled the baby boy to tears. The little girl frowned at her as she picked up her baby brother, shushing him.

Melanie struggled to lift her head to the kids, barely seeing them through her knotted hair. She clawed at some filthy clothes nearby to lift herself up. The little girl's frown was still on her, and she held her little brother that much closer to her as Melanie finally stumbled over to her.

The place was quickly darkening with the early sunset. The first sign of winter's coming. Melanie was late with the rent again, which included the power and water, so they would have no way of seeing each other besides the streetlamps outside once the sun was gone. But at least the place was quiet now. The little girl preferred this. The place was stuffy and sloppy, but at least it was quiet. For now.

She never knew when the loud and angry monster would come back to grab her mother, and Melanie would just...go right along with it. She never fought back or anything. She would just cry whenever she could and go along. The only protest the little girl saw was when the man said something really ugly, then Melanie would remind him of the kids in the room, but that only made him raise his voice louder and say something even uglier to spite her and them.

Melanie lifted her son from her daughter's arms. "It's alright, Le Le. Let's get him changed."

* * * *

"So you grew up with a single mom," Diana says. I lift my frowning eyes to her. "Hold your questions 'til the end, Miss Diana," I correct her. "Lemme just get all the way through the story and get it over with." I suddenly catch myself, realizing I'd snapped at her, and lower my voice. "No, I didn't grow up with her. That's my only childhood memory of her. HRS took us away right after that."

* * * *

Michael Tonio Harper. Leila came to know the monster's name. Her grandmother would roar it the moment he set foot in her house. In her elder eyes, her little boy was always in trouble. This particular time, Grandma Alice brought Leila into the kitchen to confront him. He never did like facing Grandma Alice, but he didn't have a choice.

She would always start the same way: "Now you a grown man, so I really can't speak for what you do on them streets, but I got the final say on what happens under my roof."

That's usually when he would turn to face her.

She had Leila's face in her hand, and she turned her to him. Even on her dark skin, the large weal around her left eye was visible. "What happened here?" She raised a finger to his face. "And don't you lie to me, boy."

All he could do was scowl. He looked down at Leila, then at his mother. "Yeah, I did that. That's what she get for givin' me them dirty looks."

Grandma Alice put her free hand on her hip and popped her neck at him. "Like the one you got on your face right now? Great example, Daddy."

Leila's eyes lowered. Grandma Alice spat the word out with such anger. *Daddy*.

"You ain't never known me or your daddy to do this to you," she continued, still holding Leila's face in her hand. "Ain't nothin' wrong wit disciplinin' ya kids, but you spank 'em on they bottom, or slap they hands, or pinch 'em. Not this."

Michael gave Leila one last look before turning around to his business again. No apologies, no nothing. Leila took off to her room and cried to herself. It was always like that with him. Nothing Grandma Alice said ever swayed him. He'd do it again tomorrow.

Not even tomorrow. Later.

High school was agonizing. The hormones were so high, Leila could practically feel them slapping her as she walked through the halls. She especially hated lunch period, which she noticed was only five minutes away as she stared up at the analog clock from her back row desk. She packed up as quickly as she could in the last sixty seconds, and just stared at the clock. Nothing the teacher said sank in. She stormed out the moment the scratchy bell rang.

For the first time in months, she was able to find a spot remote enough to buy her the time to wolf down all of her food. She didn't bother to savor anything. It was on her way back from the football field, back into the thick of the student population, that her nemesis found her.

Tawana Miles.

This junior nag made Leila feel so...subhuman. And it didn't help that Leila was a freshman. Tawana was one of those early bloomers, already taller than most of the boys in her grade, and her chest already flaunted plush pillows. Even her limbs were starting to fill out some; her pelvic bone and elbows didn't threaten to stab anybody. Her skin was a nice almond cushion over it all.

"What up, Le?"

Leila didn't bother to answer, as usual. She instead turned off in a different direction, but Tawana's little fan club wouldn't let her. "Whoa, where you goin'?" one of the skinny, undeveloped girls asked, laughing.

Leila didn't answer her either. Tawana positioned herself in front of Leila again, looking her up and down. "That's mad rude, yo. I say 'what up' and you walk away? Where they do that at?"

When Leila didn't answer, Tawana finally reached for her face, turning Leila's head a little. "Oh snap," Tawana laughed. "Pissed Pops off again, huh?"

Her entourage laughed.

"What you do this time? Forget to give him a happy ending?"

Leila was tight. It was one thing for Tawana to attack her, but it was a whole other kind of ugly when she suggested such terrible things, especially in front of all those kids.

"Don't feel no way 'bout that," Tawana said. "E'r'body know 'bout your sex offender pimp daddy."

Daddy. She spat the word out the same way Grandma Alice did.

"All you gotta do is watch the news...unless y'all ain't got no TV at the crib."

The entourage roared with laughter again.

By now Leila's eyes were filling with tears. Thankfully none fell. The lump in her throat threatened to burn a hole right through her neck.

Tawana was tired of the silence, and lunch would be over in ten minutes. She threw the first punch, ready to add another bruise to this sorry mongrel's face.

But Leila dodged it.

A soft gasp rippled through the crowd, which by now was larger. Tawana threw the next punch, but Leila dodged that, too. Tawana let out a disgusted laugh. "Pimp daddy been training you the hard way, huh?"

An "oooh" traveled through the crowd. Leila snorted and spit aside in reply. Tawana's eyes flashed, and she landed a mean right hook, making Leila's nose bleed.

Usually, Leila would break down and look pathetic after a hit like that, but something in her today just wouldn't let her. She instead chuckled and just stared. And stared. And stared. Tawana balled her fist again, readying another hit, but Leila simply snorted again, and hard, drawing up as much metallic mucus as she could...

And nailed Tawana right in the eye.

The crowd exploded. Then, as if on cue, the bell rang. For the first time ever, Leila walked away from a confrontation with Tawana on her own terms. She didn't even bother to clean her nose. She kept it as it was in the next class, which she actually shared with Tawana since Tawana failed it sophomore year. She was going to flaunt her bloodied nose in that little terror's face, and force-feed her that same sick smirk she always fed Leila. No matter what her father did or said to her tonight, her day was made. She felt so bold, she could curse at him now and it wouldn't matter to her.

"Grandma, what's a sex offender?"

Grandma Alice looked at Leila with outrage, but Leila saw through the mask of surprise to the embarrassment beneath it. "Where you hear that kinda talk from?"

"A girl at school called Daddy that," Leila replied, emotionless.

Grandma Alice looked away with a tight jaw. Leila could tell this was definitely not the conversation she wanted to have with her, but now was better than later, since her dad wasn't there. "It's somebody who does bad things to women and underage kids," she grumbled.

"You mean get it in with 'em?"

Grandma Alice shot her a sidelong glance. Those words sounded terrible coming out of her mouth. "Against the person's will, yes."

Leila looked at Grandma Alice now. Grandma's eyes were glued to the locked hands in her lap. "Daddy done it before...ain't it?"

Grandma Alice lifted her eyes to the muted TV, which was playing an ad that asked the viewer about personal responsibility. She couldn't bring herself to answer Leila.

Leila took the hint and rose from the couch. "So the pimp part's true, too?"

"I pray for that boy every day," Grandma Alice confessed in a feeble whisper. "That's all that needs to be said. You need to pray for him too."

"If he would stop beatin' me long enough, I might."

This brought Grandma Alice to her feet. "You listen here, lil' girl. You may not like him, but he's still your daddy. You better respect him."

"For what, Grandma? He barely respects you."

"That don't excuse you from doin' the right thing!"

She saw the sudden fear in Leila's eyes and caught herself. "Look, Le Le. It ain't easy doin' what's right, but it's our responsibility to do it anyway. Especially when the people around us don't. That's how we shine as bright lights in this dark world."

Leila slowly shook her head as the tears came. She snatched up her backpack and ran to her room. Shine as bright lights in a dark world? What does Grandma know? How would she understand that she's been trying to do the right thing every day, in school and at home, and still gets beat up in *both* places?

A sudden shuffling noise in the closet startled Leila to silence. She turned to stare at the door as it slowly opened. "What happened now, sis?"

Her baby brother, her only oasis of sanity, sat comfortably in the closet amid scattered toys, smacking his lips on a huge wad of gum.

A quick smile broke through Leila's face. "Nothin'," she replied with a sniffle.

"Liar." Kalvin slowly lifted himself from the closet, careful not to bring the toy mess out with him, and stood over her. He gently cupped her chin and turned her face a little. "Tawana got you again. At least she ain't break your nose."

Leila made a disgusted chuckle. "At least you noticed. Grandma sure didn't."

"It's all good, though," he replied with a smirk. "I heard what happened. Dope payback. Gross, but dope."

"You start your homework yet?"

"Mine's done. You betta get on yours before Pooty Tang comes home."

"Stop that," Leila murmured, feeling half-guilty. "He's your dad. You gotta respect him."

He made a disgusted chuckle of his own. "Grandma got in your ears 'bout that, too?"

"She's right."

"To hell with him," he hissed with a sudden malice that startled Leila. "I hope one of them hookers chew his nuts off."

Leila shot upright, fearful Grandma Alice would hear. "Shh! Are you crazy?" she whispered sharply.

"How can you say that to me?" Kalvin's little black eyes glimmered all the more as tears flooded them. "After everything he's done to you...the way he treats Grandma after all she's done for him..."

Leila heart was breaking all over again. She pulled her brother into a tight hug. "It ain't fair, Le," he murmured as the tears finally fell and soaked her shoulder. "There's gotta be some kinda punishment for that. You can't be mean to your momma and your daughter. Somethin's wrong with that."

He pulled away scowling. "And he'll pay for it. One way or another."

Leila watched Kalvin as he left the room, confused and scared at his words. Was he talking in general, or something else?

The Breaking Point

Junior year was a little better. Only a little. By then, Tawana already graduated; and Michael spent even less time at home, which meant a small amount of peace for her.

But whatever he was doing on the streets, his anger was more intense than in previous years when he finally did get home. He and Grandma Alice were falling out more loudly now, and since he couldn't dare lay hands on his mother, he took his anger out on other objects in the house. Or on Leila.

June just began, and Leila was already excited for summer. The south Florida humidity and bold sunlight made it feel like summer was already here. A few more weeks, Leila thought, and then summer. Candy bars. The big pool. Movies in the theater. Sleep-ins. The crazy, happy cousins. The auntie and uncle who are actually nice and give her and Kalvin whatever they ask for, within reason. Summer break. The sweet sweaty relief.

But summer break never came.

That first Thursday in June, Leila was working on her last homework assignment for the school year. She was on pins and needles that whole afternoon because Michael was home when she arrived from school, but he hadn't bothered her up to this point. She'd just finished the first draft when he finally disrupted her. "Dinner's on you. Your grandma ain't here."

Are you kidding me?, she wanted to scream. "I'm-I'm still workin' on my homework," she stammered instead.

"I don't wanna hear that! Either 'Yes, Dad' or 'Okay, Dad'!" He stormed in, and Leila heart fell to her toes. The tears were already falling. He grabbed her by the hair. "What I told you 'bout talkin' back to me?"

He slapped her so hard, the sound echoed off the walls. Her ear rang for several seconds, as if an explosion had gone off right next to her.

"Get up and make my damn dinner!"

Only a whimper escaped her. "Yes, Dad..."

"Thought so."

A slow, soft creak sounded behind him, and before he could turn around to find the source, a muffled shot suddenly rang out. Leila yelped in terror as Michael bucked forward a little, his eyes wide with surprise. He looked down at his dingy t-shirt and found a spot of blood in the center of his chest slowly spreading wider across the white. He fell to his knees and folded backwards, and it was then that she saw it: the closet door cracked open, and a smoking 9mm, silencer and all, in Kalvin's hands. No trembling, no nothing. Kalvin's face was crumpled into a hard frown, his black eyes like diamonds with the pent up tears that refused to fall.

It finally occurred to her to check the wall, and the bullet hole was inches from her. She silently thanked the powers that be that the bullet didn't bounce off and hit her.

She barely had any breath to speak. "Kalvin..."

"That's what he get for not listenin'," Kalvin growled. "Grandma told him years ago to keep this gun outta the house."

"Kalvin!" Her tearful whisper was all terror -- no relief, no joy. Pure terror. Of all the times he could've chosen to do this, he chose now. On the eve of their yearly break of joy and freedom and hope, he kills a man. Right in front of her. And their father at that. Her eyes widened in deeper fear as she saw the carpet slowly staining red. "Kalvin, we gotta do something! He can't stay here like this!"

Kalvin calmly held up his cell phone. "I already texted Grandma to come home. She on her way."

She let her emotions take over completely. Her hands shielded her frantic face. "Why did you do this, Kalvin?" She was so hysterical, she was almost wheezing. "This is terrible. This is awful..."

Kalvin stepped over his father's body and came to her, still calm as ever. He dropped the gun on Michael's chest and gently held her wet face. "You know why."

* * * *

The police never seemed to care. Despite Leila's frantic explanation and the obvious swell on her face, the officers already had their minds made up. Her heart and jaw fell as she watched them cuff her beloved baby brother and Mirandize him. She looked desperately at her grandmother, who was equally terrified, but did nothing to stop them. What happened to doing the right thing, no matter what? Why wouldn't she say something? Leila had obviously tried her best to and the cops weren't listening to her.

She looked back at her brother, who they were now walking to the squad car. He gave Leila one last look, and as he smiled at her, the angry tears that refused to fall before finally escaped down his cheeks. She couldn't speak, but her lips moved for her. "I love you," she mouthed. He nodded as an officer loaded him into the car.

That night was the last time Leila saw Grandma Alice. Leila's only remaining family numbly walked to her room, and despite desperate little Leila standing at her door calling for her in the hopes of finding comfort, Alice closed the door in her face.

No summer break came that year, just police interviews and crime scene photos and fingerprints and funeral arrangements and rumors around the neighborhood. Leila was in a prison of her own. The only TV in the house was the one in the living room, and Alice hogged it. Leila stayed in bed most of the day and barely bothered to eat, crying as loudly as she could in a hopeless effort to quench her pain, but no amount of tears helped. Alice didn't bother to scold her like she used to. These days, she just turned the TV up.

Senior Salvage

Senior year began, and all Leila cared about anymore was graduation. She knew she was weak in science and math, so she enrolled in afterschool classes. It doubled as a useful excuse to stay away from the house longer.

Her afterschool tutor was Christie Lockheart, a petite white woman with bright blue eyes and shoulder-length blonde hair that was always in a ponytail. Green was her favorite color. She reminded Leila so much of Tinker Bell, she silently nicknamed her that.

Christie was impossibly positive. Even when Leila would kick herself for her mistakes while doing homework or reviewing for an exam, Christie would stop her. "You're still learning, Leila," she said. "And you have to remember you're doing a lot better than most of your other classmates. You're doing great."

One early release day, not even two full weeks into the school year, she received a note from the guidance counselor during the last class of the day. She entered his office when the class dismissed and found a familiar duffel bag, ready to burst at the seams, sitting in the chair across from him. "Your grandmother dropped that off," he said. "...Um, what's going on at home, Leila?"

Her confused look gave way to a tight jaw. She shouldered the bag. "Nothin' now."

"Uh...she said to tell you there's a note in the main compartment."

"Thank you, sir."

She sat outside her tutor's classroom door like she always did before the scheduled 3:15 time, and pulled out the note.

Leila,

If you tried to come into the house before reading this, I'm sure you realized that your keys don't work. I'm sorry, but the peace in my house has been gone for many years now, and after losing Michael, I have to restore it. Kalvin's gone now too, and he says he did it for you, so I decided it's time for you to be on your own. You turned eighteen yesterday, so now you're officially grown and can take care of yourself. I'll be praying for you as I always have, but it's time to get my house back in order and drive all these unwelcome demons out.

Love,
Grandma Alice

Unwelcome demons? Leila shook her head to herself as she refolded the note and buried it at the bottom of the compartment. She checked the rest of the contents: mostly clothes and shoes, all her books and writing supplies for school, and a birthday card in one of the side pockets. She opened the card, and a small folded piece of paper fell out. She unfolded it and her eyes immediately began to tear up. She knew that handwriting anywhere.

Le Le,

Things mad crazy in here, but I can't forget your birthday. It's the one day of the year I always look forward to, whether I'm with you or not. Last year was a blast. I loved the look on your face when our cousins showed up at school to pick us up. You looked like you died and went to heaven or something. I hope you have a moment like that this year. I made it happen last year, but I can't this time. Maybe Grandma will cook your favorite dinner or something.

Anyway, love you. Visit me when you can, okay? I'm tired of seeing Grandma's depressed face. I love her too, but she ain't coping well. You might be a little stronger than her. I miss your smile.

~ Kalvin

Leila wiped her eyes repeatedly, but they just mocked her with more tears, until she finally surrendered to them, burying her face in her arm. She could feel the brick wall every few seconds as each sob sent her back against it. Some eighteenth birthday this was. No party. No cousins. No friends. No meal.

No home.

How was she going to finish school now? Why did she have to be a statistic? It wasn't fair; she was studying hard. She was doing the right thing, no matter what. Was Alice wrong about that? Was it all just a lie to protect her own pride in her son?

"Hey, hey!" Christie's alarmed whisper startled her. "What's the matter?"

Leila finally looked up to the six familiar faces, but didn't answer. She didn't need the other five afterschool students knowing her business. Christie picked up the birthday card and looked inside. "It's your birthday? You never told me you were born in September. I am too."

"It was yesterday," she mumbled. "I ain't tell you 'cause I forgot. Too busy studying for the today's physics test."

Christie handed one of the other students the room key so they could head inside. She folded Kalvin's letter, closed the card, and placed both in the open side compartment. "What's going on, Leila? These your clothes?"

Leila perched an arm on her knee and rested her forehead in her hand. "That's my whole life."

Christie's eyes widened. "What happened?"

"I don't know. The bag was waiting for me in the guidance counselor's office."

Christie closed her eyes regretfully. "Wow. Okay, just -- let's get inside and get you started. We'll go one step at a time, okay?"

"For what? Where Imma go? How Imma get to school every day?"

"Just...don't worry about that right now. I'll take you out for a birthday meal after we're done here, okay? Let's go kick some Calculus butt first."

It was more difficult for Leila to concentrate than ever before, and it didn't help that some of the other students in the class kept looking at her as they whispered to each other. She ended up being the last student left in Christie's classroom, but she managed to get her homework done. "See?" Christie said. "You barely even needed my help."

Yeah, if she didn't count the half-hour she spent working with Leila on one problem.

Leila chose to remain silent as she packed her backpack. One look at the duffel bag brought the truth back in her face. The tutoring was over now. Where was she going to go?

"You ready?" Christie's happy voice threw Leila off.

"What?"

"Birthday dinner, remember?"

"Oh. Yeah. I'm ready."

A steakhouse. Christie asked Leila where she wanted to go, and it took some serious prodding to get the answer out. She watched her with a warm smile, tickled by Leila's awe, especially when she started admiring the very table. Her fingers pressed against it, checking that it really was that nicely polished. She even tilted her head to see the reflections of the television screens against the shiny surface.

"You've...never eaten at a restaurant before, have you?"

Leila lifted her head in embarrassed surprise, but immediately shrugged it off. "Only a couple times." She started to look around her again. "And never a steakhouse."

"Smaller places?"

"Not really smaller, just less interesting. Buffets, fast food joints, that kinda thing. And only in the summer when I stay with my cousins."

Christie gave a curious look.

"They got money like that," Leila said. "They're not really rich, but well off."

Their food came, and Leila ate quickly but carefully, mindful that she didn't come across like a UNICEF poster child.

"So what happens after this?" Christie asked. "Where will you go?"

Leila fell silent for several seconds. Her eyes and voice lowered. "Don't know. Maybe someplace out front or in the back by the dumpsters and sleep."

Christie's heart suddenly sank, as did her utensils. She rested her chin in her hand as her mind flailed for words it couldn't find. She instead shook her head and let her heart speak in her mind's place. "I can't let you do that."

Leila stopped eating as well and looked up at her.

"I had a feeling it would come to this," Christie admitted her eyes slowly filling, "but I was hoping that maybe someone, some family member, would call you or something."

"So all of this was you stalling?"

Christie knew Leila was a clever girl, but the question still gutted her. "Not really. I really did want to celebrate your birthday. And I'm glad we're here."

"You got a full house, right? Husband, kids, all that?"

"...Not exactly."

Leila winced, looking around her, then leaned in. " 'Not exactly'? That's a yes or no question, Miss Christie."

"No." For the first time since she met her, Leila could see the agitation in her eyes. "It's just me. Anyway, I'm glad you were concerned enough to ask. No one ever does."

"Probably 'cause you always so bubbly. People won't ask if they don't think nothin's wrong."

"Yeah, but you know it shouldn't take something wrong to ask how someone's family's doing."

"Everybody ain't raised like me, Miss Christie."

"You're definitely right about that."

Christie got to relive Leila's awe as they entered her ranchland style home. There was space upon space upon space.

The bedrooms had nothing smaller than queen beds; they were that big. Leila had never slept on a bed by herself before, let alone a queen, so this would be interesting. Christie led her to the last bedroom closest to the front door. "This one's got you written all over it."

Leila entered and smiled. "Thanks." She examined the drawers and found them empty. Her sympathy deepened. Whatever happened in this house must've been bad for the kids to empty everything. "Um...did your kids move out?"

She immediately gave Christie a sorry look, but Christie only smiled. "You eat ice cream, Leila?"

"Rarely," she replied, flinching at the randomness of the question. "I had to earn it by keeping my grades up and staying out of trouble."

"Then why was it rare? You're doing great."

"I wasn't always outta trouble. Used to get bullied a lot."

A thoughtful nod. "You a Rocky Road fan?"

"It's my favorite flavor."

"Make yourself comfy and meet me in my bedroom. It's the only part of the house you haven't seen yet."

The Rocky Road ice cream was sticky and thick and freezing cold and heavenly to taste. The perfect end to that big steakhouse meal. Christie had her own bowl, but she barely ate, satisfied to observe Leila some more.

Leila looked all around the master bedroom again as she ate. The wall to her left consisted of sliding closet doors that doubled as one large mirror; and in size, the room was two of the other bedrooms put together. They were sitting on a loveseat as it was. How does someone manage to have a loveseat in a bedroom? "How can you stand it? Being in such a big place alone?"

"I try not to think about it," Christie said. "I usually watch TV or a DVD, or put on some music. And that's if I have time. I'm usually bogged down with papers to grade and can't think about it anyway."

"What happened?"

Christie told Leila the heartbreaking story of her youngest son, who had severe depression, and despite receiving frequent counseling and not being abused, decided to drown himself in the bathtub one afternoon. Her husband put her out of the house as a result. "That's why I couldn't let you spend the night sleeping by a dumpster. It's a terrible place to be."

Leila was almost speechless. "Thanks. I'm...sorry about what happened."

Christie shook her head.

"But wait, if he kicked you out, how are you here now by yourself?"

Christie explained that her children threatened to call the cops on him if he didn't bring her back. He complied, but then legally separated and moved out. The kids were in college now.

Leila let out a sigh. "That's a lot. How you always so happy at school, then?"

"Things happen that we can't control, sweetie. I chose to move on and be happy. My house is empty, but I know my kids are safe; I talk to them every week. Plus I love helping brilliant kids like you tap into your potential.

"And really, that's the best way to overcome any situation, Leila. Helping other people. Seeing the thankful smile on someone's face or hearing them say it -- just knowing that you made their lives better -- that's a high you can't buy."

From that night, the floodgates opened, especially since Christie allowed Leila to live with her until graduation. Leila put out her best effort in every class. While she and Christie didn't grow much closer thanks to Christie's increasing workload, Christie would still offer an encouraging smile when Leila left an A+ physics or calculus exam on the kitchenette table for her to see.

Besides, for the first time since she started high school, Leila finally started having a social life. She allowed herself to have a small circle of three or four friends, all connected by their weirdness. And since they were all nerds, Leila got all the help she needed to do her homework and study for tests, so she quit the afterschool tutoring.

She ended up filling that time with a job at the local library. It was a tedious one, cataloging and stocking books, and it didn't pay much, but it was money. Bus fare. Food money. Treat money. Clothes money. And anything else she could save up for. For once, she felt...real. Independent. Adult. Human.

Reunion

Christie made sure to buy Leila a cell phone for easy contact, and she immediately passed the number on to Kalvin in a letter, which reminded her of what she owed him. Two months later, when an early release day doubled as a day off from work, she rode the metro to the county jail.

The air was heavy in that place. She followed the guard through heavy door after heavy door to the visiting area. The guard pointed her to the correct booth and she sat down.

Within moments, a blue jumpsuit entered the room, but she barely recognized the face. A long, ugly scar ran down the whole left side, dangerously close to his eye. His right eye showed echoes of a past swell; and despite only being in here a few months, his head was already a small sponge of thick, wavy hair, caught back with a rubber band.

Everything in her wanted to pound the glass until it broke just to be able to touch him. She so badly hungered for a hug. He sat in his seat and grabbed the phone receiver with a tilted head and a smirk, already ready to crack a joke, as he always did when they were home together. "Come on, sis, you ain't come all this way to look like Grandma, did you?"

Puberty wasted no time with him in here. His voice was deeper now.

Leila's yearning eyes hardened. "Never. And she ain't no 'grandma' to me."

"Hold up, I ain't mean to get you tight," he said with deep concern. "What happened?"

"She kicked me out the day after my birthday, and didn't even have the nerve to do it to my face."

"What?"

"Packed my summer bag with all my things and left it with the guidance counselor. A note was the best she could do. Talkin' 'bout she had to clear the 'unwelcome demons' from her house."

"Unwelcome demons?" he asked with a chuckle.

"The only good thing that came outta that was your birthday letter. She put it in the bag with her card. Sorry I ain't smilin' for you right now, but you right about me being stronger."

"So where you been? That was months ago."

"My afterschool tutor found out, so I'm living with her 'til graduation."

"Oh word? What she tutor?"

"For me, physics and calculus."

"What! That's what I'm talkin' 'bout! Look at my lil' genius. I knew your head was big for a reason."

"Shut up, man," she replied, laughing. "Your head bigger than mine, anyway."

"That's aight, though. I'm fillin' it up."

"With what?"

"Books that matter. The Bible, books on Malcolm, Martin, Carver, Tavis, Spike, all them dudes. And yeah, the school stuff, too. Algebra and all that. Mad boring."

Leila laughed again. "I'm glad you good. What happened to your face?"

He shrugged. "A little misunderstandin'."

"Misunderstandin'?"

"Dudes thought I was weak since I'm a kid, so they tried somethin'. And failed miserably. This scar's nothin' compared to what I did."

"Do I wanna know?"

"Let's just say the dude that cut me is...not quite a man anymore."

Leila closed her eyes. She couldn't imagine the kind of pain that would cause.

"Anyway, I'm glad you came. I got somethin' for you. I was gonna send it to you in my next letter, but since you here..." He pulled a piece of paper from his pocket and held it up against the glass. "Write that phone number down."

"Who's Melanie?" she asked as she pulled a pen and a piece of paper from her pockets.

"Your momma."

The words smacked her upside the head so hard, she froze. She'd been so busy trying to keep her sanity all this time she didn't even realize she had a mother. "You seen her?"

"She been here, like, three times in the last couple months."

She finally brought herself to write the name and number down, putting everything away.

"Thanks for sendin' me your number, by the way," he said. "I'll call you when I get a chance."

She was still a bit stunned. "Good."

"You be good, sis," he said, smiling.

"I should be tellin' you that."

"You know I'm aight."

She put her hand up against the glass, and he followed suit. Despite the thick cold material, she could still feel the warmth of his hand on hers. "I miss you so much, Kal."

"I know. Miss you too, yo."

The security guards appeared on either side of the glass -- one for her and one for him. "Love you," she whispered. He smiled in return, just like he did the night he was arrested. There were no tears this time, though, which helped her fight hers back.

* * * *

Leila held the phone to her ears, forcing herself to take deep breaths. She had no idea what kind of voice to expect on the other line. Would it be high and girly, or soft, or deep, or raspy? Would she have to deal with an attitude? Four rings went by, and Leila lowered her phone, ready to hang it up.

"Heh-hello? Hello?" High and girly.

Leila quickly lifted the phone back to her ear. "Yes, hi. Is this Melanie?"

"Le Le?"

Leila took another deep breath. "Yeah, this is Leila."

"Hey, girl! Yeah, this is Melanie, but you can call me Momma, it's alright."

Leila made an "are you serious?" look. "Um, with all due respect, Miss Melanie, I ain't got no momma. You my egg donor? I mean, thanks for sacrificing one to bring me into the world, but..."

"Well, I ain't sure what you talkin' 'bout, but how you doin'?"

Leila gave her a very vague summary of her high school life, and only the positive parts, at that. She allowed Melanie to get in some reactions, but she spoke quickly to make sure Melanie got the impression she was busy.

They hung up, and Leila rolled her eyes to herself. Melanie was everything she expected her to be: self-centered and self-conscious. All she kept talking about was what she's got and what she did with her hair, and who she's been with, and who she can't stand. Nothing intelligent or valuable. Leila suddenly realized who Melanie reminded her of, and her jaw locked so tightly her teeth began to hurt.

Tawana.

As the former junior bully's sneering face haunted her, she made a silent promise to herself: come hell or high water, so help her God, she will never, *never* be like Tawana.

Or her mother.

"I sure hope you never get pissed off with me." The familiar booming male voice shook Leila from her ugly thoughts.

Bryce Livingston.

She looked up at the only other person in her life who made her happy besides Kalvin and offered a smile. "I hope so, too."

"You on a break or something?"

"Nah, just...had to make a quick call. I'm headed back in."

The two headed inside the library, and as usual he followed her around as she combed the isles with her cart, putting books back in their proper place, and conversed with her.

She loved those conversations, and looked forward to coming to work every day to have them. He only went off on his own to get his studying done or to work on a project, and even then, she would follow him and have him explain his studies to her, or explain the project he was working on. She asked him every question she could think of about college life, his courses, his career goals, and his general knowledge of the world. She inhaled everything he told her, and he was happy to have an eager ear to share it all with.

She would catch herself sneaking little glances at him while he worked on his own or with his schoolmates, his dark brown eyes wide and beautiful and bright, reflecting his never-ending energy. And that smile... His perfectly even white teeth were a source of light against his dark skin, and his dimpled cheeks made him look all the more adorable. His smile always brought a smile out of her, even when he wasn't smiling at her.

The Home Stretch

Bryce made those last few months of school much more bearable than they could've been, and the final week of school snuck right up on Leila. However, upon the start of that final week, the clock seemed to fall into quicksand and stay there.

Monday was the worst. Melanie made the stupid mistake of calling Leila while she was in class, so out of good courtesy Leila called her back after school, and the conversation was more of the same shallow girly garbage she had no patience for, so after a while, she politely cut her off and said her goodbyes. Leila passed a trashcan and was tempted to drop her phone in it, or toss it against the nearest wall and watch it fall to pieces.

Bryce wasn't at the library that day to help her lighten up, so that ugly cloud loomed over her all the way home. But she couldn't relax even then. The house seemed too quiet tonight. She snuck around to Christie's room and found the door cracked open as usual. The TV was off, and her cell phone was on the nightstand. She had to angle her neck in an uncomfortable way to see her, but she spotted Christie sitting Indian style on the floor on the far end of the room, her head lowered and her fingers clasped together. Was she praying?

Then Leila heard a telltale sniffle, and looked more carefully at the woman's pale face. Christie's eyes were red and irritated from constant rubbing.

Leila finally knocked on the door. Christie's head popped up in alarm. "It's all right, Miss Christie, it's just me," Leila said.

"Of course," Christie replied, smiling. Her voice cracked a little. "Come in."

Leila entered and immediately noticed the difference in the place: one corner of the room was loaded up with boxes, the walls were bare, and all the trinkets and picture frames that were on her dresser and nightstands were missing. "You movin' out, huh?"

Christie released a heavy sigh. "Kicking and screaming, but yes. The day after graduation."

Leila's heart skipped a beat. She knew her time was almost up, but she'd forgotten how close that was.

"My...soon-to-be-ex-husband is finalizing the divorce process, so this house has become collateral damage. He's sticking me for almost everything I have, so in order to survive, I've gotta sell this thing."

"I'm guessin' you already got a buyer, then, if you already got a moving date."

She paused. "Yes."

"Aight. I'll be packed before the week's out."

"What will you do? Where will you go?"

"That's for me to worry about, Miss Christie. The more important question is, where *you* goin' after this? You got a pretty important job, and gas ain't cheap 'round here."

"A motel room for now. I've been hunting for an apartment the last couple weeks. Haven't found a decent one yet, but I'll keep looking." She rose and slowly approached Leila, pulling her into a tight embrace, which scared her, because she'd never experienced one before. It felt awkward that Christie didn't pull away after the first few seconds, but just stood there, silently holding her. Leila could hear her racing heartbeat. "I have my physics and calculus finals tomorrow," she managed to say.

"You'll blow them out of the water."

"Only 'cause I found some smart friends, which never happened before you moved me in."

Christie started sniffling again. Leila shook her head. "Don't go missin' me," she said. "You got your own family."

"And you're part of it now," Christie corrected.

"No. I'm just someone you were nice enough to rescue. I'm the fish you gotta toss back."

Christie finally pulled away to look her in the eye. "When will you understand, Leila Sudders? You had me from the moment you first walked in my afterschool classroom."

That sounded creepy. "What you mean?"

"Because I saw in you what you should see in yourself. Unlimited potential."

Leila rolled her eyes. Alice used to tell her that crap, too.

"Leila, did you notice something about yourself in that class compared to the other students I tutored?"

"You mean the token black part? Yeah."

"Not just that, but do you realize you were the *only one* who stepped up for tutoring in two of the hardest subjects? The others were getting help in easier things and coasting by with B's and C's. I've seen kids improve by one or two letter grades, but you...you went from F's to A+'s. And considering what was going on with you at home, that's impressive.

"You're more than just someone I chose to rescue. You're a brilliant soul I couldn't let go to waste. Which is why this--" she gestured to the boxes. "This whole thing bothers me to no end. I feel like I'm just adding to your torture."

"A deal's a deal, Miss Christie."

"If I had a choice, I would just extend your stay, Leila. That wouldn't be a problem for me. I see you're a hard-working girl."

"Well, I'm alive, ma'am. Take comfort in that."

"Believe me, I do."

Having only exams and going away parties in class meant longer workdays for her at the library, which she was glad for. Bryce was working hard on his final projects for the end of spring semester, but he was kind enough to make time for her. She asked him about his summer schedule to get an idea of what he would be doing and where: he was headed out of town for summer break, but he was already enrolled for fall semester, so he'd be back. She smiled and congratulated him, wishing him a fun summer. That news immediately killed her eagerness for the season, since her cousins were most likely out of the picture now.

However, she faced a more pressing issue at the moment: her graduation was in twenty-four hours and she still didn't know where she was going afterwards.

Post-Graduation

Despite graduating with honors, Leila couldn't celebrate. Her mind was running over all the different shelters closest to her job. She knew the first option and set her mind to head there after work.

She worked harder and faster than usual tonight, practically panicked. She barely noticed Bryce at the table with his schoolmates, though she wondered what they were there for, since their finals were over, too.

She stayed focused and got as much done as she could stand, to the point that she successfully stowed all the books that needed to be stowed, including the backlogged ones. Her coworkers were as amazed as she was. They let her off on a one-hour break just to allow some time for book returns.

She finally strolled by Bryce's table, smiling and nodding on her way out the door. Bryce's friends all smiled at each other and then at him. "You betta follow that ass before it's gone," one said.

Bryce shot him a sidelong look. "It ain't like that, Sean."

"Maybe not for you," Sean replied. "But she been tossin' it at you left and right since you first met her."

Bryce shook his head.

"Well, if you won't catch it, I will."

"You'll fail," Bryce said sternly. "She don't know you like that."

"She ain't got to, playa. I can get it anyway."

"Says the dude with the worst game ever," one of the other friends said.

Bryce laughed. "That's 'cause all Sean sees is ass." He gathered his things and rose to leave. "Which is why he's one."

"Ooooooh!" the guys jeered.

"I'll catch y'all back at the dorm," Bryce said as he left.

Bryce nearly did miss Leila. She was already two blocks down the road by the time he left the library. "Ayo, Leila, wait up!"

Despite Leila's embarrassment at having to tell him where she was going and her reluctance to walk back to the library with him, Bryce drove her to the shelter. She hit a brick wall right away. The shelter closest to the library was full, and the next closest was another half-hour away. Bryce was nice enough to drive her there, too, but there was no joy there, either. She was denied on the basis of her current employment status -- that shelter only took in people who were in totally dire straits: no job, no home, no vehicle, plus kids to feed. "Whatever," Leila grumbled as she got back in the car. "We gotta go back to the library. My break's over."

He brought her back and parked. "You know, you could...crash in my dorm while I'm gone...if you comfortable with that."

"Your friends your roommates?"

"One of them is."

"Lemme guess, the horny pervert?"

Bryce sighed in dismay. "Yeah. Him."

"In that case, thanks, but no thanks. I'd rather sleep on the streets."

"You risk worse things out here, Leila. People can rob or mug you, or even kill you."

"Beats bein' raped," she replied.

"Nah, take it easy, babe. Sean's not like that."

"You don't know that, and I ain't 'bout to find out the hard way. He look like a rapist or wife beater, and with you gone for two months, that's way too much time for him to be tempted to try somethin' stupid." She saw the surprise in his face and caught herself. "Look, I really do appreciate your kindness, but I also gotta think about my safety, and I just don't trust him."

He was silent for a while, deep in thought. "Aight, tell you what, take this." He pulled a small stack of one-hundred-dollar bills from his wallet. "This can get you a motel room for the week, at least. Beats bein' in the streets, and it keeps you away from him."

She hesitantly took the money. "But...don't you need this?"

He shrugged. "I'll earn it back where I'm goin'. It's a summer job."

"Well...okay. Thanks. So you come back at the end of August?"

"Mhm. The day before classes start."

She put the money away in a pocket and opened the door. He gently grasped and rubbed her left hand, surprising her. His voice was sultry. "I'll miss you, Leila."

She was thankful her skin was dark enough to hide the blush. "I'll-I'll miss you too, Bryce. Just...just make sure you come back."

The bright dimpled smile emerged. "Of course, yo. I gotta keep my commitments."

"Yeah. You already paid to reserve your classes."

"I wasn't talkin' 'bout that." He stared her in the eye for a long moment.

"See you." She nervously pulled her hand away and finally got out of the car.

"Hey, hold up a second." He pulled out his phone. "Lemme get your number."

"Why you need it?" she asked after they exchanged numbers.

"So I can know which motel you're staying in."

"Why you need that? You'll be hundreds of miles away."

"Just trust me, yo," he said with a smile.

She smiled back, and finally headed back inside.

On the plus side, the motel stay bought her time to learn about a shelter she hadn't noticed before: a nearby apostolic church with a community outreach ministry. She entered the humble church sanctuary and immediately ran into a face she least wanted to see: Bryce's friend Sean. As expected, his eyes stripped her several times as she approached him. She swallowed her disgust to ask him who she needed to speak with about the shelter. He pointed over his shoulder. "Right through that door back there." She gave him the polite thanks and went about her business.

As she spoke with the church elder responsible for the shelter, Leila could feel a stare on her and finally looked behind her in time to catch a pair of black eyes and a subtle nod. Whoever this man was, he was quite important: he wore a tailored dark blue suit with gold-bordered diamond cufflinks and nicely polished dress shoes. He was the stuff of teen girl dreams -- tall physically toned frame, clear cinnamon skin with a head full of wavy black hair. "I'm guessin' that's the pastor," Leila murmured. The elder gave her an enthusiastic nod and smile. "Apostle Randall Thompson."

Leila studied him as he went about his business and mentally compared him to Bryce. The two were opposites in almost every way. Apostle Thompson carried himself with all the pomp of his position, while Bryce, who was a leader in his own right among his schoolmates, was very casual: t-shirts, v-neck shirts, crisp jeans, clean sneakers, fresh haircuts. Thompson was wearing five rings between both hands, including a wedding band. Bryce couldn't stand that stuff. He always said rings were -- what was that long word that made her laugh all the time -- flamboyant. Sure enough, she chuckled to herself at the thought of it, amazed that even Bryce's memory could make her smile. "You're all signed in," the elder said. "Follow me."

She was led out the church's rear exit into a strip mall parking lot. "This whole strip is church grounds," the elder explained, pointing. "The children's day care is right next door to the church, the community center is next to that, and the shelter is directly across the parking lot."

Leila's heart sank. It was impressive that the church owned so much real estate, but the shelter itself wasn't very big. The elder explained that she could only stay a maximum of two months, since the shelter doesn't believe in turning new residents away. He even went so far as to suggest she find work and save up for a motel as a backup.

A wall of noise met them as they entered the lobby. Two residents were holding a young girl about Leila's age back as she spewed hateful words at another girl who was doubled over, covering her nose with a hand as blood ran down her lips. "That's what you get!" the wild one yelled. "Keep that Bible out my face!" The elder was leading Leila past the embarrassing scene, but she took a good look at the girl's angry face and two-inch-high mohawk.

Leila's heart broke at the sight of the poor victim who was now beside herself. The little girl wasn't even upset because of her broken nose, but because the Bible in question was in pieces on the floor in front of her. The two residents wrangled the wild one away, giving the victim some peace. She wiped her bloody hands in her clothes and slowly picked up the pieces, apologizing to God and begging His forgiveness in sputtered breaths. Leila stopped the elder and went to her. Without a word, she lowered herself and helped her clean up. The poor kid reminded her so much of herself after one of Tawana's lunchtime attacks. Her wet, feeble eyes looked up at Leila. "Th-thank you." Leila handed her the pieces she'd picked up with a timid nod.

As Leila rejoined the elder, she felt eyes on her again. She looked behind her and spotted Apostle Thompson in the corridor across the room. He gave her another nod, glanced at the victim and gave her a nod as well, then took off down the corridor.

The Fall

The ring felt strange on Leila's finger, but she was beside herself with excitement as she sat in Bryce's car, staring at it. Not only did she get to see him again, but he bagged her. They'd be together permanently, and for once, she'll have a man who actually loves her. She looked over at him with tender eyes. "Thank you, Bryce." He simply smiled back, holding her hand as he drove. "Oh, don't thank me yet. That'll come later." She laughed, embarrassed.

Leila was too nervous to open up to her husband the first night. Just the sight of his face hovering over hers was uncomfortable for her. Not for lack of love or desire -- she loved Bryce, and it was still unbelievable to her that he proposed in the first place, but seeing his lustful face bothered her. He was clearly frustrated with that, but being the gentleman he was, he didn't force himself on her.

She instead curled up in the curve of his body, facing him as he faced her. As he gently caressed her downcast face, he finally realized an important truth he'd overlooked: for all that he found attractive about Leila, she was still a child. And although he didn't know her whole story, he knew it had to be a very dark one for her to be so afraid to give herself to him.

"Were you...raped, Leila?" He watched her jaw tighten. A single tear fell from her left eye. "It's alright," he whispered. "That alone says enough. Wait, it wasn't Sean, was it?"

She slowly shook her head.

The next two months saw her equally timid. Fortunately, Bryce's fall semester had him nose-deep in his books, but he was still a man, and still wanted his wife, so she made a gradual effort when she could stand it. He settled for their little make out sessions, always just shaking his head and smiling at her when she closed herself off again.

Then his birthday came. He entered the apartment, exhausted from work and taking his final exam for that month, and found a meal already waiting for him. "Leila?" he called. No answer. He walked the entire apartment and didn't see her, but saw that she pulled out all the stops: the bathtub was filled with hot water and soap for him, a fresh pair of pajama pants were laid out for him on the bed, along with his neatly folded, freshly washed laundry, and the apartment had the subtle refreshing scent of cleaning chemicals. She'd scrubbed the whole place down and vacuumed the carpet.

He decided to go ahead and enjoy her surprise. It wasn't until he put on the PJ's and put all his laundry away that he finally saw her. She silently leaned in the doorway watching him, wearing an oversized black button-up shirt. He smiled. "That's my interview shirt, baby girl. You gotta be careful with that."

She smiled back. "It's only been on me for the last five minutes."

"Where were you -- Were you here this whole time?"

She nodded, smirking.

"Where were you hidin'?"

"The one place you didn't look." She pointed to the closet as she slowly approached him. "I just moved around whenever you did."

He noticed a resolve in her eyes he'd never seen before as he caressed her face. "Thanks for the meal. For all this."

She nodded, grasping his hands and moving them to the shirt buttons. He raised curious eyebrows. "You gonna hang this up, or am I?" she asked. "I ain't tryin' to mess up your good shirt."

The dimpled smile emerged as he unbuttoned it. "I can always iron it again."

Leila finally let herself go, and closed out the night with the gift he'd always wanted.

* * * *

A knock on the door interrupts my story. Diana answers, and a white guy pokes his head in to check on us. This must be another newbie; I've never seen him before either. I'd call him cute if he didn't look so...corporate: hazel eyes, rich coffee-colored hair parted on the side, clean shaven, like they all are around here, long-sleeved plaid button-up pushed into charcoal slacks with a leather Kenneth Cole belt thick enough to make me wonder if he was going to spank me in a minute. His shoes are about the only cool thing about him: he's rockin' all-black sneaks instead of the usual shiny, pointy, boring dress shoes.

"We all done in here?" he asks.

"Not yet, Dr. Isaacs," Diana replies.

He looks at me with raised eyebrows and then back at her.

"I told her she could take her time."

He makes an empty chuckle. "Oh, of course. But you must have quite a story, Leila," he says to me. "Two hours and still not done, huh?"

I don't bother smiling back. "Almost. I could've finished in the time you've been here."

"Leila," Diana says in a big sister tone.

I turn back around to her and stay that way. "I only diss people who diss me, Miss. Dr. Isaacs ain't here for me. He just here to make sure I ain't done nothin' to you."

She gives him an embarrassed look.

"Sorry you thought I was dissing you, Leila," he replies. "Not all of us are out to get you. I just came in here to time check you folks, nothing else. Lunch break's in an hour. Just make sure you finish up by then."

"I'll be done in the next fifteen," I reply without looking at him.

"Sounds good," he replies as he closes the door.

I glare at Diana for a few seconds. "Who the hell is that? You bring him with you? I ain't never seen neither of y'all before."

"You speak as if you've been here a long time, Leila," she replies with that knowing smile. "He and I are actually regulars at this home. We visit once a month."

"To do what?"

"Exactly what we're doing here." She gestures between us.

"Make us relive our nightmares all over again? You call that useful?"

She tilts her head a little and gives me a cautious, caring look, helping me realize I'm losing my temper again. I take a deep breath to calm down.

"So you finally got intimate with Bryce. That's where we left off. What's next?"

I look down at my belly, and immediately felt tears coming. "God -- or the devil -- stirred the pot."

* * * *

Leila hated the doctor's office, but the cramps were worse; and the puking wasn't fun, either. She had to know for sure what was up. Thankfully all the poking and peeking was done, and she sat quietly on the chair, fully dressed, awaiting the doctor's return.

He returned with a stern look on his face, which told Leila she was not going to like the news. "You...mentioned that you've been sexually active in recent months."

She nodded.

"Well, your efforts have paid off...if this is in fact what you wanted." He perused her medical file, then looked up at her. "You're sixteen weeks pregnant, Miss Sudders."

"What?" Leila looked down at her still flat belly. "Sixteen weeks..." she whispered to herself. The news avalanched her: sixteen weeks was four months, which means she was already in her second trimester. Just like that, she was going to be a mom. She was finally going to have someone to love. And soon.

"Do you know who the father is?"

Leila knew the answer, and seeing his face in her mind sapped all the joy out of the news, caving her face in despair as she nodded. She covered her mouth to quiet herself.

The doctor gave her a sympathetic look.

"Thank you, Doctor."

"Well, um...considering you've gone this long without prenatal care, I suggest you make time for it, Miss Sudders," he said. "For your child's sake and your own."

She could only nod. "Okay."

Leila got back in the car and stared straight ahead without a word. Bryce was instantly concerned. "Everything aight?"

She nodded.

He took a deep breath with raised eyebrows and drove off. "Okay."

Leila's heart was in her mouth as they entered the apartment. She silently wished he had class to attend, but he'd been let out early thanks to a two-hour-long power outage at the college. She sat -- more like fell -- on the couch. Bryce watched her, ready to catch her if she passed out. She lifted her worried, watery eyes to him. "Bryce...I'm pregnant."

His eyes spread. "Word? Get outta here! You ain't even showin'."

"I know, it shocked me too."

He hugged her. "That's crazy! I'm 'bout to be a daddy!"

His excitement actually surprised her. She expected him to get mad at her and kick her out, which made things harder for her.

Bryce noticed her look wasn't any happier. "Then what's wrong? You don't want it?"

"I do," she replied, her composure falling apart. "But..."

He stared expectantly, confused.

"I'm already four months along, Bryce."

His face slowly hardened as the truth set in. "It ain't mine."

She shook her head.

"You were that lonely while I was gone, Leila?" His voice fell low with anger. "You couldn't wait the two months for me to come back?"

She started crying miserably, much like she did before Mike would explode at her. The sound of her own sobs annoyed her. When was this curse going to end? "I tried to..."

"Tried to? How you try to wait on somebody and get knocked up anyway? Whose is it, then?"

She finally looked up at him in shame. "It's Thompson's. Randall Thompson's."

"Apostle Randall Thompson?" The shock only worsened his fury.

She nodded. "I was stayin' at the church shelter, and he..."

"Don't blame him!" he screamed. "That's all y'all bitches ever do! Throw it at us and then blame us when we take it!"

"No, Bryce! That's not what happened!" She screamed with every ounce of desperation in her. Any hope of a good life she had was slipping away. Again.

"Don't you say my name!" he screamed, grabbing her throat. "Don't say nothin'!"

She fought and struggled like a dying fish in his grip. Her voice squawked between sobs and chokes. "No! Bryce, please!"

"I loved you, Leila! Took you off the damned streets when nobody wanted you!"

She kept struggling. "Stop!"

He grabbed a nearby pillow and shoved it on her face, pressing down as hard as he could.

She screamed and flailed and kicked, but he didn't budge.

"Evil bitch. Made me wait two months to get it, when you already gave it away."

"No!" She screamed from beneath the pillow. "I didn't!"

Bryce held his position until she stopped struggling. Her body lied still on the couch. He pulled the pillow off and saw her empty eyes looking up at him, and in that moment, the reality of his action finally set in. He not only killed this woman, but the baby, too. His face crumpled in shock and disgust at himself. He leaned in closer to look at her face, ready to say something...

And then a leg kicked him hard in his crotch. Leila smacked his face as hard as she could, kicked him repeatedly in his crotch and chest to get some distance between them, and raced out the door. He rolled on the couch, gripping himself and groaning in pain.

Leila managed to find a way back to Thompson's shelter, looking behind her every second for fear Bryce would suddenly appear like some demon, and demanded to see Thompson. The elders kept turning her away, but she was manic -- wild, like the girl she saw the first night she was there. She crossed the parking lot to the church and asked around for him, but no one had seen him all day. She made a beeline for his office, and Sean was leaning in the doorway, wearing a smug look. "He ain't here," he said.

"He feed you that script, too?" she snarled, sweaty and breathless. "Thought you were better than that."

He frowned in disbelief. "Who you talkin' to like that?"

She came up close to him. "Get mad if you want to. I've already survived two others like you. Take a damn number."

"Back up off me," he said, erecting himself. "And stop cussin' in church."

"Chasin' skirts on church grounds is just as filthy, you dog."

Sean laughed. "Don't go there with me, lil' girl. You don't wanna do that."

She finally stepped back.

"Like I said, he gone. He at a conference in Cleveland. Won't be back 'til next week."

"You got a number for him?"

"I ain't givin' you that."

"Fine, I'll find it another way."

"Ain't no other way," he replied. "I'm the head elder, and the associate pastor ain't on church grounds right now. He's still at work."

"There's always another way," she replied, storming off.

Her stomach sank as the tears came. She told Sean off, but knew he was right. She had to tell Thompson what happened, and whether she liked it or not, she would need Sean's help.

The thought angered her all the more, and she just kept walking. She was nearly at the door when she heard him again. "Hey, hold up!" he called from behind her. She turned to face him, not even bothering to wipe her face. His look was mingled with horror and pity. Leila's eyes were tearful but intense with fury and desperation, her jaw tight and grinding. "You look like you need a hospital or somethin', though," he said. "You 'bout to fall out."

"Thanks, Captain Obvious," she snapped. "Did you stop me for a reason?"

"Yeah, here." He pulled out his phone and gave her Thompson's number.

"Why change your mind?"

" 'Cause I seen that look on your face before," he said. "Girls like you need help. That's what he's supposed to be doin'."

"*Supposed* to be doin'," she muttered as she saved the number. "Thank you." She turned to leave.

"Wait, hold up, not so fast," his voice was finally back to its usual greasy lilt as he gently grasped her arm.

"Back up off me." She spat his words back at him, yanking her arm away. "I'm already knocked up."

His jaw hung in surprise as she left.

Leila made a point never to return to the church, especially after telling Sean she was pregnant. She called Thompson from a shelter landline phone instead of her cell. He was silent on the line for several seconds after she broke the news. She thought he hung up on her.

"You have to help me, 'cause I'm keepin' it."

Silence on the line again for several seconds.

"I...I really hate to tell you this, but you can't. Neither of us is ready to take care of a child."

"What you mean? You got money! You show off your fancy clothes and your fancy car and all them rings on your fingers. You ain't poor. Plus you told me you and your wife were gettin' a divorce--"

A heavy exhale met her on the other line. "Look, Leila, I can't do this. I can't father that child with a family of my own.

Now, if you know what's good for you, you'll abort that baby and move on with your life."

"How can you say that to me?" she cried, her desperation breaking through. "This your child, too! Don't y'all always protest abortion as a sin? Come on, Mr. Thompson, please. I got nowhere to go, and no help. You gotta help me."

"This is the last time you call me, Leila. The last time. Do what I said, or deal with it on your own."

Click.

* * * *

I finally wipe my face, mad at Diana again for making me share all that. Now she knows all my failures...and that I am a failure, just like all the other losers in here. Just another pregnant black girl with a dark history. "Anyway, I wasn't showin' up for work often enough anymore, so the library fired me. Five shelters and many sleepless nights later, I finally managed to get a space in here."

She stares at me for a while with what looks like deep empathy. Not sympathy, *empathy*, as if she's been through the same thing. She slowly leans forward, interlocking her fingers. "Let me ask you something, Leila. Earlier, you said, 'God or the devil stirred the pot'."

"Mhm."

"So you believe in both."

"That goes without sayin'," I reply. "If you believe in one, you gotta believe in the other, 'cause one created the other."

"So you're not atheist...but would you say you're agnostic?"

"No. I seen enough evidence that God is real, Miss." I can feel that nasty anger rising in me again. "What I am is pissed and apathetic. I could give a damn about Him, 'cause He sure don't give a damn about me. Or my family."

"That's where you're wrong, sweetie," she says tenderly. She nearly reminds me of Christie, and it pisses me off even more because I know if Christie were here, she would *actually* care.

"You not recruitin' me, Miss. If you here to witness, witness to somebody who don't know Him or don't believe in Him. Don't waste your time with me."

"It's about more than just letting people know He exists, Leila," she pleas. "It's about letting people -- about letting you know He loves you and wants to help you."

"Yeah. Hypocrite Alice told me that too before she shut me out for her dead womanizin' wife-beatin' son. God don't love a unwelcome demon."

She slowly closes her eyes and sucks a bunch of air in, embarrassed for Alice.

"Maybe He loved me when I was a kid, before my daddy and Tawana started beatin' on me and makin' me damaged goods. Maybe He loved me before that lowlife pastor raped me and then lied to me about being divorced to cover up his lust, then lied some more to lure me into an affair with him because he knew I was hurtin'."

The fury raises my voice louder. "Dude's wife was *sick*. Fightin' breast cancer at that. That's the only reason she wasn't at the damn church. Anyway, maybe God loved me before this baby. Maybe He loved me when I married Bryce. But not now."

Diana looks ready to cry. "If He didn't love you, why would He give you the child? And give you a determined heart to keep it?"

"To give it up to a family that needs it," I snap back. "That's the best answer I can think of, 'cause nothin' else makes sense. Love ain't got nothin' to do with that. That's logic."

"And what about escaping Bryce? He could've killed you."

"Bastard should have!" My voice bounces off of every wall. "Then I wouldn't have to tell this embarrassing story to every Tom, Dick, and Jane that's so fed up with their own lives they gotta come hear somebody else's sob stories to feel better about themselves!"

She's taken aback.

"I'd be in some pit pushin' up daisies and free of this mess!"

She slowly shakes her head, her eyes full of water. "You'd be much worse off, dear," she replies quietly. "Which brings me back to His love. He could've let you die and enter a place far worse than this."

"Don't sugarcoat it, Miss Diana, I know what Hell is," I snap again. "But you don't see I'm already in it. It don't get much worse than this."

"That's what everyone says...until they hear someone else's story."

Throwing my words back at me, huh?

"For what it's worth, I'm glad He's kept you," she continues. "And the child. He has a great plan for both of you if you would just let Him back in."

"I never shut Him out! That's what pisses me off! He turned His back on *me*!"

"Did He?" She looks at me in the same motherly way Christie used to when she would force me to think out a difficult physics question myself. It forces me silent. "You seem like you know a lot of things, Leila, and judging by your kindness to that girl with the tattered Bible, you value the Word."

"What that gotta do with nothin'?"

"Listen to the way you speak of these people. There's one thing they all have in common. You think about that." She finally rose from her chair and headed for the door. "And remember what I told you." She opens and holds the door open for me to leave. "I'll be praying for you, Leila Sudders. God doesn't make junk, and He doesn't waste anything He creates."

I finally get up. "Good. Maybe He'll listen to your prayers, 'cause He sure ain't hearin' mine."

"There's a reason for that," she softly says as I reach her.

"We're done."

"Yes, we are," she sighs, disappointed. "Thank you for your time."

"You're welcome. I'm sure you'll be well-paid for it."

She chuckles and shakes her head. "You're educated far beyond your level of humanity, Leila."

"What's that supposed to mean?"

"You're so lost in your head, you've abandoned your heart."

I'm so tired of this woman, and I let it show when I look her in the eye. Even after everything I told her, she still doesn't know a thing about me. "I didn't abandon it. It was *destroyed*."

I finally walk out and check my phone clock. Fifteen minutes until lunch break. The corporate clown would be proud.

2

Speak of the devil, I pass a counseling office with the door half-open and see him slumped in his chair, rubbing his face with a hand. He makes this heavy sigh -- a lot like the one I heard Thompson make when I told him I was pregnant. My legs mysteriously draw me to his door and I lean in the doorway. He gives me a curious look.

"I see your girl had quite a story too," I say. "And obviously worse than mine, if you lookin' like that."

"Like what?"

"Emotionally drained. Miss Diana got you beat."

"That's good," he replies. "She's new to the game, so she's hungry."

"And what? You tired of it?"

"Nah. I never get tired of this."

I'm tempted to repeat my whole "feel better about yourself" spat, but I don't bother. Corporate Boy's got to have a boring story and feel better listening to ours.

"She reads me," he murmurs with a playful smile, revealing perfectly even white teeth. It looks like he used to wear braces. "What are you looking for, Leila? What are you asking yourself about me?"

"I'm actually awestruck at your presumptuousness, sir."

He raises his eyebrows in surprise.

"Yeah, I said *presumptuousness*. We ain't all illiterate, dude."

"You're as guilty as I am, Leila. You still presume the worst about us. Remember, we're the ones helping you. Don't bite our hands."

"We? The home is helpin' me. You just amuse me."

He laughs. "Glad I can hold your attention long enough to do that."

Did he really just say that? "Am I supposed to read between the lines there, Doc?"

"No. I was speaking plainly. Most of the residents assume, as you do, that we're just here to ridicule them, or whatever other negative expectations they might have, so once the counseling's over, they don't acknowledge us at all. They forget we're people too, so I'm being sincere when I tell you I'm glad you stopped by, even if only to have a laugh at my expense."

"Actually, I just came in here to tell you I managed to finish up before lunch break. Thought that might make you proud or somethin' shallow like that."

He laughs again. "You're a class act, Leila. Well, thanks for the memo."

"Mhm." I step off to leave.

"By the way, when you're interested in playing for real..."

I poke my head back in, ready to chew his head off for hitting on me.

He catches the look and smiles it off. "I see you live on that phone when you're not in counseling. But nothing beats a real checkered board with real pieces and a *real opponent*. You've gotta be tired of beating the computer so many times."

My heart skips a beat. There wasn't another soul in here who connected with me on that point.

"Must be lonely, knowing that the game's so available to you the matrons allow you to keep the board and all the pieces in your room, despite the facility's rule about residents not keeping extra property in their rooms."

This weirdo's been stalking me.

"How you know 'bout that already? You just got here today."

He rises from his chair and comes around to the other side of the desk, leaning against it with folded arms. "Actually, we got here two days ago, you just didn't notice; and your little friend wasn't gonna say anything ahead of time because she knows you wouldn't care. Besides, your game play's no secret. The matrons are actually happy you found such a good outlet, and so quickly."

"You were saying before?"

"When you're interested in playing for real, let me know. We're here for four more days."

"On one condition."

"Name it."

"You bare your life while we play. Just like we've had to in this hell. You shrinks might find this torture cute, but we don't. It ain't nothin' nice to relive our failures this often to so many different people. People who don't care."

The smug smile is gone. That same look of deep empathy I saw on Diana's face is now on his. "Fair enough."

I look at my phone again. "How five minutes from now sound?"

"Your little friend might object."

"She can watch. And get in on your dirt, if there is any." A smirk breaks through as I walk off.

Sure enough, my little friend quietly watches as the Doc and I play. She frowns at the pieces, not knowing which is which and why we're moving them like we are. He and I notice her discomfort and smile. "It's aight, baby girl," I tell her. "I could explain each move, but it might bore you."

"Mhm," she replies, munching. "Doc's been kinda quiet, though."

I laugh, looking at him. "You heard the lady."

"Well, we've only just started playing, but okay." He moves a knight and takes my pawn. "My story starts in the U.K., actually."

Wow, dude hides his accent real well. Thought he was from some super-white place like L.A. or Orlando.

"Came to the U.S. to study psychology and psychiatric medicine."

I move my bishop and take the knight that killed my pawn.

"A little hasty, don't you think?" he asks.

"I ain't worried 'bout it. You won't take the easy move I just left for you."

"You're right about that." He moves a pawn on the far end of the board its first two spaces. "Once I finished school, I worked with private practice doctors, you know, gained some experience."

"Where you lived at?"

"Went to school in New York, moved to Boston for a little while after graduation, even stayed in Charlotte for a spell. That's actually where I caught the social work bug."

"How long was all this?"

"About a decade," he replies.

My friend makes a weird face. "How old are you, den?"

"How old do I look?" he asks, smiling at her.

"Be nice," I warn her in a soft voice as I take a pawn. "That's a trick question."

"You ain't lyin'," she replies, laughing. "I don't know, like, thirty-seven."

"Thank you, ma'am. You just made my week."

"So how old are you really?" I ask.

"We'll stick with thirty-seven."

"So you're more like forty-two."

He takes my last pawn with a rook, giving me a sly look. "That's not very nice. Check."

"But more accurate." I take his rook with my knight without taking my eyes off his.

From the corner of my eye, I see my friend look at the board and back at me in amazement.

"If anything, that's a good thing," I reply. "To be in your forties lookin' like thirties. It means you treat your body right."

He makes another move without breaking his gaze on me. "Check." If I ain't know better, I'd think he really was tryin' to hit on me.

"So no dirt, huh?" I finally ask.

The smile returns as he makes another move. "Most of my dirt happened back home. I've kept my nose clean since I came here. Checkmate."

"I guess I'll have to earn that," I reply, finally looking back at the board.

"Yeah," he says, tipping my king over. "When you defeat my king, you can hear all about it."

We stare into each other's eyes again, smirking. *Challenge accepted, Corporate Boy.*

Diana appears, breaking our little tension. "Excuse me, folks, but your next resident's ready for you, Dr. Isaacs." She spies the chessboard with tickled curiosity, and looks at him and me.

"Thank you, Miss Diana." He gathers his lunch stuff and rises from the table. "Excuse me, ladies. Good game."

"Thanks for caring enough to challenge me."

Both he and Diana look at me with concern. "We already talked about that," he finally says with a smiling wink as he walks off.

My little friend shyly eyes Diana. "Who he counselin'?"

"Oh, you know I can't share that information, sweetheart," Diana says. "We keep your privacy, right?"

"Y'all don't have to," she replies with a shrug. "I don't care. I'm as curious as anybody else."

For some reason, Diana looks at me before she looks back at her. "Well, we have to be fair to everyone. What applies to one applies to all."

"When's your next session?" I ask, wondering why she still has time to stand over us right now.

"Not 'til this evening."

"Good luck, then."

"No luck needed, dear," she replies with a knowing smile. "God's with me. I'll be fine."

"His bein' there don't equal success," my friend says. Couldn't have said it better myself.

"You ladies have a good day," Diana says, laughing to herself as she walks off.

Counseling session aside, today's no different than any other for me since I got into the home. I leave two hours after lunch and walk at least three miles, filling out as many job applications as I could get my hands on, making copies for myself at a nearby college library. The more I fill out, the better my chances of finding work; and real talk, I ain't tryin' to be cooped up in that place all day.

I'm halfway back to the home, waiting at a crosswalk and carefully watching my back now that it's nighttime, and a black sedan with tinted windows makes a left turn and pulls up on me. I turn, ready to run, when the window slowly rolls down. "Looks like you could use a ride, huh?" Dude looks drunk, and much less corporate -- he's wearing a t-shirt with jeans, his hair's fussed, and he seems a lot more relaxed. His cheeks are flushed.

"Um...no thanks, I'll hoof it back. I'm almost there anyway."

Doc shrugs. "I can get you there faster. Besides, the more you dog your feet, the harder it'll be to walk in the days to come. Might as well take a break when you can get it."

"Ain't there some kinda rule against this?"

"No. I'm helping a resident, and no money's being exchanged for any services."

Ugh. He had to go there with it. "Aight, whatever." I get in, silently reminding myself that if I push too hard, I might hurt the baby. Forget my feet.

As he pulls off, he rolls up the window and locks the doors. "Relax," he says before I can freak out. "Just a safety thing. I'm not gonna try anything."

The trip back is quiet...until we pass the library. "That's where you used to work, right?"

"Mhm."

"Tried applying there again?"

"No reply so far. Guess they still mad at me."

He surprisingly doesn't dispute my statement, but instead turns onto a street I've never seen before. "Relax," he says again. "Again, nothing bad." He drives another four blocks and makes another turn, pulling into a small mom-and-pop restaurant on the corner. He finally unlocks the doors and pulls a mini gym bag from the back seat. "Come on."

I follow him to the restaurant's back patio and we sit at a wooden bench table out there. He sets his cell phone on vibrate and places it on the table to the right of my right arm. I want to ask him what the hell he's doing, but I just watch him fiddle in the mini gym bag. He pulls the load out and it finally makes sense: he sets the chessboard in the center of the table and hands me my pieces. "You know, you coulda just asked me."

"Not sure you would've said yes, though," he says. "You did turn down the lift altogether." He then gestures to the menu at my left hand. "Find what you want on there. The waiter should be here in a few."

This experience reminds me of my first steakhouse dinner with Christie. This seafood joint is another first for me, and has a sports bar kind of feel to it. The patio's got little flat screen TVs hanging from the beams, each on a different channel: some on sports, some on political news, some on music video channels with whack reality shows and half-naked chicks. The other customers, mostly men, are chillin' at their tables, crowded with empty beer bottles or pitchers, minding their own conversations. It's mad relaxing. "Um, I dunno what to get. I'm not a big seafood person."

"You like shrimp?"

"Yeah."

"Can't go wrong with that," he shrugs. "Better yet, I'll order us a platter of prawns."

My eyebrows fly up. "Prawns?"

"They're just like shrimp, but bigger."

"O...kay. I'll take your word for it, then."

The smile finally appears. "Like spicy food?"

"I guess. I rarely eat it. My folks had to cook without it, mostly."

"Willing to try some here?"

I nod.

Doc's timing is perfect. The waiter shows up less than five minutes after that. He places our order and orders two sweet teas. I don't know how he knows I like that, 'cause I sure didn't tell Diana, but whatever.

I thank him and the waiter, and we dive into the game as soon as the waiter's gone. This round of blitz chess was more interesting 'cause of all the distractions, like the waiter bringing us our tea, then eventually our food, plus the weird feeling of using the phone as a play timer instead of having an old fashioned clock to press after each move.

We're munching on the prawns, and both down to five pieces on the board each when he drops a bomb on me. "The chess is fun, but that's not the real reason I brought you here."

I literally stop chewing, despite the big chunk in my mouth. "What?"

"Feel free to finish that," he says, pointing at my mouth and laughing. "It's nothing bad, just interesting."

I gesture for him to tell me as I finish chewing.

"It's my after-lunch resident."

"What about her?"

"She's a single mom. And apparently you two have met."

Say what? "Who is this?"

He leans in closer and lowers his voice. "You may not recognize the name, but it's Sabryna Hodges. She's only a couple years older than you."

I take another bite, hesitant to say what I want to say next. "So what's her story?"

"You heard Miss Diana, Leila."

"Heard that conversation, huh?"

"Barely, but yeah."

"If you agree with her, why you told me 'bout Sabryna in the first place?"

"Just thought you'd find it interesting."

"Told y'all 'bout that torture stuff, man. You say somethin' like that, Imma wanna know more."

He smiles to himself as he makes his move. "Can you keep a secret?"

"When I'm not forced to tell a counselor about it, yes."

He laughs. "Touche. Alright. We'll be here a while, though. You know that."

"I'm not the one who gets paid by the hour, Doc."

"Neither am I, right now. You've been warned."

SABRYNA'S STORY

What would a kid know about the lesser of two evils? All sixteen-year-old Sabryna knew was she had an ugly choice to make: she could move to Fort Hood with her mom, which she already didn't like considering that ugly mass shooting that just happened there, or stay here in halfway-upscale Tamarac with her super-Christian uncle who rubs her forehead with oil one too many times and speaks in those terrifying tongues.

Going to Fort Hood would mean she'd be close to her mom, but then she'd have to leave school, and all her friends, and her fine basketball star boyfriend...

Devaughn was a tough catch, too; she had to game hard to get him. Mr. Bookworm wasn't trying to get sidetracked from his scholarship goals, and he had to get those grades up. She had to play smart and actually study with him to get past that wall and break him down. On the plus side, her grades went up, too, but none of that was as exciting as his kisses, or feeling his warm, hard fingers all over her, or catching dirty looks from all the girls who wanted him for themselves.

In fact, Sabryna actually stole him from his girlfriend at the time. Little Miss Lead Cheerleader Shanice Houston didn't know what hit her when Devaughn dumped her. Shanice was fine with him studying because she knew his goals, but was clueless about his study habits or who he studied with. All she knew was his grades were getting better and she was happy.

Until she let things go to her head.

In typical elitist fare, Shanice and her snooty squad decided to harass Sabryna, who was totally exhausted from the girls' basketball team tryouts. "I hope you don't think you makin' the first cut if you that tired after tryouts," Shanice sneered. "You won't last a single game."

Sabryna didn't even acknowledge her. She tied her shoelace and got up, slowly heading for the basketball rack. Of course, Shanice didn't appreciate being ignored and waltzed over to her. Her big mistake? Putting her hand on Sabryna's shoulder to turn her around. "Hey--"

Without a word, Sabryna immediately grabbed her hand, spun around, and twisted her arm backwards. Shanice roared in pain. Sabryna released her hand and gave her an intense stare. "If you know what's good for you, you'll never touch me again." The other girls backed off, but Shanice snarled and lifted an arm to punch her. The fist froze inches from Sabryna's face. She looked to her left in shock at the dark brown hand gripping her arm. "Devaughn..."

Her boyfriend was less than pleased. "What the hell you doin', Shanice?"

"Who you talkin' to--"

"Someone I thought knew better," he replied. "You bigger than this. And if you knew who this was, you wouldn't mess with her."

"Excuse me? What's she to you?"

"The girl responsible for gettin' my grades up."

Shanice looked at Sabryna in disgusted disbelief.

"She's my study partner."

She gave him the same disgusted look. "Let me go."

He instead pulled her away from Sabryna and toward him. "Leave on this side of the gym with me. And bring your goons with you."

She yanked her arm away from him and stormed off with her posse in tow, pointedly not using the doors he told her to. Not that Sabryna cared. For her, that was the nail in the coffin. He was pretty much hers from there. There was no way she was leaving such difficult prey behind to go to some Army base in Texas with a mother she barely knew anyway.

Sabryna pulled out her cell phone and typed her decision: "I'M STAYING. ENJOY FT. HOOD. DON'T GET SHOT."

It wasn't until weeks later that the gravity of her decision hit her: she was parentless. She'd never met her father, and that mother she barely knew was really out of the picture now. Uncle Gus was no daddy substitute, either. He was just extra. It was freeing, but still a little unnerving. She had no real support system.

So she chose to become one for herself.

She never did make the girls' basketball team, so she went any and everywhere with her friends, and spent much of her time with Devaughn and his family, telling herself that her own judgment was good enough.

She started staying out later and later each night, ignoring her uncle's nine o'clock curfew, and when she crept in, he was always waiting up for her, Bible in hand. He would sit her down and read scriptures to her explaining the wrong she did. "Honor thy mother and father, that your days may long on this earth." She always wanted to scream, "you ain't my daddy!" but never bothered to. He would always follow with Proverbs 1:10: "My child, when man entices you to sin, consent thou not." The long, calm lecture would stretch on for at least an hour, then he would have her get on her knees with him to pray.

The very first time she snuck in at midnight, she expected him to lose his mind and spank the skin off her, but instead he did what he always did...just for much longer than usual. The thought scraped her mind over and over, *why can't you just beat me and get it over with?*

The Bomb

By junior year, Sabryna grew antsy. Devaughn was a senior now, so she didn't have much time left with him before he shipped off to college. But they'd been together for a year, so he grew quite comfortable with her, which was a relief considering what was happening back home with Uncle Gus.

One night after studying, she and Devaughn lied down on a blanket in his family's backyard, watching the full moon and stars. It was boring for her, but she was just happy to be with him and hang around his Jamaican parents. They were strict when it came to schoolwork, but they were cool about everything else, and didn't choke her to death with the Bible. "My mom really likes you," he told her. "She said if you ever want to stay over, you can."

She looked up at him total surprise. "She'll let me do that? Even though we datin'?"

"Well, obviously we can't try nothin'," he replied. "At least not here at the house. But yeah, she's cool with you stayin' overnight once in a while. We got a extra room."

"Sound good to me," she said.

" 'Course it does," he replied, chuckling. "You like her cookin' and she likes havin' you around as the daughter she never had."

"...Um, that would make us brotha and sista, though."

"You know what I mean, man. She don't look at us like that."

"Well, what happened? She try havin' a girl?"

"She don't really like talkin' about it, so never ask her, okay?"

"O...kay."

"Yeah, she tried. Twice. And miscarried both times. Dad gave up after that 'cause he was concerned for her health, so she had to, too."

"Sorry to hear that. She ain't do too bad, though. Two sons is good."

"Tell that to her," he murmured. Sabryna could hear a certain longing in his voice. "Don't get me wrong, she proud of us and everything, but...we can always tell she still got that hole inside her. She gets this faraway look in her eyes sometimes, even while we talkin' to her. The only time she don't do it is when either you or Alexis is around."

"Your brother's girl?"

"Mhm. Mom spoils y'all."

"I ain't complainin', though. I'll definitely take her up on that."

They held each other closer.

Shortly before Christmas break, Sabryna's life capsized. One of her younger friends, "Tiny", ended up in a fight in the cafeteria with a girl twice her size -- a tall, chunky creature that looked like she should've graduated three years ago. She got there in time to see the huge crowd and could barely make the two of them out. It wasn't until the bigger girl punched Tiny and knocked her to the floor that Sabryna realized who it was. The crowd howled in shock, but rose to a roar as the 4'11" Tiny stood back up with a bruised cheek, determined to go at it again.

The big one swung again, but Tiny slid between her legs and climbed unto her back, punching her in the neck. She was ruling the crowd for a few seconds, until the girl clawed her off her back and flipped her onto hers on the hard floor.

Tiny couldn't get up this time. She tried, but writhed in pain on the floor. "Help..." she croaked. "Somebody help me up. I can't...I can't get up."

"Not so brave now, huh?" the big girl snapped. "My space is mines! Nobody sits in mines!" She moved toward Tiny's helpless body, only to meet Sabryna's scowling face. Sabryna kept walking forward, merely inches from her face, despite being shorter, forcing her to back up. "So you like 'em small, huh?"

"What?"

A swift right punch was Sabryna's answer, knocking the girl to the floor, unconscious. Some of the other kids loomed over her, realizing she was knocked out. Sabryna then knelt beside Tiny, who was still conscious, but in a world of pain. "I'm sorry, Tiny," she whispered to her friend. "I shoulda came in sooner."

All Tiny could do was look up at Sabryna as a solitary tear ran down her face, and smile.

Uncle Gus was already home by the time Sabryna dragged herself in. She looked at the letter in his hand in sheer dismay. She already knew what it said. He silently looked up at her as she hesitantly approached him, which was odd for him -- he always had something to say when she got in trouble. She leaned in the living room entryway, dropping her backpack at her feet. Her eyes silently commanded him to get his lecture over with, but he still said nothing. They simply stared at each other for several minutes.

He finally rose and walked past her into the kitchen. "Your dinner's ready," he murmured. "If you're going anywhere, I suggest you eat first."

"You're allowing me to leave the house? Even with this suspension?"

He turned to face her, wearing the same sad look he had when she first came in. "You're not exactly a homebody, Sabryna. Even if I grounded you, you'd disrespect my authority and sneak out anyway. You do it every night when you break curfew."

Her eyes hit the floor. For the first time ever, she actually regretted her actions. "I was just tryin' to defend my friend. The chick broke her back, I had to do something."

"Did you?" His eyes pierced hers as he calmly spoke. "God is our vindicator, Sabryna. Vengeance is His alone."

Her eyes rolled before she could stop them.

"The fact that the girl broke your friend's back was enough to get her in trouble. There were plenty of witnesses. But now you're both hammered." He sighed to himself as he shared Sabryna's meal on a plate. "At least you were only suspended. She was arrested and expelled."

A chill scraped Sabryna's spine. That would've been her too, if she'd let her anger get the better of her. "Can you do me a favor? Please?"

He stopped what he was doing and looked at her.

"Just...don't...rub my head with oil...or come into the room in the middle of the night talkin' in tongues. Please. That stuff scares me."

He stared at her for several seconds. "I wasn't going to."

"Thank you. And thanks...for dinner." She grabbed her backpack off the floor. "I'll be right back, I'm just puttin' this away and washin' my hands."

Contrary to his expectations, she didn't use the opportunity to disappear. He sat in the living room watching a televised sermon by someone with an unusual and raspy voice -- either a deep-voiced chick or a high-voiced guy. Sabryna peeked over at the TV to see that it was an older woman. "You really love that stuff, huh?" she finally said as she ate.

Uncle Gus almost didn't answer. "Anything having to do with the Word of God, yes."

"You don't listen to nothin' else?"

"Don't need to anymore. I'm happy with this."

"Oh. Thought you was gonna say it's all demonic or somethin'."

"No, not everything is. Some things are amoral, and some things are immoral. Anything that inspires a person to sin is immoral. That's what I'm against."

"That why you and mom disagree so much?"

He hesitated again. "No. Our disagreement is about something far more specific."

"About me."

"And your little sister."

Sabryna stopped eating. Her voice shrank. "My what?"

"Exactly." He turned in the couch to look at her. "She never told you about her, which I think is very unfair."

"Why...why would she do somethin' like that?"

"I don't know, sweetheart," he replied with a heavy sigh.

Sabryna's throat was starting to burn and her eyes were full. "Who is she?"

"Kimberlee. She's five now. Born from a different father." He rose from the chair with his wallet in hand, and pulled out a small portrait of the child. Sabryna wiped her hands clean in her napkin before taking it from him. She immediately spotted the familiar large eyes and wide smile. All of Kimberlee's other physical traits favored the father, including the lighter skin. "Where is she now?"

"Fort Hood. It's why your mother moved down there. I'm guessing she finally wanted to come clean with you, so she invited you to move there with her."

"The dad there, too?"

"Yes. He's an Army Sergeant."

Sabryna could only nod repeatedly as she handed Uncle Gus the picture. No words came. The gravity of her decision to stay was hitting her again, this time with a galling burn in her gut.

She finished her meal with a resolve Uncle Gus had never seen before. "Thanks again for dinner, Uncle Gus," she said as she rose from the table and put her dishes in the sink.

"You're welcome, dear." He glanced at her in amazement as she washed the dishes, which she never did before. "Are you okay?"

"Yeah," she sighed. "Thanks for tellin' me about Kimberlee."

"Sure...But it's bothering you, isn't it?"

"Yeah. But I'll be alright."

That night, since she'd stayed home, Uncle Gus prayed with her and turned in early. She checked her phone: 9:47 p.m.

Mrs. Ellis was putting the finishing touches on supper when the doorbell rang. She opened the door in surprise at the long, wet face before her, with a backpack on her shoulders. "Sabryna? What's wrong? Come in."

Sabryna silently entered, numb as ever, and hugged Mrs. Ellis. "Is it still okay for me to sleep over?"

The hug and weak voice, cracked from screaming or crying, melted Mrs. Ellis' heart. "Of course it is. Come, I'll walk you to the room."

Devaughn leaned in the doorway, watching her unpack a few things, his brow heavy with concern. She finally saw him as she rose. "Oh, hey. Thought you was sleep."

"Too early for that."

"Ten-thirty's too early?"

"These days, yeah. School projects and tests and all that. Senior year ain't no joke."

"Yeah."

"What happened?" he asked after an awkward pause.

"Nothin', just takin' Mama up on her invitation," she said.

"You lyin'," he quickly replied, coming into the room. "Think I don't know what cryin' look like? Your eyes swollen. And you sound like a frog."

She couldn't resist a laugh, but still didn't reply to him.

"You could just say you don't wanna talk about it."

"I don't wanna talk about it. I just want to be with you."

He pulled her into a hug. "Well, here I am."

Christmas Confrontation

Christmas found Sabryna torn. She already had her mind set on dinner with the Ellises, but apparently Uncle Gus had some neighbors from nearby homes coming to his house for dinner too, and she had to at least respect that. No family members flew in, and Sabryna's mother already called that morning wishing her and Uncle Gus Merry Christmas. Sabryna nearly didn't talk to her, but swallowed her pride to do it. It took everything in her not to mention Kimberlee, or ask about Kimberlee 's father. She kept the conversation short, and passed the phone off to Uncle Gus as soon as she was done.

Sabryna washed the dishes so quickly after dinner, Uncle Gus kept watch in case she broke something. "What's the rush?"

"Well...I have another Christmas party to go to."

"Oh." He made no effort to hide the dismay in his voice.

"You can come if you want. It's a Jamaican family. They mad cool."

"Um...thanks, but no thanks," he replied. "I've had enough food and people for one day."

"Okay," she said in a cautioning tone. "But you missin' out on some good grub. They throw down."

"I'll take your word for it," he said with a smile. "Just be safe."

She watched him walk off into his room with slumped shoulders and turn the TV on to watch another televised sermon, keeping the door ajar. Her heart fell to her stomach. It never occurred to her until now just how lonely the man really was. With his wife deceased, Sabryna was all the company he had in the house, and she clearly made him know on a daily basis that she'd rather be elsewhere.

She stood in his doorway and stared at him as he watched the screen, sucked in by the speaker's words. "Uncle Gus."

He flinched back to reality and looked at her. "Oh, hey. What's up?"

"Come with me. Please."

"...Why?"

"What you doin' in this house on Christmas Day by yourself? There's more to life than just watchin' some pastor or apostle or prophet or bishop on TV. Come outta the house with me. You ain't gotta eat if you don't want to, but you gotta get outta here. At least for a while." She gestured to his clothes. "You still in your dinner clothes, anyway. Let's go before you crush 'em up."

He laughed to himself. "If you insist, Sabryna."

She navigated him to the Ellis' house, whose reggae bass could be heard from all the way up the block. The driveway and sidewalk were fully occupied; Uncle Gus had to parallel park across the street. Sabryna rang the doorbell and waited with a small smile, excited to spend the rest of the day at her favorite place. Mrs. Ellis answered the door and lit up; Steel Pulse's music spewing out. "Sabryna! Merry Christmas, darling, how are you?"

Sabryna exchanged pleasantries and introduced her to Uncle Gus, who respectfully shook her hand. "Pleased to meet you, Mrs. Ellis."

"Please, come in."

The house was so full, the atmosphere was actually hot. Jamaican Patois flowed from every room, followed by explosions of laughter. Short, stubby, dark brown beer bottles mobbed the tables, and the plates were a rainbow of bright yellow curry chicken, steamed mixed vegetables, rice and red beans, candied sweet potatoes, potato salad, and jerk pork.

Uncle Gus snuck Sabryna a look. "I'm sold on the food," he said only loud enough for her to hear. "This stuff looks good."

Mrs. Ellis introduced Uncle Gus to her husband, who shook his hand with a look of relief on his face. "Are you her guardian, Mr. Gus?"

"Yes, I am."

"That's good," he said, nodding. "She, uh, never mentioned a father, and we know her mother recently moved."

Uncle Gus looked at her. Her eyes lowered in embarrassment.

"So...we were just curious about who was taking care of her. She's a bright young lady. She's been a big help to my son Devaughn."

"That right?" Uncle Gus was still looking at her.

"Oh yeah. They study all the time, and both have really good grades."

"They better, or else they couldn't be under this roof," Mrs. Ellis added.

The three of them laughed. Sabryna managed a small smile.

"Anyway, Miss Thing, your knight in shining armor's pretty occupied this evening," Mrs. Ellis told her. "The boys' cousins are here, and they're all in Marlon's room playing the Xbox to death."

"That's fine, I can watch," she said.

"You've been warned," Mrs. Ellis replied, gesturing to the hallway. "You know where it is."

Marlon, Devaughn's younger brother, was extremely competitive, and very territorial. He only let Sabryna in his room once during her first tour of the house. She leaned in the doorway, amazed that so many people could squeeze into a single room: there were about fifteen souls in there, all with their backs to her, since the TV was directly opposite the door. Some were sitting on the floor, on the bed, in front of the TV, and the rest were standing.

Her eyes searched the room for Devaughn, who she finally spotted sitting on the floor against the bed, in front of the TV, with an arm around a young girl's shoulders. The two of them were laughing together and cracking jokes on the game players in Patois. She barely understood what they were saying, but it didn't matter. She was already getting mad.

"Oh, good evening." The tall, deep-voiced young man closest to the door greeted her. She admired his dark skin and tight muscle tone. She could see the family resemblance. "I'm Marlon's cousin, Winston," he explained, offering a hand.

"Sabryna," she replied, shaking it.

Devaughn looked around in excitement. "Sabryna, you made it!" He got up, signaling the girl to rise with him, and they both came to the door. "This my cousin Nikki. I been tellin' her all about you."

"Oh, word? Hi, Nikki." Sabryna shook her hand.

"Pleased to meet you," she replied. Her Jamaican English accent was soft and professional. "He said I reminded him of you, or you reminded him of me, or something like that," she said, giving him a playful look.

"How's that?" Sabryna asked, giving him the same look Nikki did.

"Well, you provin' it right now," he replied. "Y'all both lookin' at me crazy."

Sabryna refocused on Nikki. "You must be younger."

"How can you tell?"

"Just a guess. You kinda that baby sister, right? He always standin' up for you and all that?"

Nikki and Devaughn glanced at each other. "Yes," she answered. "I don't have any brothers, so these two decided to adopt me, I guess."

"And we'll kill a man, too," Marlon yelled from inside. Everyone in the room laughed.

"Yeah. I know the feelin'," Sabryna told Nikki. "I'm like that with mines too."

Nikki gave Devaughn another look and removed his arm from around her neck. "I'll leave you guys to it. Nice meeting you, Sabryna." She returned to her spot on the floor.

Devaughn led Sabryna out to the back patio. "That was unnecessary, Sabryna."

The sudden authority in his voice caught her off guard. "What?"

"Nikki's my cousin. She's *family*, not competition."

She glared at him.

"Don't look at me like that. You came to *our* house. You see how happy everybody is? I don't know what kinda day you had, but these are people we ain't seen in years, some of 'em decades. Couple of 'em flew up here from Jamaica to see us, includin' Nikki."

The glare disappeared.

"Look, I'm glad you're here. And I see you brought a date." He nodded to the kitchen, where Uncle Gus and his parents stood talking.

"I had to get him outta the house," she explained.

"Good idea," he said, smiling. "You see he's havin' a good time, too."

Sabryna looked more closely and saw that he was munching from an already half-empty plate and laughing with the Ellises. Mrs. Ellis even called another gentleman over to meet him. "This is us, Sabryna," Devaughn said. "We all about family and havin' a good time. When you ready to do that, you lemme know." He opened the door to head back inside. "No more givin' girls the evil eye, okay?"

"Aight," she replied, following him inside.

Mr. Ellis and a relative were having another laugh with Uncle Gus when Mrs. Ellis' cell phone rang. She excused herself and took the call out front. "Hello?"

"Is this Mrs. Venise Ellis?" the female voice on the other end asked.

"Yes, speaking."

"Hi, I'm calling from Plantation General Hospital, ma'am. I tried calling Sabryna Hodges, but got her voicemail and she listed you as her emergency point of contact."

Mrs. Ellis was taken aback. Why didn't she list her uncle Gus? "What's wrong?"

"Well, Sabryna's friend was admitted here last week after suffering a back injury during a fight at school," the lady explained. "The young lady said Sabryna was her best friend and wanted her to be the first to know the news."

Mrs. Ellis covered her mouth in shock at what she heard. "Oh my goodness. I'm so sorry to hear that. I'll let Sabryna know."

"Thank you, ma'am."

Mrs. Ellis re-entered the house as if nothing happened, smiling and laughing as she headed for Marlon's room. Devaughn caught his mother's look from the corner of his eye and she beckoned him. He smooched Sabryna and went to her. "Be right back."

The look on Mrs. Ellis' face spooked Sabryna, so she left the room to snoop on them. Mrs. Ellis brought Devaughn into the kitchen and politely asked their relative to excuse them for a moment while they talk to Gus.

Her voice was low, but Sabryna could make out what she said. "Stick around afterward, Gus," she said with soft concern. "We'll need to talk to Sabryna."

"What's goin' on?"

"Plantation General just called me about a friend of hers."

The men looked at her in shock.

"We'll catch up later about what's going on."

"Why'd they call you?" Mr. Ellis asked.

"Something else we'll need to ask her," she said. "I don't mean to kill the good vibes, though. I just wanted to give all of you the heads up."

Waiting up was no small feat. Sabryna and Gus learned the hard way that Jamaicans party long. The last guest didn't leave until almost 3 a.m. Devaughn delayed the meeting even longer to help his brother clean up. Once he was done, he finally joined everyone in the den. Sabryna was on needles as she watched him sit down.

Naturally, Mrs. Ellis spoke first, and gently. "Why don't you tell us what happened last week, Sabryna."

Uncle Gus took a deep breath. He already knew where this was going.

"Um...my friend Tiny...got into a fight with this big girl..." Sabryna began. "I think she a senior. Anyway, they was in the cafeteria. By the time I got there, the big girl already punched her down, but Tiny was defendin' herself, so I ain't do nothin'. But then..."

Sabryna's eyes started watering. "The chick body slammed her on the floor and broke her back. That's when I stepped in."

"What did you do, sweetheart?" Mrs. Ellis asked.

"Knocked her out. I couldn't just...let her get away with somethin' like that. Tiny..." Her voice began to croak. "Tiny couldn't even get up."

Devaughn slowly rubbed his face with both hands.

"You didn't know about this?" Mrs. Ellis asked him.

"No," he replied at a lower volume than usual. "This my first time hearin' 'bout it."

Sabryna lowered her head. "I'm sorry."

"Anything else happen?" Mrs. Ellis continued.

Sabryna's mouth refused to open for several seconds. "The girl got arrested and expelled. And I, um...I got suspended."

The Ellises collectively inhaled.

"That's why I looked so sad that night," she confessed to Devaughn.

"And you didn't...you didn't think it was a good idea to tell me somethin' like that?"

"I said I didn't want to talk about it at the time," she replied. "It had just happened."

"Okay," Mrs. Ellis softly cut in, eyeing her son. "We know now." She looked back at Sabryna. "I know that's uncomfortable to admit, Sabryna, but I had to ask, because Plantation General Hospital called me tonight. They told me you listed me as an emergency contact."

Uncle Gus frowned in surprise.

"Anyway, they called because your friend -- Tiny -- wanted you to be the first to know that she's paralyzed."

The room fell silent. Sabryna's jaw hung.

"The broken vertebra cut her spine. She can't move from the waist down."

Sabryna buried her face in her hands and cried. Cried for Tiny, kicking herself for not stepping in sooner, cried for embarrassing Devaughn and Uncle Gus, and cried out the pain and betrayal she felt at her mother for starting another family without her.

At first, the others were frozen, wondering who would move to console her first. But the sobs soon gave way to unstoppable wailing, and Uncle Gus finally wrapped his arms around her. Mr. Ellis gave his wife a disapproving look, but she simply eyed her son, who numbly watched Uncle Gus console his grieving girlfriend, in concern.

Fixing Loose Ends

Devaughn stayed with Sabryna until he graduated, but their relationship was never the same after Christmas. He cheated on her with his books and sports, slowly closing himself off from her. Sabryna had never really been rejected by a boyfriend before, so Devaughn's behavior made her a little desperate. They were arguing after school now. Every time she would ask to chill at his house with him, he would give her some new reason why it was a bad idea; and it didn't help that her grades were falling as they fell out of love. She knew the Ellises took school performance very seriously, and they treated her differently too: the already territorial Marlon *really* didn't have any patience for her at this point, and Mr. Ellis was a little sterner with her than he used to be. Only Mrs. Ellis gave her the time of day anymore.

After Devaughn's graduation, the family had another house party, and though Sabryna was glad to be there, she knew she was the extra wheel. During a moment when she and Mrs. Ellis were alone, she asked her if they could chat on the back porch real quick. Mrs. Ellis gave her a weird look, but decided to go with her.

"Do Devaughn hate me or somethin'?"

Mrs. Ellis was taken aback at first. "What? No. Why would you think that?"

"I ain't been here in months, Mrs. Ellis. I used to come here all the time."

"I was wondering about that."

"I always ask Devaughn if I could come here with him on the way home from school, but he turns me away most of the time."

She lowered her eyes in dismay.

"What did I do?"

"I think he..." She sighed heavily and rubbed her brow. "I really hope I'm wrong about this, but I think he feels...kind of...betrayed about what happened on Christmas Day."

Sabryna's stomach fell to her toes. She swallowed hard to recover. "That goes for all y'all, don't it? Marlon don't even talk to me no more, and Mr. Ellis can barely look me in the eye."

"I apologize for Marlon's behavior," she said, clearly offended by Sabryna's blanket statement. "I raised him better than that. As for Mr. Ellis...he's in the same boat as Devaughn. But he just wants what's best for his son. You have to understand that."

What's best for his son... "Devaughn already made that choice," Sabryna replied, totally dejected. "Thank you, Mrs. Ellis. Just...tell Devaughn to enjoy the gift Uncle Gus and I bought for him. I already told him congrats."

She pocketed her hands and walked away from Mrs. Ellis, headed around the side of the house. "Wait," Mrs. Ellis called, "How will you get home?"

"The same way I always do, ma'am. Catch the bus."

"At least show some good manners and tell Devaughn goodbye in person."

"He don't want nothin' to do with me, Mrs. Ellis," her sadness was quickly transforming into anger, and it was already showing in her voice.

"Ever thought to ask me?"

The ladies looked at the patio door in surprise. Sabryna's look melted into disgust. "What do you think I was tryin' to do, Devaughn? How many times you lied your way outta bein' with me instead of just tellin *me* the truth? You think I betrayed *you*? I never once lied to you!"

He looked at her in surprise, then glanced at his mother.

"My friend's a cripple now, and I got suspended for defendin' her, which is the same thing you and Marlon would do for lil' Nikki, but I'm the one who gets dirty looks now and brushed off everybody's shoulders just because I didn't jump right up and tell you the night it happened. Really?"

"That's enough," Mrs. Ellis said with firm finality. "I don't tolerate any disrespect in my house, Sabryna. Either calm down, or say your goodbye and go."

"Hold on, Mom," Devaughn said. "We gotta clear somethin' up before she goes." He stepped out onto the patio and slid the door shut behind him, catching his brother and father's looks as he did. "You wanna know the truth, Sabryna? You right. I felt betrayed by that, but not because I felt you lied to me by not telling me the night it happened, but because I honestly didn't think you would do that. Knowin' what you know about my family, and knowin' how long we been together, why would you try somethin' like that?"

So that's what you were really worried about, she wanted to say. "And you couldn't just explain that to me? You had to silently push me away instead? You pretty much dumped me from that night." Before he could fire back, she looked at his mother. "Sorry, Mrs. Ellis. I ain't mean no disrespect. Y'all have a nice day. Good luck, Devaughn."

She pocketed her hands again, shoulders slumped, and left around the side of the house without looking back. She silently cried her eyes out in her bed that night, realizing that was the last time she would ever see that family. Her only real family.

* * * *

With Devaughn gone, Sabryna had no reason to maintain the act anymore, so she stopped going to school altogether. She knew she wanted to be a hairdresser though, and started attending cosmetology school using the money she'd saved up from her various birthday and Christmas cards from her mother and Uncle Gus, and the monthly allowance her mother electronically deposited into her account. She stayed gone all day and would tell Uncle Gus her homework was already done when he asked her about it.

Though the cafeteria fight caused the silent breakup between her and Devaughn, and perhaps even in spite of him, she never abandoned Tiny. She cheered her homegirl on and helped her with any schoolwork she could, and in turn Tiny would catch her up with the school gossip and what she was learning in class, despite her disappointment in Sabryna's choice to drop out.

Sabryna's loyalty paid off. Two months into her cosmetology studies, Tiny scheduled an afternoon meet-up and texted Sabryna the address. Sabryna did the search on Google Maps to get the directions and her jaw fell when she arrived -- Tiny had led her to her hairdresser.

Sabryna stepped inside, careful to wear her confidence mask with all the pride and drive she used to win Devaughn in the first place. Tiny's stylist, Shai, was a man almost as petite as she was, standing at five feet and four inches, and slim as ever. Tiny introduced the two and explained Sabryna's studies. "So you wanna intern," Shai said with a smile. "If it's a paid internship, yes," Sabryna replied, grinning back.

Shai narrowed his eyes at her for a split second, but smiled again. "Well, as you can see, my shop's still kinda new, which means my funds are short, so I tell you what. If you ain't too proud to start on a unpaid basis, then work your way to paid, then I'm cool with that too."

Sabryna shook his hand. "Deal."

A handsome caramel brother with long limbs and suckable lips knocked at the open door. "Can I take your lunch order, Shai?"

"How many times I done told you there's no soliciting in my shop, Benji?"

Sabryna's eyes met his for a second, and a smirk surfaced as she scoped the rest of him.

"Am I sellin' somethin'?" he replied to Shai with a smile. "I'm offerin' to get your lunch for you."

"Yeah, from *your* restaurant."

"Technically my aunt's restaurant, but who's checkin', right?"

"Mhm. Well, the answer's no. You can't take my order. Maybe one of these ladies want somethin'."

"Oh no, I'm good," Tiny said. "I ordered the last time I was here anyway."

Benji finally looked over at Sabryna. "You wanna order somethin', Miss?"

"When your shift end?" she asked as she studied his face and curly black hair.

"Six-thirty."

"I'll come see you when I'm done here." The devious smirk resurfaced.

Tiny and Shai stole a glance at each other as the pair said goodbye.

Sabryna took the world by storm. By the end of her first two months under Shai's wing, Sabryna was earning good money. From the *customers*. Shai never even needed to pay her for the internship; he handed off the more basic styling customers to her and let her collect their payments. Sabryna styled both women and men with equal confidence and skill, which was a relief, considering she chose to quit cosmetology school, too. Though the shop policy was for the three stylists to give Shai forty percent of their take, Sabryna gave him fifty percent, which blew him away.

The salon kept Sabryna busy all day, which kept Uncle Gus off her back, but a deep chill ran down it as her mind nagged her of the truth she was running from: since he thinks she's still in high school, he's still looking forward to attending her graduation.

She sprung into immediate action, requesting to skip her lunch breaks and instead leave work an hour earlier, which allowed her time to go to the library to study for two hours. Tiny even managed to give her parents a good excuse to leave the house that late in the evening to help her study. She readied herself relentlessly for the GED exam, researched the nearest location to take the computer-based test, which was in Sheridan, just northeast of Pembroke Pines, and set the date. Since the results were a five-to-ten-day wait, she scheduled her exam for the last week of May. On the day, she took her test and went straight to work as if nothing happened. It was so easy she wondered whether she took the right test.

By the week of graduation, she was ready to face her uncle. She never reversed her arrangement with Shai to skip lunch and instead leave an hour earlier, so she took the opportunity to go home to him. It was a perfect flashback: at the stroke of ten, she entered the house to find him peacefully awaiting her in the plush barely-sat-on couch in the Florida room with his hands clasped together near his face. However, unlike before, Sabryna felt no sinking stomach or fluttering heart. He immediately noticed, silently gesturing to the matching chair across from him. She looked him square in the eye as she sat down. Only then did he move his hands from his face. "Now, I'm not trying to dig deep into your business, Sabryna, but it's pretty obvious that things have been different since your suspension ended."

She remained silent.

"What have you really been up to?"

"You went to the school."

"What did you expect?" He paused in case she would answer, but she chose not to. "Your grades fell steeply before you dropped out, but you're always gone all day and felt the need to lie to me. But that's not even what bothers me most." He pulled his smartphone out, cued something up on the screen, then held it up to her.

The screen showed Sabryna's bank account transaction history. Her guts finally twisted at the sight of her daily three-figure deposits. Uncle Gus's voice was still calm. "I'll ask again. What have you really been up to?"

She held up a halting finger and dug into her backpack, pulling out a small black sack. Uncle Gus's face tensed. "Relax, Uncle," she said. She opened the sack, holding out a pair of small hair clippers and a straight razor for him to see. He reclined in his seat and exhaled in relief. "Shame on you for expecting the worst," she murmured as she repacked the sack.

"I didn't judge you, Sabryna," he corrected. "I asked the open question to give you the choice to explain yourself."

"What *were* you assuming?" she pushed.

"I was fearful, yes," he admitted. "I saw the money in the account, and the usual ideas sprang up. But I shot them down every time, reminding myself you were always protected."

"Still didn't answer my question--"

"Neither did you, and I asked first. The shears don't explain everything."

"Actually, they do." The anger was seeping into her voice. "Remember Tiny? The girl you and the Ellises silently called me stupid for standing up for?"

"We didn't--"

"They shut me out for defending the only friend I have left." She held the sack in the air. "She led me to this job, Uncle. She hooked me up with her stylist, he hired me, and I've been hustling there ever since."

"What was the big payout from your account?"

"Beauty school. Dropped outta that too, once I caught on at work."

Uncle Gus fell into an amazed silence.

"Trust me, I knew what I was doin'. I knew you'd be upset about me droppin' out, but I already handled my business." She put the sack in the backpack, pulled out a folder, and handed him a stack of crisp white papers. He read the documents with a puzzled look.

"I know enough about this place to know that if I'm not in school, I need a job, and the only way I can have one is to either have a diploma...or that." She pointed to the documents in his hand.

"But...why didn't you just finish school and save yourself some money and time?"

She released a heavy sigh and looked him in the eye, but said nothing. She knew he wouldn't like the answer.

"Come on, Sabryna. You might as well level with me. Now that you've obviously jumped headfirst into adulthood, I don't know when or if I'll ever see you again after we have this conversation."

It was her turn to fall into a stunned silence. She was feeling the weight of her choices again. This man had a knack for acting convincingly ignorant, despite knowing the truth, and these little heavy moments were getting on her nerves. Why didn't he just confront her sooner, then? "You right," she quietly confessed. "I don't know, neither."

His face fell.

"Figured you'd be glad," she said. "You gettin' your freedom back."

"You never took it from me, Sabryna," he fired back. "I enjoy having you here--"

"Anyway, I'm aight. I make good money *legally*, and I ain't doin' nothin' stupid."

He let out a heavy sigh as he handed her the papers in an effort to fight back tears. His voice was much lower. "Yeah.

Thanks for at least covering your tracks. Congratulations on the job. We could've celebrated that."

She looked up at him and realized he was being sincere about his offer.

"And for the record, I never thought what you did for Tiny was stupid. I don't think the Ellises did, either. But it was a bad decision, and you know it. I'm glad she was able to help you get this job, but I think she would've even if you hadn't defended her."

"Actually, maybe not."

"Why?"

Sabryna hesitated, realizing the corner she just put herself in. "She only helped me out because she knew I dropped out. She was the only one who even cared, the only one who even reached out to me." Her eyes lowered to the floor.

"Are you tellin' me..." Uncle Gus's voice was suddenly trembling with restraint. "You're tellin' me the only reason you left school was because of that boy? Because he dumped you?"

"You noticed he dumped me that night too, huh?" she replied with a bitter smile. "He didn't seem to notice. His mom even tried to deny it. But in his defense...he was the only reason I bothered trying."

His face crumpled. "What? You hung your whole education, your whole future, on one boy? Who left you over a fight?"

"I did what I had to do," she replied, stonefaced. "He's outta the picture now, and I moved on. You should, too. Just know that I'm good." She got up from the chair and started for her room.

"Sabryna...wait."

She turned to him with an annoyed look, which melted away as he approached her. In the growing light of her room, she saw up close the damage she'd done to this man: his brow was wrinkled in more ways than was natural for his narrow forehead; his previously full and relaxed lips were pursed thin and trembling as his deep black eyes, twisted in pain, threatened tears. "I'll probably never get this chance again. Just...come here." He pulled her into a hug. "Maybe this is where I went wrong," he whispered.

Her eyes widened as another weighty truth hit her. She simply held him tighter.

The Ghost of Christmas Past

Sabryna was making a killing at the salon now. That late night conversation with Uncle Gus set her free -- no more lies, no more strict assumptions from him, no more curfew. Since she was behaving as an adult and had a good paying job, he treated her as one. She was the first stylist to show up, and closed the shop with Shai.

One afternoon Sabryna was restocking the display case at the rear of the shop with a new batch of hair care products with her back to the door. She suddenly heard Shai laughing with a very familiar woman's voice, and it wasn't Tiny's. It was deep, sultry, professional.

Jamaican.

Sabryna froze for a moment, then slowly stole a glance from her eye corner. Heat exploded throughout her body; she immediately turned back around to her work and continued stocking the shelves. "Oh, you're only getting a hair wash? Cool, I'll have my girl do that for you," she heard Shai say, sending a chill down her spine. "She'll have you outta here in less than half an hour."

She quickly finished stocking. By the time she was ready to work, her customer was reclined in the chair, her long thick black crown already in the sink. The almond eyes slid over to her. "Be gentle with me, Sabryna," Mrs. Ellis said with a smile. "My hair is rather demanding."

Sabryna gave her hair one thoughtful look and laid out the supplies she would use. "Wow," Mrs. Ellis said as she watched her. "That's exactly what I use at home. How'd you know?"

Sabryna opened the tap and got to work hosing her hair down. "Months of practice. We got a few clients who rock natural hair."

"How long have you been working here?"

"Five months now."

She hesitated. "You were working here while you were in school?"

"Mhm."

Mrs. Ellis went quiet.

"How's the family?" Sabryna's question fell cold.

"Everyone's alright. Marlon's a junior now and Devaughn just started college--"

"And Mr. Ellis?"

A pause. "He's the same. Still working ungodly hours. Stressed out."

Sabryna massaged the 5-minute leave-in treatment into her scalp. Mrs. Ellis took a deep breath and closed her eyes, smiling. "You have gentle hands indeed, Sabryna. This feels great, thank you."

"Don't thank me yet."

Mrs. Ellis's thought was shattered before it could escape her lips. "Mrs. Ellis, it's been a minute! Where you disappeared to?" Her eyes moved to the lively young man drawing closer to her, whose mustache and beard were neatly rounded out; his sideburns tapered to perfect points just below the ears. "Well, you have Shai to blame for that, Benjamin," she replied, laughing. "The hair care products he sold me do a great job."

Benji stole a smirking glance at Sabryna. Her eyes caught his immediately. "Nice shave. You look sharp."

"Yeah. I got a good barber."

Mrs. Ellis' eyes bounced between them, but she said nothing.

Despite Sabryna and Shai's jeers, Benji got an order from Mrs. Ellis. She gave Sabryna a curious look as he left. Sabryna wrapped her hair in a towel and led her to the hair dryers. "I don't know what was going through your mind the day you left, Sabryna," she said softly after she sat down. "But I want you to know my offer is still open."

"How? Your family can't stand me."

"You're wrong," she replied with a chuckle. "They were upset with what happened, but they've moved on."

" 'Til I show up on your doorstep." She lowered the dryer dome over Mrs. Ellis's head and reached over to turn the machine on.

Mrs. Ellis stopped her hand. "You can choose to believe me or not. But I just wanted to tell you that."

"Tell 'em I said what's up," she replied as she finally started the dryer. "You'll be done and outta here in fifteen."

Shortly before Mrs. Ellis left, Sabryna spied her talking privately with Shai as they both fiddled with their cell phones. Shai stole a glance at Sabryna.

Marlon's eyes rolled. His father arrived and his first words were a complaint. The longer shifts made him less loveable, and this faultfinding became the new norm. Thankfully Mrs. Ellis had no patience for the petty foolishness and called him on it. Her replies were always a relief to him, especially in his brother's absence. Devaughn was always the stern voice of reason for the family. He finally finished his homework and jumped on the Xbox 360, not even bothering to leave his room to greet his father.

The doorbell rang. Marlon didn't think twice about it since his mother usually answered it, but they were still bickering, and the bell was on its third ring. He slammed his controller on the floor and went to the door with a mouthful of venom ready.

But the guest forced Marlon's jaw shut.

The two stared at each other for several seconds. "Hello, Marlon," Sabryna said firmly. His jaw contracted several times before allowing him to speak. "What's up, Sabryna."

Mrs. Ellis's head suddenly poked out from behind the center hallway wall. "Sabryna! Hey!" Marlon glanced over his shoulder at his mother before finally opening the door wide enough to let her in. She kept her eyes on his as she entered. He locked the door and returned to his room without another word.

Sabryna met her next wall in Mr. Ellis, but she tore it down by trimming his facial hair and cleaning up his hairline. Marlon looked on from afar, waiting for a mistake that never came. She had another happy customer under her belt and earned her stay.

On to the Next

Sabryna barely began her second year at the salon and things went south. She was grooming Benji's hair first thing in the morning as usual when a disgustingly perfect sister with freshly bleached skin stormed in bathed in expensive perfume, name brand clothes, and two heads of hair. Sabryna's head snapped to her, her eyes alight. "So it's you," the girl snapped.

"What about me?" Sabryna was already popping her neck, her straight razor nestled in the hand on her hip.

The girl lifted Benji out of the chair by his arm. "We leavin'."

"No he ain't," Sabryna snapped back. "You crazy? You really want him walkin' the streets with his head half-cut? How dumb is that?"

"I don't give a damn 'bout that!"

" 'Course not, your dumb ass ain't the one gettin' the haircut! I know you wouldn't walk outta no salon with your weave half-done."

The girl spewed an f-bomb and called her a name she hadn't heard since middle school. Sabryna's hand gripped the straight razor more tightly, and the hand slowly moved off her hip. Benji caught it. "Ayo, Sabryna...chill. It's aight."

"Oh, you wanna stab me?!" The girl pushed past Benji's protective arm and got in Sabryna's face. "I wish you would!"

Sabryna shook her head and dropped the razor on the floor.

"Thought so."

With only a smirk for warning, Sabryna grabbed the girl's hair and yanked her neck back. The girl was suddenly a wounded beast, flailing and grunting in shrill, whiny tones. Sabryna spun her body around to face Benji. "You settled for this?"

Benji's eyes softened. "Let her go, man. She think we got somethin' goin' on, she don't know no better. She jealous of every girl I know, don't worry 'bout it. Just let her go."

The door slowly opened, as did Shai's jaw. "What the hell is goin' on in here?!"

Sabryna shoved the girl toward Benji. She carried on like a baby sibling caught stealing. "It was her! What kinda people you got workin' in your shop, Shai? You just lettin' any ol' thang in here!"

"Stop it, Katiya," he said firmly. His eyes bounced to Sabryna. "You gonna answer my question?"

Sabryna stole a glance at Benji, whose eyes were still pleading with her. "Your girl bust up in here ready to fight 'cause she saw me cuttin' Benji's hair."

"You cuttin' more than that!"

"That's what this is about?" Shai demanded in disgust. "Go take a walk, Katiya. You don't see me 'til noon. Benji, you get out too. Now."

Benji left the shop with his tail between his legs. He didn't even bother to take his girlfriend with him. Katiya gave

Sabryna the evil eye as she left. "You need to watch your people, Shai. Bitch almost cut me with that razor."

Shai looked at Sabryna in disbelief once Katiya left. "Are you crazy?"

"I ain't stupid, Shai," she replied. "I wouldn't cut her."

"That doesn't matter. If she goes to the cops with that, I'm screwed, Sabryna."

"She won't."

"You don't know her like I do. She might. I barely opened this shop by the skin of my teeth, it's only two years old. I can't afford the risk."

Sabryna's jaw fell as reality hit her. "You gettin' rid of me?"

"I don't have a choice."

"This the first time this happened, and you shook already?"

"You weren't listening." He shook his head with a smile. "But yes. I'm lettin' you go. I'm grateful for the work you've been doing, but you gotta go."

Sabryna didn't hide her disgust as she cleaned her area and packed her things. She walked right past him as she left. No eye contact, no goodbye, no "thank you", no nothing.

Her solo journey was short-lived, though. On her way to the bus stop from the convenience store the very next day, a black '98 Honda Accord pulled up to her and slowly rolled, the dark-skinned driver hissing after her. She looked over, ready to cuss him for stalking her, until she saw his face. "Oh, what's up?"

His half-Indian eyes undressed her. "You tell me."

Another Caribbean man. His accent sounded Trinidadian.

"You only came by the shop one time. What happened, you ain't like the cut I gave you?"

"I did. That's why I'm back." A smile peeked two gold teeth. "Get in. I can take you where you need to go."

She got in without a second thought.

Landscaper and moonlighting deejay Keyshawn Francis stole her heart and body with ease. She hung on his every word. She savored every sweaty encounter, staring at the wall, ceiling, or window, imagining Devaughn's disappointed face as Keyshawn amorously stabbed her. A smile would spread across her face with each shove; she let her noises out with abandon, forcing her would-be onlooker to hear her full pleasure. In her mind it was the sweetest vengeance, especially since momma's boy Devaughn never let her truly have him.

Sabryna celebrated her twenty-first birthday pregnant. Keyshawn promised her more where that came from, despite already having five kids with three different women. The two toddlers he had custody of were already warming up to Sabryna and calling her "mommy". She was beyond excited, exalting Keyshawn as a great father.

Except that she could never ask him about the other three. He would always become Mr. Hyde and start throwing hands -- with or without the kids present.

When people asked, she just lied and told them she didn't know who the daddy was, and instead said she went to a party and had a train run on her by four guys, so it could be any one of them. She even added that she didn't know their government names or where they live. She just saw them around her cousin's way, and only knew them as Black, Peanut, Fat Boy, and Man Man. The shock on their faces made her day every time. She simply walked away confident as ever, knowing that her boo loved her and she madly loved him. He was the first guy who could get her pregnant, and that was all that mattered to her.

Though she didn't work at the shop anymore, she would stop by when Tiny told her she was there. During her visits, Sabryna caught wind of rumors that Keyshawn had another baby mother after her.

She was bold enough to go to the restaurant. Benji was disappointed to see her pregnant, but he echoed the rumor. "How you know?" she asked.

"Dude deejays," he said with a shrug. "I seen him with her at a couple parties."

"I don't believe that. I can't."

He answered her with a cautious look.

"He always with me. That's impossible."

"Why you with him anyway?"

"What you care? You still datin' weave chicks, ain't it?"

"Nah. I dumped that one after what happened at the shop. I'm single now. Anyway, I'm just askin' 'cause he a dog. Treat shorties like dirt."

"You let me worry about that. He don't treat me that way."

"Yet."

"Least I got somebody," she fired with a nasty look and headed for the door.

"Better to be single than illegal."

She turned to face him. "What you mean?"

"Oh, Prince Charming ain't told you? He been here for like four years now, with no green card."

"How you even know all that?"

"He come in here sometimes. He and my aunt mad cool, so he told her."

His words stayed with her after she left. She shoved them to the back of her mind, but they never went away.

The rumors started to sting when she gave birth. He wasn't there at all that day. When she was able to call him, he apologized and said he had to take his son to a doctor's appointment.

When he finally came to see her and his newborn daughter, he had so many flowers she forgot about him not being there and even forgot about the rumors. In her mind, he was the best thing that ever happened to her.

She finally collided with the truth two months later. Uncle Gus wasn't pleased with the relationship or unplanned pregnancy, but he embraced little Simone and babysat her from time to time. She caught the bus one Friday afternoon to drop Simone off with him, and as the bus passed the Aurora Boulevard and 5th Avenue intersection, she spotted Keyshawn walking hand-in-hand with a tall brown woman who was either mixed or Indian. She didn't look black. The two of them turned to walk towards a record store and that's when she saw the bump.

She made sure Keyshawn saw her upset when he came to pick her up from Uncle Gus's place. "What's wrong with you?" he asked as she plopped herself in the seat and slammed the door. His voice sounded innocent, which only angered her more. "What's wrong with *you*? How you walkin' the streets with your new baby momma and then got the nerve to act all innocent with me?"

He calmly laughed. "Wow..."

She gave him an ugly look.

"Did you get a good look at her?"

"Yeah."

"What does she look like?"

"She look Indian."

"Exactly. She's Trini like me. That's my cousin Karen Covington."

"...Covington..."

"Just like we named Simone, remember we talked about that? Covington's my birth name."

She looked away. "Who the daddy, then? Ain't she supposed to be married? Indian girls don't get down like that."

"Unlike me, she was born here," he chuckled. "Don't assume anything about her culture. And I don't know who the father is."

She thought carefully before she spoke again. "You deejayin' tonight?"

"Mhm."

"You mind if I sleep over?"

"I guess you can. I dropped the kids off at their grandparents for the weekend, so you'll actually sleep."

"What time's your gig?"

"Eleven-thirty. Late night pool party."

"Hm. So you'll be gone long, then."

"Won't get back 'til maybe three of four in the morning. Thank God I'm off tomorrow."

In her usual take-action fashion, she made a beeline for his room once he left. She searched the place top to bottom to spy his Trinidadian passport amid his private files. She entered his closet and found it had a small door in its ceiling similar to an attic door, minus the string. She carefully pushed against it, and it lifted. She slid it to one side and popped her head in the cramped space, then crept high enough to freely move her arms about. She finally found the thing in a glutted manila folder sandwiched between old, stained papers. She pulled it down and opened it, and her blood scurried away from her face as she read the name inside the cover next to his face: Ravi Keyshawn Patel. No Covington anywhere. She flipped through to the Visa pages at the back, and the most recent stamp was made on October 25. Four years ago.

All the rumors she'd heard came crashing down on her. Whose name did she just give her child? Did she just name Simone after another woman?

3

Corporate Boy and I are sitting in the car in front of the home with the engine running and our to-go boxes empty. Sabryna's story took him that long to tell. And yet... "I thought you said she met me before."

"She did. Let me finish."

"The story still ain't done?"

"Well, we're at the tail end of it. After she found out what happened, she took off. Never told her uncle or anything, and never talked to the little girl's father again. She ended up at an apostolic church shelter soon after."

My jaw drops.

"She said there was a girl there that took sharing the Gospel too seriously. Wouldn't shut up about it, according to her. So one night, she flew off the handle, grabbed the girl's Bible, and clocked her in the nose with the spine."

The little girl's face flashes in my mind, and my blood suddenly flares.

"She smacked her with the broad side a couple times and then tore it up. That's when she saw you walk in with the elder." He looks over at me. "Apparently you guys crossed paths a lot while you were there. Gave each other dirty looks. She knew you felt a certain way about what she'd done to the girl, and she was waiting for you to start something, but you never did. Thankfully."

My jaw locks on me as I stare ahead at the building. I don't remember seeing any mohawks in this home, but she might've grown her hair out. I dare her to step to me now, though. She'll get her chance to see me start something. "What about her daughter?"

He shook his head. "Still no contact."

Deadbeat. Just like my mom. Girls like her need to be shot in the head. Several times.

I get inside and find a war zone. Diana's huddled over a dark-skinned woman hugging her knees on the floor, pouting like a child, with two girls off to the side sulking at her with bloodied faces -- one got popped in the eye, the other in the mouth. Several other girls have formed a circle around them all, as usual, whispering and cackling like the shallow dummies they are. People love watching people hurt each other. Makes me sick.

I'm instantly reminded of Tawana and start walking toward my room, grilling every face that dares to look at mine. I catch the wild beast's eyes as she spies me over Diana's shoulder and grill her too. The last thing I glimpse before I'm out of view is a house arrest anklet around her left ankle.

Good job, fool. Whatever you did.

About ten minutes later, I get a knock on my door, and it's Diana. Right away I'm cranky 'cause my time with this woman is done. Plus she's interrupting my chess game, which I pause. "What you want?"

"To invite you to tomorrow's business course. It starts at seven in the cafeteria. You just barely missed tonight's class."

"You teachin' it?"

"No, but I give a few pointers about getting into the business world from Section 8."

"You talkin' like you was on it."

"I was. For a short while."

Playin' that nice card again, I see. "Not interested."

She gives me a digging look, but nods. "Okay, but you'll be missing out on some valuable info. All the other girls attend."

"Exactly."

"No one improves their own lives alone, Leila. We were made to help each other."

"That's a lie," I chuckle. "Ain't nobody helpin' me."

"Because you won't let them. There's a difference between being offered help and wanting to be helped. If you don't want the help, don't complain." Before I can snap back at her, she leaves.

Against my better judgment, I go to the class. Diana wasn't joking -- the place was packed. My eyes start looking through the audience for Sabryna, but I can't see her yet. My little shadow nods me over to a bench at her left that had enough space for maybe two more butts. Unlike the other girls, I sit with my back to the table, not caring to look at any of them. The brown chick to my left glances at me from the corner of her eye, and I realize it's her.

Sabryna. With permed, shoulder-length, brownish-black hair.

Both our jaws tense as we stare at each other. My first impulse is to slide over a little to get away from her, but screw that. I ain't weak or scared. I dare her to try something.

The instructor starts the class, which is apparently about debate and public speaking skills.

Really? Boring.

Anyway, I sit through the whole lecture, letting everything go in one ear and out the other. Many of the girls are writing away, hanging on the instructor's every word.

"Now, we're gonna set up a live debate here as an example," she says. "Mandisa, why don't you come on up?"

"For what?" the deep voice demands near the front of the room. "I ain't got nothin' to say."

"Everyone has something to say," Diana replies from the wall by the door with her arms folded and smiling. "Show us what you've got."

"A whole lotta nothin'. These meds y'all feed me got me numb."

The other girls laugh.

"A numb genius is better than a silent fool," the instructor says.

The girls hiss their teeth and roll their eyes, including me. That was a whack compliment, if that's what she was going for.

"Aight, I'll come up there if you promise not to repeat that."

Another round of snickers.

"Thank you." She pauses as Mandisa, the wild house arrest beast from last night, walks up.

"Leila."

My head snaps to the instructor, and I give her the ugliest look.

"Come on up here."

I look over at Diana, who looks equally surprised, though I doubt she really is. I steal one more look at Sabryna as I get up. She's sneering at me, silently hoping I screw this up.

Mandisa's eyes latch onto me like Velcro. If her meds numbed her, they missed her eyes. Those joints are wide and glassy, like she's just waiting for me to breathe on her before pouncing on me. My fists clench on their own and my eyebrows dive to my nose. Is this a setup? Last time I checked, this was a women's home, not a prison.

A stocky female guard suddenly enters the room. Mandisa tenses up even more and shoves her hands in her pockets. She's visibly sweating now.

The instructor clears her throat to break the tension. "Alright, ladies. The topic for debate is whether low-income women have an equal chance at success as low-income men in the business world. Leila, you'll argue for women's success, Mandisa, you'll argue the point against it."

Is she serious?

"You first, Mandisa."

She closes her eyes and takes a deep breath. "I really could care less if women have an equal chance of success."

The room gasps. She then lifts her dark eyes to me again. "Women are freakin' evil. Every last one of 'em."

"A woman ruined your life too, huh?" The words fell from my mouth, causing hushed oohs and whoas across the room. I catch the tender, borderline regretful look on Diana's face.

"Like you wouldn't believe," Mandisa snarls.

MANDISA'S STORY

The unborn baby's kick caused Mandisa to buck. She gave up on reaching for the pesky new shackle choking her left ankle. "I really don't need you yellin' at me too," she said to her belly. "This damn thing ain't my fault." She looked out her window as her supposed husband drove her home from the courthouse. She already knew what was up when they get there, especially since her parents weren't there.

Her mind shifted to their 2-year-old son in the back seat, who mimics him. What kind of kid curses and beats up his mother?

Hers, she reminded herself. *Only* hers. Only she could be so weak. She brought it on herself.

Her husband wasted no time giving little Cody his iPhone as soon as they got to the house. "Daddy got your game all ready to go," he said. "You can play in the room. Just make sure you don't tell Grandma and Grandpa, okay?" Cody smiled and obeyed without a word.

He gripped her arm and pulled her toward the bathroom. "Let's go."

"Ow?"

"Quit bitchin'. This is nothin'."

He shoved her into the bathroom and locked the door behind them. Mandisa's heart slammed to her toes as he pressed her against the wall. She knew this was coming, but she hated it every time. He saw the shift in her face and hardened his. "Am I gonna have to do this the hard way?" She neither replied nor made eye contact with him. He grabbed her face and turned it towards him. "I'm talkin' to you." She still didn't look him in the eye. "Just do what you gotta do," she finally mumbled.

"You damn right I will." He turned her to face the wall.

He yanked her pants down and shoved himself inside her, completely ignoring the child in her womb -- which also belonged to him. She had to brace her arms on the wall to protect the baby from the shock of his thrust.

She was relieved to see him leave fifteen minutes later. She cleaned herself up and emerged from the bathroom. Her son sat on the couch wearing the stern look she came to hate. "I wanna watch TV, but you broke it," he mumbled. His statement nailed her right in the chest. He wouldn't understand what caused her to do what she did. To this day, her parents haven't forgiven her for it, either. "Grandpa will replace it," she replied as she came around to him. "And even if it worked, that's not how you ask for anything."

"I wanna watch TV!"

"Oh well, you can't. What you gonna do 'bout it?"

He jumped up and punched after her, but missed. "Beeetch! It's your fault!"

Before she could stop herself, she caught his punching hand and clutched his throat, shoving him back down into the couch. "You evil little--" she caught herself. "You ain't gotta like me, but you *will* respect me. You a kid, and I'm your *mother*. You not cursin' at me, and you not hittin' me."

His struggling face went pale. His teary terrified eyes aroused the terror in her and she finally released him. "Honey, I'm sorry," came the feeble whisper.

He slapped her hand away. "I hate you!" He ran to the room and slammed the door. His chant continued through the walls. "I hate you! I want my Daddy!"

Mandisa collapsed on the couch and let her tears run, silently kicking herself.

Before she could get too deep into it, her parents returned. She didn't even bother to fix her face. Her mother acknowledged her with a glance, and in her usual fashion, called for Cody. "Grandma!" He ran to greet her with the brightest smile, wrapping himself around her in total bliss. She picked him up in the air and smooched his cheek. Mandisa shot them a sidelong glance and looked away again, feeling like an extra wheel. "Hi, Grandpa," Cody said, adorable as ever. "Hey, kiddo," her father replied, giving him a simple hug. Cody returned to his grandmother, who was now sitting in the loveseat next to the couch, and sat on her lap.

"So you're okay with this too?" her father started, gesturing at the house arrest anklet. "You want to just throw your life away completely?"

"Dad--"

"First you drop outta school, and now this?"

Her eyes impaled him. This was the last thing she wanted to talk about, especially in front of her son. She stole a glance at him as he sat quietly nestled under his grandmother's arm. Her eyes bounced up to her mother, who held them hostage. "Have you scheduled your prenatal appointment?"

Mandisa's eyes fell as a familiar face flashed in her mind -- a woman whose face she prayed she'd never see again.

"What's going on with you?" she said. "Why would you not want to see the doctor about your child?"

She stayed quiet.

"You're teaching your son bad manners right now, in case you don't know," her father murmured. "You might want to answer."

"I'm fine," she muttered. "The baby's fine. He kicks me often enough."

"How do you know it's boy?"

"I don't know. I'm just guessin'."

"Well, if you're not going to school, you have to get a job. We don't keep bums under this roof."

"Honey," her mother softly chided him.

"You want her to just sit here? She still owes us a TV and a window."

She glanced at the broken TV screen in front of her, then the window. Her anger had made her quite strong. She'd tossed the remote hard enough to pierce the screen. The window tattled a long, nasty crack from her rock toss.

"Please, Mandy," her mother said. "Talk to us. You know I'm worried sick about you."

She really was. She was beside herself when the cops had carried Mandisa away, screams and all.

Mandisa reclined herself in the couch, extending her left foot to look at the anklet. "You guys believe the cops, don't you? That I was stalking her?"

"You wouldn't be wearing that, if that wasn't the case," her father said.

"She stalked *me*, Dad," she insisted. "Took photos of me in areas near her. When I would take Cody to his pediatrician." She looked her mother sharply in the eye. "When I would go see my obstetrician."

Her parents glanced at each other, worried for their daughter. "Honey, those photos prove you were following the victim, not the other way around," her mother explained.

Mandisa continued as if her mother never interrupted. "The usual supermarket too. She was the one stalkin' *me*."

"What are you not telling us, Mandisa?" her father pushed.

Mandisa's eyes stabbed him again. "Why you always treat me like a criminal, Dad? Why you can't trust me?"

His head twitched. He slowly sat up and leaned forward, resting his elbows on his knees. "My daughter who was doing very well in school decides to drop out out of nowhere, and doesn't tell us why. Oh, let me go back further than that. My daughter is in youth ministry at church, we're thinking she's receiving the Word of God, and out of nowhere, we find out she's pregnant. And doesn't tell us who the father is until I force it out of her." He tilted his head to force her eyes back on him. "Now ask me again why I can't trust you."

Her throat became a ball of acid as she stared at him with welling eyes. "You wouldn't even understand..."

Her mother's face twisted in despair as she looked over at her husband. She knew something was wrong. Something deep. They knew the truth of the case, but Mandisa kept insisting on her version of the story.

"I would if you would communicate with me," he replied. "You're my only child, Mandisa. My one baby girl. I care about you, but I can't help you when you don't tell me what's wrong and instead lash out and break stuff. *My* stuff. You know what that kind of behavior tells me? That you're mad at *me* about something. Unplanned pregnancy, college dropout...That looks like rebellion."

Mandisa closed her eyes and slowly rubbed them, taking another deep breath. Her mind drifted back to the tipping point -- a mental journey she never wanted to take again.

The professor's freckled face, in all its pale splendor, invaded her mind. Blonde hair and blue eyes. Soft skin, slightly wrinkled from her hourly affair with slim cancer sticks. Thin, supple lips always colored blood red. Lips that always fell away in a bright white smile for Mandisa. Skinny fingers, always nicely manicured with French tips. Fingers that always managed to find their way to Mandisa's hand or arm or back or shoulder.

Maegan O'Reilly. The one professor whose class Mandisa grew tempted to skip. The class itself was useful -- Excel Methodology taught her how to use Microsoft Excel in ways that most laymen wouldn't know, taught her how to master complicated formulae to quickly control and streamline data input. But after every class, Maegan would ask to speak with her privately, always asking her little uncomfortable questions. Whether she's ever made out. Which base she'd made it to. Whether she's ever been with a man before.

Once she saw that Mandisa was still making time for her, she went deeper, asking whether she'd been with a woman before. Whether she enjoyed having sex.

Mandisa was ready to drop the class then, but for her parents' sake -- like everything else in her life -- she chose to continue attending. By then, she made it clear she wasn't interested in talking to Maegan after class, and Maegan clearly picked up on it, so she moved in for the kill. "You're such a beautiful girl, Mandisa. So innocent," she meowed, grazing Mandisa's hand as usual. Her eyes bounced between Mandisa's eyes and lips as a smirk warped her mouth corner. "I really like you. I want...I want to open your mind. Show you some things."

Mandisa panicked. She left the class and never returned. The sight of Maegan's face terrified her. She couldn't bear the thought of seeing her again.

The cotton-thick silence hung between Mandisa and her parents for several minutes. "Did you...did you ever report that?" her mother finally asked. She could always tell when Mandisa flashed back to the incident. She would get quiet and antsy, and grind her teeth.

"The harassment? No."

Her father rolled his eyes in disbelief.

"I was scared, Dad! Scared of what you guys would think of me, scared of what she would do to me, didn't think anybody would *believe* me... I was eighteen, for God's sake!" She got up and walked around to the back of the sofa and leaned forward on it, pointing to him. "That's why I never tell you anything. That right there. You always react like I'm an idiot. Nothin' I do is ever good enough for you. Nothing I do is ever right. You don't even realize I stayed in the class as long as I did for *you*."

"For me."

"I woulda dropped out as soon as she started that nasty mess, but I knew you'd be mad, so I stayed as long as I could."

"It goes back to communication, Mandisa," he said matter-of-factly. "You should've told us something as soon as it happened. We could've helped you. And as soon as her car came here, we would've known it was her and called the police on her."

"It wouldn't matter. The cops woulda came for me anyway. They questioned me about our sexual conversations, so I told them yes, we talked about that stuff. I was trying to come clean, but that's when they pegged *me* as the stalker. She was the one who set it all up, gave them and her lawyer all those pictures of me, then set them on me."

Her mother looked ready to cry. "That's not how it happened--"

"So you see, Dad? Even if you called the cops on her, she woulda had me screwed anyway. She been plannin' this probably since she first started hittin' on me."

Her father simply played along. "So is this how you ended up pregnant?"

She gave him an outraged look.

"I mean, you had no place else to go after the harassment, which Professor O'Reilly denied in court, by the way. You didn't tell us, didn't report it, stopped going. We never saw you cry or anything. You had to have some kind of outlet. Was DeAndrae it?"

"No, Dad," she said, her voice heavy with disgust. "My pregnancy had nothing to do with that."

"I'm just trying to understand--"

"Life ain't that black and white, Dad! This bitch was set on me. If she didn't get me, she'd bring me down. Why me, I don't know. There's no explanation for that."

"And DeAndrae?"

She looked away and sighed. "There's no explanation for that, either. We've known each other since you first forced me to join the youth ministry."

"I didn't force you--"

"You didn't?! You didn't accuse me of being young and not knowing anything or not knowing any better? You didn't make me go because you couldn't trust me to be home alone? That I would invite some friends over and have a party while you guys were gone? That we would get drunk and do something stupid? You didn't say those things when I turned thirteen? I didn't even have any friends!"

He was about to bark back, but her mother gripped his hand hard. He looked at her in shock, but her sullen eyes told him all he needed to know. He relaxed himself.

"On that note," her mother calmly said, "you should come to church with us."

"For what?"

"For your son's sake. For your soul's sake. I still think somebody worked some kind of voodoo on you. You're going nuts. Always so quick to get mad now, so destructive, so...you're all over the place. You're not the child I remember."

"People change, Mom. And if you got set up by some creepy lesbo, you'd be pissed too. And don't even--" She took a deep breath to catch herself. Maegan was a big enough can of worms to spring on them. They wouldn't be able to handle the truth about DeAndrae.

"What?"

"Nothin'. I'm done stressin'. It ain't good for the baby." She glared at her father. "You got what you wanted outta me." She headed to her room.

Return to the Background

Mandisa hated church. Hated the coloring book the old women's dresses created, the obnoxious largeness of their hats. Hated their fake smiles as they shook her hand and said the same old "Good mornin' sista, God bless you." Hated the everlasting repetition of each song. Hated the pastor's yelling. Hated the constant sitting down and standing up.

She looked at her son next to her, who was leaning on his grandmother's arm. She resigned herself to the truth: Cody knew who his mother was, but he'd found his true mother.

Her demeanor fell.

Her eyes returned to the pastor, but they glazed over, and he blurred. All she could see was the altar itself, with her and DeAndrae standing there. Cody, not due for another four months, deformed her dress. She looked around her with those glazed eyes to find an empty church. Her parents were their only audience. Her father's eyes scolded her as she stood at the altar. It was his idea anyway. He wasn't about to have an unwed pregnant daughter. This was to be their punishment for their irresponsible behavior.

"Mandy." Her mother's whisper brought her back to reality. She followed her mother's glance behind them and spotted DeAndrae three rows back. He fired a wink. She simply turned back around and nudged her son to look back there. He gave an animated wave with a smile brighter than any light in the room.

The pastor made an altar call, inviting people to receive salvation and prayer. Her parents looked back at her as they took Cody up front. She simply stared at them.

DeAndrae snuck around to the seat next to her since its previous owner left during the altar call. Her father caught him and eyed him coldly, nodded for him to step forward. Much to Mandisa's surprise, he obeyed. The entire group looked back at her once more, spiking her blood pressure. She got up and stormed out.

She leaned against her parents' car sulking with folded arms. The ground crackled in the distance as a car slowly approached. She lifted her eyes and saw the evil chariot -- the white Cadillac CTS coupe rolled past her. Maegan was never this bold before. Their eyes met, but Mandisa's look was altogether different now. Her eyes told of certain torture, dared

Maegan to stop and step out of the car for even a minute. After Maegan passed, Mandisa took out her phone and snapped a shot of the car with the camera. Even the license plate was clear.

The Second One

Mandisa's obstetrician let her have it for waiting this long to come see her. She warned her that at five months along she might have missed any chance of early detection for any infant health issues.

The doctor checked her belly and hesitated at a large greenish spot to the left of her belly button. "What happened here?"

Mandisa sighed. "I hit a wall."

The doctor gave a hesitant look. "Were you pushed?"

"...Yes and no."

Her eyebrows jumped.

"My husband... We were having sex against a wall. He...he likes it rough."

She didn't push any further. She ran the ultrasound and completed the necessary tests. Things appeared to be okay, and she cleared her. "Don't wait so long to see me again, Mandisa. Especially considering..."

Mandisa stared her in the eye.

"Look, just... If you get hurt, get help. For your daughter's sake."

Mandisa's stare changed to slight shock.

"Call somebody. Call me if you have to. Please."

Mandisa flung her hood over her head and left the room without saying goodbye.

She quickly got in her husband's car scowling hard. He made a U-turn to leave, and sure enough, the blasted Cadillac was parked on the next block. "Wait, slow down a second."

"Since when you tell me what to do?"

"DeAndrae. Seriously."

He slammed the brake to spite her. She shot him a nasty look but didn't let his pettiness stop her from taking the shot she needed with her phone. "Done."

"What's that for?"

"Bitch has been stalkin' me since I dropped outta school."

DeAndrae spotted a stocky man in the driver's seat of the car she photographed, but said nothing, instead laughing to himself. "What you do?"

She looked at him in disbelief. "You think I did something to deserve that? She sexually harassed me!"

"Wow."

"Oh, but I deserved it, right? Ass."

His slap rang in her ear for several seconds. Her cheek went numb. "You musta forgot who you were talkin' to," he snapped.

"No, I just stopped caring."

He smacked her again.

"Some Christian you are," she murmured to herself, laughing.

He swung at her belly, but she caught his arm. He instead slapped the center of her face with his free hand.

"Beat me all you want to, but you ain't beatin' your daughter." She shoved his hand away from her stomach.

He finally let up. "So it's a girl."

She looked out her window.

"You so miserable, yo. You supposed to be happy 'bout that. And that's your problem. You always been like that. Always tight. So damn frustratin'."

"You don't live with me, so you don't know," she replied. "The fact that you ain't even allowed at the crib should be a hint-and-a-half."

"You Daddy's little girl, that's all."

"More like Daddy's little pitbull on a chain leash."

"So what's wrong with havin' a girl?"

"Nothin'. I just thought it was gonna be another boy."

"Why? Ain't one good enough?"

"Cody's yours."

"What that mean?"

"Means he's yours."

She could feel his stare as he drove, but she kept her eyes on the scenery through her window.

* * * *

Mandisa's daughter showed no mercy. She sent her into labor only nine weeks later. Her parents rushed her to the hospital. Thirty-six hours of labor later, the little one was finally born, and the doctors had to take her immediately. While Mandisa found that strange, she didn't argue with the worried look on their faces. They clearly knew something she didn't.

"Mandisa, your baby's excretory system -- her urinary tract -- is slightly underdeveloped," her obstetrician had told her a week before the birth. "And her kidneys are uneven."

The words went in one ear and out the other. Only her son's vulgar screams filled her ear. "No!" "Beeetch!" "I want Grandma!" "Liar!" "I hate you!"

"Mandisa..." Her doctor sensed her distraction and reached for her chin.

She clutched her wrist with wide eyes. "What you doin'?"

"Ow!"

"Do your job and nothin' else," Mandisa said. "Your hands ain't supposed to be nowhere near my face."

"Sorry! Just...let me go!"

She released her hand and quickly dressed.

"I was just trying to get your attention. You weren't listening to me."

"Then say my name."

"I did."

"Yell it next time."

"Did you hear what I said before?"

"Somethin' wrong with her urinary tract, right?"

A heavy sigh. "Yes."

"That all?"

The doctor looked at her in disbelief. "Yes. That's all."

Fetal hydronephrosis. It all sounded like garbled syllables when the doctors were explaining it to her the day after the birth. They had to repeat it at least three times for her to get it. The more specific condition was ureteropelvic junction obstruction, or UPJ. "Your daughter's left kidney is larger than her right," one doctor explained, "which led to a slight blockage in the left ureter tubes -- it basically makes it more difficult for the left kidney to send waste to her bladder."

"So...what does that mean? I mean, what's gonna happen to her?"

"Well, we're examining her for now," he said, "and if it's mild, then we'll send her home with some amoxicillin. It's an antibiotic. If it's something a bit more serious, then you'll need to take her to a specialist regularly to monitor her progress."

"Worst case scenario?"

"Well, worst case, she'll need to be on dialysis or have a kidney transplant."

The words sucked the air out of the room. Mandisa couldn't think.

"But that's worst case," he assured her. "We're keeping an eye on her, and from what we've seen so far, her condition isn't severe."

Sheltered

Within days of her return from the hospital, Mandisa got a knock on the door. She opened it to find a stout young Black woman in business casual wear with a clipboard in her hand. Her jet black weave looked ready to fall off her head thanks to her growing roots. "Mandisa Burrell?"

Mandisa wanted to slam the door in her face. "Yes."

"Brittney." She extended a hand for Mandisa. "I'm your social worker."

"Social worker?" She finally shook Brittney's hand.

"Yeah. Today's your first anger management counseling session. Remember?"

"Oh. Wow, totally forgot about that. I was too busy freakin' out 'bout this stupid anklet. Anyway, is there a set time I gotta go? 'Cause I can't leave now. I'm here alone with my kids."

"Kids? I was told about your 2-year-old son."

"Yeah. I had a baby girl couple weeks ago."

"Oh." Her voice was flat. "Congratulations."

Mandisa gave her a curious look. "Thanks. Uh, my mom will be home in about a hour, can you come back then?"

"I'm sorry, I can't. But you can bring your kids with you. I'll look after them."

That news was sweet relief. She was itching to leave the house anyway.

Godhand Women's Home. What a name. Mandisa entered the place and was immediately uncomfortable. Most of the girls she saw were either Black or Latino, many of them pregnant, and the ones who weren't were scoping her out. The few White women peppered throughout the place barely lifted their eyes to notice her.

Brittney led Mandisa to her counselor, assuring her that she would notify Mandisa's mother of her location and text her when she came to pick the kids up. Mandisa watched as she ushered a very fussy Cody to the main activity area. For the first time, Cody actually looked at his mother with loving dependence. Mandisa gave him a reassuring nod with a wry smile.

That barely sufficed.

The thirtysomething Latina counselor welcomed her. She entered the room and slumped in the chair, rubbing her brow. "Um, why am I here?"

"Well, you tell me, Mandisa."

Mandisa winced. "Who are you?"

"Forgive my manners," the counselor replied with a chuckle. "I'm Carmen. Carmen Colon."

"Well, Carmen, I don't know." She extended her left foot for her to see. "I'm on house arrest for supposedly stalkin' somebody who was actually the one stalkin' me."

"Can I ask you something?"

"You just did."

"Something personal," Carmen replied, smiling.

A shrug.

"How are things at home?"

Mandisa tilted her head a little. "How *are* things at home for me, Carmen? Look at me and tell me what you see."

"Are you...sure you want me to do that?"

"That's what I said."

"Okay." A deep breath. "Well, I see a woman who's undervalued."

Mandisa's brow surged.

"You disagree?"

She shook her head.

"Want to know how I know that?"

"No, but I'm sure you'll tell me."

"Because of how you carry yourself. We're careful with the things we take pride in. Undervalued women in turn don't value themselves, so they occupy the extreme ends of the spectrum. They either overdo their appearance for desperate attention, or they don't care how they look at all." Carmen eyed her from head to toe. "You're on the latter end."

Mandisa's eyes pierced hers as she took a deep breath. "And?"

"You're socially detached. I'm guessing you don't have a close relationship with your son. You didn't hug or kiss him before you came in."

Mandisa's gaze finally faltered as she shook her head.

"He doesn't value you either."

Mandisa's jaw locked as her eyes pooled. That truth was painful enough when she realized it in church all those weeks ago, but to hear it from a stranger who knew nothing about her was more than she could take. She shook her head.

Carmen didn't dare push any further. She took a deep breath of her own and moistened her now dry mouth. "How's your temper?"

A heavy chuckle flew from Mandisa's chest. "How you think?"

Carmen thoughtfully nodded. "Would you like to share anything with me today? I know it's your first session, so I want to give you that option."

"First day free trial, huh? No obligation?"

Carmen smiled and nodded. "We get deep from there."

"When we meet again?"

"Same time tomorrow."

"And if I can't?" She pointed her thumb at the door behind her. "I'm stuck at home with the kids 'til, like, four."

"Brittney will take care of you."

Her phone suddenly vibrated. Sure enough, Grandma had come by to grab the kids. "How long these sessions supposed to be?"

"An hour, unless you have more to share."

"We might as well get into it. We got forty minutes to burn."

Mandisa unloaded the stalking case, DeAndrae's abuse, and her son's disrespect. That was more than enough for her to relive in one sitting.

Carmen took a deep breath. "Everything you've told me points to one thing." She paused. "You're not going to like this, though."

Mandisa shrugged. "Can't be any worse than what I hear at home."

Schizophrenia. The word made Mandisa gawk. Carmen ran down the list of characteristics Mandisa displayed: neglecting basic hygiene, trouble focusing, lack of pleasure from daily life, delusions of persecution -- like her unflinching belief about Professor O'Reilly stalking her -- and hallucinations, withdrawal and extreme agitation.

"It...it never even occurred to me...that I might have a mental disorder."

Carmen sympathetically shook her head. "It never does with schizophrenics, only someone on the outside, usually family or friends, can see the signs and seek help. So I'm glad you're here."

They nodded farewell, and Mandisa left the room.

She went to the activity area and realized Brittney wasn't there, so she sent a text to her mother to pick her up. The sun had finally disappeared below the horizon, leaving the once warm-colored space a sickly greenish from the wall paint and the fluorescents overhead.

As she awaited her mother's reply, two young women stood over her. She fiddled with her phone to avoid looking at them. "What your name is?" The one on the right had a deeper voice than even she did, and hers was pretty deep for a girl. "My business," she muttered.

The two girls looked at each other and snickered. The one on the left squatted to force her eye contact. "It's ours now."

"I'll tell you if you back up off me."

Some passersby began to pay attention and murmur to each other. Mandisa spotted Carmen leaving her office, giving her a concerned look as she went further down the hallway. "I ain't the one, ya'll, I'm tellin' you. Back up off me."

"We just aksin' your name," the squatting one said. "Nothin' else."

She finally looked her in the eye. "Mandisa."

"Pretty name for a pretty girl."

"Too damn pretty," said the right one, reaching for her head.

Mandisa slapped her hand away and jumped up. "Don't touch me!"

Carmen heard the yell and hurried back.

"Why? Scared we'll do somethin'?" the left one jeered, rising and poking Mandisa's rib.

Mandisa gripped her arm and twisted it almost out of joint, head-butting her in the nose.

"What the f--"

Mandisa clocked the right one in the eye before she could finish her thought.

The girl was ready to come at her, but Carmen gripped her arms behind her. "That's enough!"

The left one ran behind Carmen and locked her neck in her arm.

"Get off her!" Mandisa swerved to the girl's side and mashed her ribs. The girl's holler traveled all the way down the hall. Mandisa yanked her off Carmen, who finally released the other one. She laughed. "Pretty girl can fight, I like that. 'Bout time we got a bitch with some fire 'round here."

The one with the bruised ribs punched Carmen. "Puta! Mind your business!"

Mandisa rotated the girl's neck to face her and punched her in the nose again. The second girl came at her, but she landed a chop to her chest to knock her back, and managed a solid hook to her left jaw.

"Ladies! That's enough!"

Everyone obediently froze at the sound of the voice, even the onlookers, who had now formed a circle. Diana nodded for the two girls to step aside as she went to Carmen, whose lip was busted open and bleeding. "You alright?"

Carmen nodded.

Diana scowled at the onlookers. "No disrespect, but you ladies need to make yourselves useful. Someone help her out of here."

The other girls looked at each other for several seconds, but one finally emerged, wrapped Carmen's arm around her neck, and walked her out.

Diana finally directed her attention to Mandisa, who was now sitting on the floor by her chair, hugging her knees with wild eyes. "What happened?"

"I told 'em not to touch me," Mandisa growled breathlessly. "I told 'em."

"It's okay, it's okay. They won't bother you again. It's alright."

"Who the hell are you?"

"My name's Diana."

"What you did to 'em? They turned marshmallows 'round you."

Diana smiled. Her voice fell soft. "I chose to care. Respect goes a long way." She looked back at the two girls and hardened her voice again. "A lesson they clearly forgot."

"You betta tell 'em again," she said, giving them a murderous gaze.

The main entrance doors creaked open. Diana glanced at the dark brown mom-to-be who sauntered in wearing the ugliest frown. Some of the others scoped her as well, falling into a curious silence as her eyes threatened them. Mandisa finally glanced up at her over Diana's shoulder as she walked away from the scene. The girl finally looked over her shoulder at her, fury to fury, and walked away.

Mandisa noticed the hush around her. "Who the hell is that? And why she mean-muggin' me?"

Diana couldn't resist chuckling to herself. "A new girl, just like you, but she's been here a bit longer. Don't worry about her, she's got nothing against you. She's mad at the world."

Mandisa glanced at her antagonists again. "So am I."

Diana helped her up. "You don't have to be. We're not all out to get you."

The home's designated psychiatrist, Dr. Turner, a Caucasian in her early forties, appeared with a small white paper bag. "This is Tuinal, it should stabilize the anger and anxiety. Take your first dose first thing in the morning. You should feel the difference by the time you meet with Carmen again. But make sure you keep that out of your children's reach, whatever it takes. It's a very strong sedative."

* * * *

As Mandisa stared her debater in the eye, she realized she needed another pill. The first one threw her for a loop -- she hadn't been that calm ever, not even when she was drunk. Nothing anyone did or said upset her. Not even DeAndrae with his nasty self. He didn't bother to wash after his last tryst before sneaking in and boning her. Unlike him, she made sure to shower and cleanse herself immediately afterwards.

At this point, however, she was fully sober again, and it seemed her anxiety was heightened, unrealistic. She felt like a different person. Like her jittery mother.

And it didn't help that her probation officer was in the room.

4

This girl must be one of them fiends. She looks...way out of it.

"Don't worry, I ain't diggin'," I tell her. "Your business is yours. Just know we in the same boat."

"Why you mean-mugged me last night?"

I laugh, something I haven't done in a long time. "I got some bad news before I came in. Wasn't tryin'a be messed with. Everybody got the point. Wasn't nothin' against you."

She sniffles. "So what's your point?"

"Excuse me?"

"I made my statement, you gotta disagree."

"Oh. I think we got a level chance 'cause we all at the bottom of the barrel together. In everybody else's mind, we all shit anyway. The crap that claws up the walls has a better chance of being cleaned up than the ones that stay in the tank."

The rest of the room inhales and goes quiet, even the officer at the door. Mandisa laughs. "Can't front, you right 'bout that. But I can tell you we gonna stay in the tank."

"Speak for yourself," I reply.

"If a woman ruined your life, the last thing you want is to see another one come up."

She killed whatever clever thing I was going to say with that point. "Can't front, you right. But you gotta choose to get over what anybody else doin'. Damn 'em. They don't care 'bout you anyway, they won't help you. All you got is you."

She winces. "You mad corny, yo."

The other girls laugh.

"Corny or not, she's right," Diana says, shooting me a smile. I don't return it.

"My turn?" Mandisa asks.

I nod.

"You know why I don't care if women succeed? 'Cause I don't care 'bout nothin' period. I'm done. When I get this piece of shit off me--" She looks down at the house arrest anklet. "I'm fallin' off the map. Won't nobody find me."

"You got kids?"

She tightens up again. I'll take that as a yes.

"You just gonna drop 'em like that?"

She looks at my belly. "You won't know 'til you pop one out yourself. Heard what you said before? Don't worry 'bout nobody else 'cause they don't care 'bout you anyway?" She nods with a tight jaw. I'm betting five seconds before the tears come. "It's true for them too. They don't care neither."

...Dag.

"So why should I?"

I look at the instructor, silently commanding her to stop the debate. I don't know this girl from Adam, but she's putting her business in the streets right now, which none of us need to hear. This stuff should be between her and her counselor.

"The men don't care, either, so what the hell we workin' so hard for? Who the hell we celebratin' with? I sure as hell ain't poppin' bottles with none of y'all 'ho's."

The girls hiss and snicker again.

"I was wrong," I declare after a pause.

The room suddenly goes silent again. Even she's curious. "What?"

"I was wrong. We not in the same boat. You in the same boat as most of the girls in here, and most of the girls in the streets. You hang your life on other people. I ain't got nobody extra to compare with. I got *me*. I ain't got no degree, but I got me, and I know I ain't stupid. I'll wipe the damn floor with any hood dude that wanna come up on me, even if he *is* smarter. Screw him. I'm surprised you ain't like that, you beat the fire outta them girls last night."

She looks out to the audience to spot them. Her eyes fall in shame.

"Any woman who can fight like that can't be no damn pushover. If that's what you wanna be, that's on you. Ain't nobody else's fault but yours."

"You don't think I know that?" Her voice cracks. The five seconds are up. She gives the instructor a dirty look and walks past her P.O. out the door. I give the instructor a nasty look too as I return to my seat. I'm not even mad about her calling me up there anymore. I would want to kill her if I ended up putting my business out there like Mandisa did. And knowing the shallow chickenheads up in here, they'll use it against her.

"I see the Apostle rubbed off on you," Sabryna sneers as I sit down, breaking my concentration.

"Go to hell, Sabryna."

"You first, pastor." She hesitates. "And how you know my name?"

"How you know 'bout the Apostle?"

"Who doesn't?" she asks, laughing. "Dude nasty. You were younger than me, and he got you. He went for younger ones, too."

I don't give her the chance to go any further. "We done or what?" I holler at the instructor.

She clears her throat. "Yeah, that's it. Thanks for volunteering, by the way."

"Mhm." I get up and leave the room, barely acknowledging Diana with a glance.

As I get dressed the next day my mind remembers the child growing in me. She's coming in less than five months and I'm still not showing at all. Crazy. What's worse, I'm still not prepared for her, still don't have a place of my own or a job.

A sudden hard knock on my door sends my heart through the ceiling -- one of those SWAT team kind of knocks. My eyes scan the floor on my way to the door and I notice a small note a few feet from it. I quickly grab it.

I realize it's Diana and immediately shut the door on her, but her hand stops it. "The leadership class is in session. Thought you might want to know."

"You might want to tell me about a morning class the day before so I don't show up on CP time, Diana."

She smiles. "Better late than never."

"Better on time than late. And quit knockin' like you five-O."

"You could be getting dressed in the time you're taking to fuss me out."

"It's more fun to fuss you out. Anyway, don't y'all have some kind of printed schedule or somethin'? Imma need you to leave my door alone from now on."

Another smile. "Come to class and you'll get it."

"There's a evening session, ain't it?"

"You're dead set on not coming with me, aren't you?"

"What was your first guess?"

"Yes, there's an evening session. It starts at seven."

"Same place?"

"Yes."

"Good. Bye." I close the door. Thankfully she doesn't stop me this time.

I finally open the note and get the best news I've had in a while: the home's agreed to extend my stay up to six months.

Oh what the hell, I might as well go to that class.

5

Diana's so excited at the podium, she needs a bib. I'm hearing her leadership lecture, but I keep fantasizing of different ways to kick her off her soapbox. I sit through an hour of preaching and cheerleading: she tells us we're smarter than we think, we're brilliant and beautiful, we can do it, and God loves us. She explains that leadership is nothing but influence, when we really get down to it, so who we hang with and the choices we make matter. That pisses me off, considering all the shitty influences I've dealt with. I thought leadership was always a good thing, but apparently it can go either way, which makes it pretty damn worthless.

Now I really don't care for it.

I storm out when the lecture ends, heading straight for my room without even grabbing my usual late morning snack from the vending machines. I pass one of the counseling rooms and overhear angry whispering. The fool doesn't realize she's still too loud. I try to zone her out as I walk by...until I hear a familiar voice that makes my heart stop. "Take it easy," she coaxes.

"It was her, not me!" the angry one insists. "She screwed me!"

I look over at the door and realize it's cracked open, so I step closer and peek in.

My God. It really is who I think it is. I know that shoulder-length blonde flip hairdo anywhere.

"Mandisa," Christie says with a sigh, stroking her hair back with a hand. "It wasn't her, I can promise you that."

"How the hell would you know? Why am I even talkin' to you?"

"Because I was with her. All the time."

Both Mandisa and I stop breathing for a second.

"What you mean you was with her all the time?" Mandisa asks.

"We were together."

"What?! Y'all girlfriends?"

Christie takes a deep breath. "We were."

My stomach falls to the floor.

"My point is she wasn't following you. You really were the one stalking her."

"What you talkin' 'bout? I saw that bitch by my house!"

"After you followed her for two straight weeks, yes," Christie calmly says. "And that wasn't her in the car."

"That was you?! Who are you to scope out my house? That's my family you messin' with, bitch!"

Christie goes red, but takes a deep breath, refusing to loose control. "She sent me because she knew you would make a scene if you saw her in the driver's seat."

"You don't even know the half, yo. I bet she ain't tell you what she did to me at school, all that nasty shit she said."

"Actually, she did. Which is why we're no longer together."

"And you ain't report her? What the hell you good for?"

"Reporting her wouldn't change much," she said. "Her only violation was sexual harassment. She'd be suspended with pay or fired. Nothing else. You were already eighteen, so she wouldn't be labeled a sex offender."

Mandisa looks all over the place in a desperate effort to calm down. "That it?"

"Yes."

Mandisa makes a beeline for the door. I run to the vending machine area, pretending to choose something. She walks back to the cafeteria, giving me an ugly scowl on her way.

I look back at the door in time to see Christie slip out. Her eyes catch mine and we both freeze, not sure whether to escape in opposite directions or approach each other.

6

Christie makes the bold choice to come to me. I'm ready to flee, but something in me keeps my feet planted. I guess I missed her. She forces a smile when she finally reaches me. "Hey Leila, fancy seeing you here. Small world."

"How's school?" I ask.

Her eyes moisten as she takes another deep breath. "Wish I knew."

"You quit?"

She only shakes her head as she hugs her arms.

"How the kids?"

"They're okay." She finally smiles again and nods a lot. "Thanks for asking."

"So you switched sides, huh?" The words just rolled out of my mouth.

She goes red again, but laughs. "You heard all that, did you?"

"Close the door next time."

"Yeah. Well, she was the only one."

"You ain't stayin' here, right?"

She shakes her head again. Her fingers fidget on her arms. "I have an apartment. You're welcome to live with me again, by the way."

"You nervous or somethin'?"

"What? No, why?"

"You twitchin'."

She blushes again as she strokes her hair behind her ear. "Just edgy, I guess. Mandisa tore my head off in there."

I see through her lie, but I leave it alone. "Well, she gone now. Get outta here. This ain't no place for you."

"I take it you're not interested in my offer."

"I ain't buggin' you with that again, Miss Christie. I ain't have a choice last time. Now I do."

Her eyes scan the floor as she nods. "I understand. You take care, okay?"

I nod back.

She walks away and I realize something real sad: of all the people in my life, this once bubbly woman, who now walks with slumped shoulders and a low-hung head, was my one positive influence. My one good leader.

Is there anybody in this world who isn't miserable? Is misery all there is? Must we all live like that?

* * * *

Seven-o'clock strikes, and I'm barely motivated to leave my room. I could give a damn about CP time at this point. Today sucked. My usual three-mile job application run was fruitless, and I wasn't lucky enough to get a lift from Corporate Boy this time, so my feet are killing me.

As expected, Diana hunts me down. I open the door and just walk back to my bed. She makes that concerned face as I sit down, but I still don't buy it. "Rough day, huh?" she says.

"That's every day in here." I rub my face with both hands.

"You're only here as long as you choose to be."

"DON'T." I grill her. "I heard your hour-long sermon this mornin'. Quit already!"

For the first time since I met her, she hardens on me. She steps into the room with a tightened jaw and lowers her face to mine. "No."

I lean back a little to get away from her.

"You may not care about you, Leila, but I do. That's my job, and I take it very seriously."

"Your job ain't got nothin' to do with me."

"If it didn't, you best believe I wouldn't waste my time with an ungrateful child like you."

"Who you think you--"

"SHUT UP."

I'm ready to punch her for that, but I obey her.

"You've been here a grand total of thirty-three days. Thirty-three long days. What have you done in all that time? Who do you think is scared of that chip on your shoulder? Every woman in this place has a story. What makes you so special? Why should I change who I am for you?"

"Get out my face."

"No. Answer me."

"You asked me like ten questions, the hell you mean answer you?"

"What. Makes. You. So. Special?"

"Nothin', alright? Nothin'! Just leave me alone."

"No. I don't give up on the young women I work with."

"Young women. You got the wrong one."

"You opened your legs, didn't you?"

I slap her so hard, my palm stings. "Bitch! You know exactly how I got pregnant, and you say somethin' like that?!"

She inhales with a tightened jaw as she looks back at me. Her voice is now much lower. "I wasn't talking about the rape, Leila. You know me better than that."

"I don't know you from Adam. You chose to invade *my* life."

"Not me." She stands tall again and heads for the door. "Not me."

"What the hell do you care? You got your good life, your payin' job, your car, your house. You probably got a man too, ain't it?"

"I'm not answering any of that. You know why?"

I don't reply.

" 'Cause I'm not feeding your sorry excuses for hating me. And that's my issue with you. All of you."

"What you--"

"You waste your time hating people like me instead of realizing you can have what I have. All you have to do is apply the information we give you, and you'll get there! You're a slave to your excuses! All of you! My heart bleeds for you girls, but I swear to God, you're all so...STUPID! By choice!"

"Who you callin' stupid?!"

"I'll never understand why you refuse a chance at freedom when it's right in front of you. Why would you want to keep your chains?" She shakes her head at me for a few seconds, on the verge of tears, and shuts my door.

Within minutes, there's another knock. I dry my eyes. "WHAT?!"

"Whoa..." the male voice says. "Never mind, I'll come by tomorrow."

I rush to the door and look both ways. He was already at the end of the corridor. "Doc, wait. I'm sorry."

He turns around and comes back. "Thought you could use a break."

I shake my head as my mind goes blank. The tears come back with a vengeance. This is embarrassing, but I can't help what's happening. Doc reaches in, but I fight him back. "Get off me!" He takes a few good hits to the chest, but he doesn't give up. "Stop," he quietly says.

I don't listen, as usual.

After taking several more hits, he grabs both my wrists and refuses to let go, despite my pulling against him. He gives me that calm teacher look. "Stop, Leila." He finally pulls me into his arms, and all I could do is fall apart.

This was unfamiliar. I can count the men that have held me in my life on two fingers, and none of them ever held me like this, not even Bryce. There's something in the Doc's embrace that Bryce was missing. The closest one I can compare Doc to is Christie. I think back to that long, teary don't-leave-me hug she gave me the night before graduation, and it brings on a whole other wave of tears.

"Should I come back tomorrow?"

"No," the word falls from my throat like crumpled paper. "Stay."

"Okay, but it looks like the chess will have to wait."

"No." This time my voice is clear. I pull away from him and rub my wet nose. "I could use a game. I'm still tryin' to find out your dirty secrets."

He chuckles. "Alright. Game on."

7

By seven the next morning I'm in class. No knock on my door, no nothing. I woke up and showed up. It's a good thing I did, too -- this lady's talking about how to save money, which is a shock-and-a-half.

I've always wondered how that worked. Not a soul in my family ever did it, at least not that I know of. I never even saw Alice with money; she always told Michael -- Dad -- to buy everything: clothes for Kalvin and me, food for the house, Alice's medications, all that. With what he was doing in the streets, I know he wasn't saving anything. After his funeral, the family looked over his belongings and he didn't have a dime to his name.

Then the instructor issues a warning. "Ladies, I'm about to get deep on y'all, so you better break out your pen and paper if you haven't already. And for those of you who don't, you'll wish you did, and end up buggin' the other girls so you can copy off them."

Compound interest. To be honest, I didn't take her warning seriously, but once I heard the term, I knew I was going to have to write it down. I'd never heard it before this morning.

She explains that that's how savings, retirement, and investment accounts work. College funds too. I put a certain amount of money in the account...and just leave it there. Then it grows over the years. By itself. The bank adds more money to it based on a set annual percentage rate, or interest rate.

She shows us the math formula to calculate it, which confuses most of the girls in the room, but the formula took me right back to Pre-Calculus class. She has us use the calculators on our phones to do an example, and I understand it on the first try. I suddenly feel a surge of some good kind of feeling. Maybe hope or excitement.

By the end of the lecture, I'd filled about six pages in my little notebook with notes. Everyone around me gets up to leave the room, but I'm still leafing through the notes, memorizing everything. I didn't realize how hungry my brain is. Maybe that's why I love playing chess so much.

From the corner of my eye I see a sheet of paper creeping toward me. I look to my right and find Diana's hand on it. "I promised you a schedule."

I'm not sure what else she's going to say, so I'm quiet for a good minute. "Thanks."

"Sorry about last night," she barely says, folding her arms. "I was disrespectful."

"That why you didn't knock on my door this morning?"

"Figured you'd want a break."

She's been talking to Corporate Boy, apparently. He said the same thing.

"Glad to see you here this morning," she says.

Something suddenly occurs to me. "This your last day here, ain't it?"

"For the rest of the month, yes. We'll be back next month."

"See you then, I guess."

She slowly nods, but I can clearly see the disappointment in her face.

"Relax. I ain't stayin' here 'cause I want to. You asked me last night what I've been doin' with my time, I've been walking three miles every day applying for jobs."

"Any takers?"

I shook my head.

She digs into her inner jacket pocket and pulls out a business card for me. "Call me when you're doing your next run. It's time to expand your search."

"That would be today, but thanks anyway."

"Thank you."

"For what?" I ask.

"For forgiving me."

"You ain't bad. I can deal with you."

She chuckles. "That's good. Honestly, though, I'll be glad for the day I don't have to see you again."

I look her in the eye. Am I supposed to read between the lines on that one?

"That's the day I'll know you're free. I'm still praying for that. And for you."

All I can do is nod.

She nods back and heads for the door. "You might want to get outta here too. The cafeteria staff wants their room back."

I'm heading back to my room to get ready for a shower and I spy two girls in a lonely corridor through its cracked door, one of those "employees only" areas. I approach the door and find Sabryna and a white girl scheming. Sabryna sees me first, then the other girl looks around and does a double take. "What you lookin' at, pastor?" Sabryna says calmly.

I shove the door open and come closer to them, and I'm hit with the familiar stink of weed. "Two idiots, apparently."

"What you gonna do, rookie, tell on us?" Sabryna's friend asks.

"For what? There's nothin' in it for me. I just saw y'all through the door you dummies left cracked open and got curious."

"Well, take it with you on your way," Sabryna says.

I turn to leave, happy to follow her advice. That smell reminded me too much of my dad.

"You could have some if you want, you know," the friend offers. "Long as you don't tell nobody."

I barely look over my shoulder. "I'm good."

"Too good, if you ask me," Sabryna said.

"Nobody asked."

She laughs, staring into my eyes as she takes a puff. "Ever wonder what happened to your little Bible-thumpin' friend?"

"If memory serves, you thumped her with the damned thing, not the other way around."

The friend perks up. Apparently Sabryna hadn't shared this with her yet.

"I asked you a question," Sabryna continues.

"Sometimes."

"Thompson nailed her, too."

Every muscle in me tenses up. I recall her innocent little face and how annoyed I was with seeing her look so pitiful, how angry I was to hear her asking a god who doesn't care about her to forgive the idiot in front of me for beating her. "You lyin'."

Sabryna slowly shakes her head as she exhales smoke. "I'm a mean bitch, but I never lie."

"When's the last time you saw him?"

"Couple weeks ago, probably. Dude on TV now. He big time."

I finally leave them and close the door, aching to punch something. Preferably somebody's face.

Preferably his.

* * * *

I reach my room and get an interesting surprise. Corporate Boy's leaning against my door. His little hazels light up when he sees me. I'm not sure why, but whatever.

I simply fold my hands and glare. He finally moves out of my way so I can open the door.

"Come to say goodbye, huh?" I ask.

"For now," he replies with a deep breath. "We'll be back in a few weeks."

"You coulda just said next month."

"Wasn't sure if you'd spoken to Diana about that."

"Well, I did."

I enter the room and start emptying my pockets, which I always do when I'm getting ready for a shower. I check everything on the bed: class schedule, check. Notebook, check. Pencil, check. Phone... Where's my phone?

I pat myself down in angered shock. "The hell..."

"What's missing?" Doc asks.

"My phone. I swore I had it with me. I always have it with me."

"Well, no worries, just work backwards. You were in the cafeteria just now, right? The finance class?"

"Yeah." For some reason, I look at him. I'm not sure what he sees in my face, but he agrees to go back to the cafeteria with me.

We return to the cafeteria and get dirty looks from the staff. Diana's already there and apologizes to the staff on his behalf. He explains the situation, then the staff shrugs him off and lets us look for the phone.

Only it's not in here, either.

"Where the hell is it?"

"Where were you before you came to class?"

"The room."

"And you didn't go someplace else after class before you went back to the room?"

I thought back to the forbidden corridor. I don't recall using the phone while I was in there, I sure didn't drop it, and none of the girls mugged me for it. "Well, I talked to a couple girls on the way."

"Where?" He leads me back to the doors.

"In a small hallway not far from--"

There's suddenly a bunch of screaming outside the cafeteria double-doors. A woman's yelling at the top of her lungs, but all I can make out is cursing.

Doc shoves me behind him and holds out a protective arm.

He peers through the thin rectangle of glass in the door to make out what's happening and I see his eyes go wide. He looks back at me and gestures for me to hide under one of the benches. I quickly look behind me before I move off, and the staff is frozen in fear and confusion. They're not sure whether to hide or scream or call 5-O.

The doors bust open, and Mandisa tumbles into the room. The black psycho who shoved her is holding a .45.

My eyes finally go wide.

8

Doc helps Mandisa aside and stares at the one holding the gun. From this angle, I can see a witness chillin' against the wall a few feet behind the psycho, shaking her head at her. "Shut up, Sabryna," the thug says.

What's Sabryna doin' there? Doesn't she know to get the hell out of a situation like this?

"Patrice..." Doc holds his hand out. "Put the gun down. Talk to me. What happened?"

"Everything," she says with a heavy laugh.

Doc risks a few steps closer, looking back at me and silently wondering why I'm not under a bench yet.

I'm too busy staring at her shaky hand. Clearly she can't manage the cannon. What the hell is she planning to do with that? This isn't a convenience store. There's nothing to stick us up for; we're all broke.

She finally sets her eyes on me. She doesn't say a word. Just stares.

"Patrice," Doc breaks her focus. "Gimme the gun. Please. What are you even doing with it?"

"Keeping you in check, obviously," she says, stepping back some and aiming at his head.

"Who pissed you off?" he asks.

She rubs her nose with an arm. Her eyes are totally bloodshot. "I hate this place and everyone in it."

"No one's keeping you here, Patrice, you know that." Doc's voice is tender, almost apologetic.

"I have no place else to go!"

"Alright, alright. Just...take it easy. Just...let me have the gun. We can talk to about this."

She shoves the gun against his forehead. "I'm tired of talkin'! You don't even listen to me!"

He gently grips her gun hand and lowers it to his chest. "Then do something, Patrice," he says softly. "Never aim a gun unless you know for sure you're gonna fire. Never hesitate with a gun."

Is he stupid?

"Coward." The word falls from my angry mouth.

He gives me a panicked look.

Her wide eyes fall on me again, and without warning, she fires.

A stabbing pain rips my chest as Doc and I fly backwards. I stare at the hole in his back on my way down.

I slam against the hard floor, and all I can see is the fluorescent bulbs in the ceiling. The screams around me turn into muddled echoes. I'm starting to feel cold and physically crushed and just all around bad, like, like...like I'm going to die.

It's getting harder to breathe by the second, and all I can taste is blood. In my breath, in my mouth...

"Leila!" I barely hear someone scream. "Leilaaaa!"

I let my head fall to the left and look towards the door, and all I can make out is Doc sliding himself toward me with a trail of blood behind him. Blood trickles from his mouth.

"Leila, hang on," he says. "You've gotta hang on. Stay awake."

I start to nod off, but suddenly feel a sting on my cheek. He's tapping it.

"No! Leila, no. Look at me, look at me! Stay awake." He looks up at someone, I'm guessing one of the cafeteria staff, or maybe Diana. "Raise her legs! She's going into shock!"

"Doc," I croak, staring at his chest. "You bleedin' too."

"I know, I'm alright."

Suddenly uniformed men enter the room and carefully lift him off me onto a stretcher, then they come for me too.

His eyes never leave me as he rolls out. They're worried and watery and bright as ever. And they're the last hint of light I see before sleep takes me.

PATRICE'S STORY

Young Patrice sat alone in the police interrogation room with a hard face. Her right cheek was cut and her lower lip cut open. She interlocked her fingers and stared at the handcuff prints on her hands.

Another confrontation had gotten out of hand.

If there was one thing Patrice had in her favor, it was courage. She never backed down from anyone who challenged her, regardless of his size.

This time it was her baby daddy's closest friend. Ungrateful bastard killed someone for a failed drug sale and was on the run from the cops, so she let him crash at her place to duck them. Once the cops left, he felt he deserved a piece of her fine and very pregnant tail.

She made sure he knew her answer -- by smacking him over the head with the biggest skillet she had.

Despite all that, she didn't rat him out for the murder. She simply presented him as a suspicious boyfriend. She'd dealt with his type before, so the shoe fit.

There wasn't much else the cops could do with him, so they let him go. And like her daughter's father, she'd never see him again.

A uniformed officer released her and she caught the bus home. The first thing she did was call her grandmother, who was babysitting her son and daughter. "I'm done now. I'll come pick them up first thing in the morning."

She called her sister Sandy next and told her everything. "You are out of your mind, Patrice. I told you stop doing them dudes favors. They'll never repay you and will only get you killed."

"You think I don't know that? I don't know why I always end up with dudes like that."

"Your poor decisions are why you always end up with dudes like that. Shoplifting? Slangin' drugs? Come on now."

"Shut up. I needed the money."

"Look, you made a statement, I'm just helping you understand."

"Whatever, CO. You think you know it all."

"I don't know it all, but you learn a whole lot workin' in a prison. Anyway, how's the new baby?"

"Still in my belly."

"Dag, that's all you can say?"

"You wanna pay for my doctor visit?"

"I'm just askin' considering the shape your body's in since you...you know..."

Sandy was skirting around Patrice's two abortions, but didn't want to upset her. She was already on edge about having a baby at twenty-seven, and after the abortions.

"Whatever, Sandy, I'm fine."

"You always act like I'm your enemy. I'm your friend, remember?"

"Mhm. Sometimes I wonder."

"Excuse me?"

"Good night, sis. I'll tell the kids you said hi."

Patrice loved and hated her big sister. Sandy was her only female friend, the only one she could trust. But lately it seemed like Sandy was getting more and more chatty, more and more opinionated. More and more like other girls.

Patrice's cell chimed with a text message from her. "SLEEP WELL."

"Thanks for the reminder," Patrice whined, rolling her eyes. Her brush with death during her second abortion caused her now recurring nightmare: she would be on the table, surrounded by doctors and nurses and technicians, ready to give birth, and die before the child was born. The high-pitched sound of the heart monitor would always jolt her awake. She began every morning in tears.

It also didn't help that she'd attempted suicide after the first abortion. She overdosed on her prescription pills and scared Sandy to death. Sandy came to her house and found her unconscious on the floor with the empty pill bottle right beside her. The doctors had to pump her stomach and revive her. Instead of smiling and being thankful for coming back to life, she broke down.

Turmoil aside, she was a Christian. She'd given her heart to the Lord shortly after she dropped out of high school. By then, she'd already had her daughter and was pregnant with her son. She gave herself away at fourteen and had her daughter and dropped out at fifteen. Two months later, she found out the daughter's father cheated with another girl and he left Patrice for her. At seventeen, she had her son. Different father. Same story.

From the age of eighteen to her early twenties, she was a girl desperate for attention and love, especially since she never fully recovered from losing her mother at twelve. She and Sandy lived with their aunt briefly, then moved into their grandmother's very full house the following year. Mama Francis had Patrice's uncle, aunt, and cousins, as well as Mama Francis' own ailing mother, who was in her final years of life. Despite the constant company, Patrice always felt alone. So during her confusing early adulthood, she'd gotten into affairs with married or committed men, hungry for whatever they could give her. They sensed her desperation and made the most of it. She was more a free whore for them than a woman on the side.

She reluctantly went to bed, already expecting the nightmare. Her mind ran over the nagging lie that always hung over her head: she told her two kids they have the same father, and she gave them her last name so they wouldn't be able to tell. She confessed that to Sandy, but she wondered if that was a good idea.

She forced her eyes shut. Morning would be here before she knows it, and she wanted it to come so she could visit her new baby's nineteen-year-old father in prison.

Number Three

Patrice had a close call during the birth, but her daughter was born safely and healthy. Dionne Francis, named after her father. Deon's mother was so excited for the birth, and became Patrice's crutch, especially once he came out of prison. The five of them were one happy dysfunctional family: Patrice, Deon, twelve-year-old Maggie, ten-year-old Xander, and three-month-old Dionne.

For the first time in years, Patrice felt better. The dark panic she had was finally gone, and the recurring nightmare was happening less and less often now that Dionne was in the world. Her obstetrician couldn't figure out what was causing them, since the baby was normal during pregnancy, but her psychiatrist monitored her behavior for two weeks after the pregnancy for postpartum depression. Fortunately, she never experienced it.

She convinced Deon to get a normal job and stay out of trouble. "Once you're in the system, it's a lot easier for them to hit you for somethin' else."

"I got you, mommy," he would say, kissing the back of her hand. "I love you."

As much as she loved to hear him say that, she was still stressed. Their public housing unit was in disrepair and the landlord refused to fix it. Doorknobs were broken, the toilet was leaking, and the back patio screen was lopsided thanks to a busted hinge. She liked the help Section 8 and food stamps provided, but she wanted to at least be in a respectable home and have a better job. There's only so much a customer service specialist at Walmart could earn.

The Break

Deon managed to land a job with a mechanic shop just off of 2nd Avenue and Mathews Street. Patrice was satisfied because he was finally doing something constructive and getting paid, which helped with some of the bills. She and Deon would normally "turn over" as their shifts overlapped. She handled things at home while he worked during the day, cooked dinner and helped the kids with their homework if she could. Once he arrived, they'd kiss, sometimes argue about the bills or what she made for dinner, and she'd leave to work the Walmart night shift. He put the kids to bed and stayed up late watching TV or watching videos on his iPhone. Until midnight.

"You better check up on your boy," Sandy warned Patrice several weeks later.

"Why?"

"He up to no good, girl. I told you stayin' with him was stupid. He's still a kid."

"Yeah, he's young and I can mold him to what I want him to be. This is his first baby, and we can make a good family for ourselves. He ain't got no baggage that I know of, and he the first faithful dude I been with. Anyway, you ain't answered my question yet."

"I spotted him down by the shop mad late. He and a couple dudes were up to something, I don't know what. I just know no shop is open after midnight."

"What you doin' on the road after midnight?"

"My job. One of our ex-cons on probation lives in that area, so I check his neighborhood to make sure he ain't up to nothin'."

"How do I know you tellin' the truth?"

"You don't have to believe me, the truth will come out."

That night, before Deon came home from work, she sat Maggie down. "What time do you usually fall asleep, Maggie?"

"Like, eleven or midnight."

"Why so late?"

She shyly shrugged. "My phone."

Patrice gave her a disapproving look, but let it slide for the time being. "Do you ever check up on Daddy? Do you see what he does?"

She shrugged again. "Usually plays videos on his phone with the volume loud. Then he leaves."

"He leaves?"

"Yeah. I don't know where, and he doesn't tell us anything because he thinks we're asleep."

"Around what time?"

"About the same time I start nodding off. I always hear the door shut and fall asleep after that." Maggie noticed her mother's thoughtful look. "Um, am I in trouble?"

"No, no. You're fine."

"Is Daddy in trouble?"

Patrice offered a smile. "Not yet."

* * * *

By the time school let out for summer break, it became obvious. Deon didn't bother to come home. Patrice had to make Maggie head of the house and tuck everybody in while she went to work, which Patrice didn't appreciate, especially since relations with her landlord was getting worse.

She switched shifts with one of her coworkers to get a night off and snuck around to the shop. The front looked fine: rolling door down and locked, building lights off. She drove up a few yards to check the back. That's where things were active. Men were huddled behind the huge commercial dumpster which faced the street, so they couldn't easily be seen. Only the random shine from a cell phone screen gave them away. Patrice looked further up the block at the two or three cars parked in scattered, random places to appear abandoned. Sure enough, Deon's old Toyota Celica was among them. She quietly reversed her car to where it was by the front of the shop so they wouldn't notice her. After about twenty minutes, she saw Deon get in his car and drive off. She followed him two car lengths behind all the way home. He looked behind him in surprise when she pulled in. "What you doin' here, babe?"

"What were you doin' at the shop so late, Deon? The place is closed."

He sighed, knowing he was busted. "Look, I met some dudes and we gamble every night, aight? Nothin' illegal about that."

"If that's true then why hide behind a dumpster using cell phones as flashlights? Hm? You better tell me the damned truth. The job was enough, what you got into that mess for?"

"You really think that job is enough? By the end of every month my paycheck gone. The hell is that? I can't save nothin', can't buy nothin' for myself--"

"Don't give me that. You ain't thinkin' 'bout savin' nothin'."

"How you know? You read my mind? Quit the drama and get inside, man."

"Not 'til you tell me the truth. That's gotta be more than gamblin'. Your back pocket's pretty fat."

"I slang for this dude, aight?" he finally admitted after a long pause. "Look, it's quick, easy money, it pays the bills, and I can get stuff for everybody. Not just myself. For you, the kids, the grandmas, everybody."

"Damn you, Deon!" she whispered, on the verge of tears. "We got three kids! What happens if you get caught?"

"What you do when I was locked up? Send 'em to grandma while you work."

"You asshole! You plan to go to jail again? You just...not gonna try to stay outta trouble at all?"

"Calm your ass down, Patrice," he said firmly. "That won't happen. Now get inside and get some sleep."

She dropped her kids of at Deon's mother's house for the week. When she returned home, she felt the need to search Deon's belongings, and found a folded eviction notice in the back pocket of one of his Dickies work pants. The two-week-old notice warned that if no response was received by that day, they would have to leave. "Damnit, Deon!" she screamed. Where was the drug money going, if not to the rent?

She suddenly received a call from an unknown number, but answered it. It was Deon, sounding low as ever. "Hey, babe. I'm down at the station."

"For what?"

"The cops caught somebody involved in some drug ring, and the dude dropped my name. So they showed up at the shop and got me."

Patrice wanted to go off on him, but she knew better considering where he was calling from. Why did she always end up with men like this? She hung up the phone on him.

She knew there wasn't enough space at his mother's house for her, and she had no desire to go back to living at her grandmother's still-crowded house. She sure wasn't about to live with know-it-all Sandy, so she could rub it in her face every day. She walked to the nearby women's home and signed in, secretly hating herself.

Clash

Once she got her room assignment and changed into a fresh uniform, she called Sandy and let her know what happened. She was amazed and angry at the drastic shift in her life. How did she go from having a family and roof over her head to losing her home and her man? It was as if things were moving backwards again.

Within a couple weeks, she was welcomed into a clique. They gave her a sense of importance and belonging, since two of the four girls had boyfriends in prison as well. They went around the home bullying everybody, from the slim, quiet one with the baby bump and bleached hair and her cranky friend, to the newbies. They only ever lost one tussle: the wild newbie with the house arrest anklet. She'd punched and elbowed them pretty good. Patrice didn't appreciate the busted lip and bruised ribs, or Diana's self-righteous front, or that cranky girl's mean mug as she walked in that night, acting like she was the untouchable queen of the castle.

She was assigned to Dr. Isaacs that week, and he gave her an eye-opening diagnosis: *borderline personality disorder*. Based on everything she'd experienced, she realized it made sense: the nightmares, her attempted suicide, her pattern of intense and stormy relationships -- including this fiasco with Deon, extreme reactions to abandonment; even that dark spell during her last pregnancy that eventually went away. He explained to her that being part of a community with commonly unstable family relationships increases a person's risk for the disorder, and people with BPD also have a high rate of having co-occurring disorders, like depression and anxiety disorders. BPD even explained her odd, unshakable tendency to have unsafe sex with unsafe boys and men, despite her faith.

Dr. Isaacs prescribed a mood stabilizer for her, and forwarded it to the home's psychiatrist, Doctor Turner, who filled it for her, and it worked. Briefly. She stopped rolling with her clique for a while and interacted with others.

Unfortunately, the cranky one hunted her down. She cornered Patrice in one of the bathrooms, jacking her against a wall. The girl hit Patrice's head on the wall so hard it bled, and nearly crushed her windpipe. "Not so tough without your girls around, huh?"

Patrice begged for mercy.

"You better not ever bother my friend again, you hear me? Try me all you want to, I can handle it. But you leave her the hell alone."

"Who the hell are you?"

"Leila. Remember my name and face. Mess with me and mines again and I'll finish the job."

As Leila left, Patrice wondered what was wrong with herself. She was always ready to take people bigger than her. Leila was shorter and managed to punk her. Then she remembered Doctor Isaac's diagnosis again: adults with BPD are usually more likely to be victims of violence. Her anger suddenly erupted, causing her to turn and punch the wall.

The next week, she returned to her clique and told them what happened. They started plotting against Leila, but Patrice stopped them. "Who can get a gun in here?"

The group's lanky white leader, Beth, stepped up. "My man's a cop. He can get me one of those guns they seize during the raids."

"I need to borrow one," Patrice told her. "I'll handle her."

"Tell you what," Beth said. "The day the gun comes, I'll ask you for your room key. You pass it to me, I'll put the gun under your pillow, and pass the key back to you."

"Deal."

* * * *

The following month, Diana and Doctor Isaacs returned, much to Patrice's delight. She could do without Diana, but she loved Dr. Isaac's company, and he was more along the lines of what she hoped for in a man: caring, intelligent, handsome, well-paid *legally*. She scoped him as he and Diana passed her. He could use a fashion makeover, but he would definitely do. She went to the snack room and found Beth by the vending machines, pretending to choose something. "Pass it," Beth said in a low voice. Patrice gave her the key. Beth nodded and left the room.

Much to Patrice's surprise, she got a text from the front desk announcing a letter for her. She opened the letter and lost her mind. In it, Sandy confessed she revealed the truth about the kids' fathers to Patrice's grandmother and Deon's mother in a desperate effort to get the fathers to help the kids since Deon was on trial.

She called her sister, who normally answers her phone, and got her voicemail. She called Deon's mother and got her voicemail. She called her grandmother and got her answering machine. Where were her kids? Did the fathers come back? Did they take them? Was her family mad at her? Patrice roared at the hallway ceiling, earning some leery looks.

The only silver lining to her day was her counseling appointment with Doctor Isaacs that evening.

* * * *

Patrice woke up that next morning pissed. She still got no word from her family, and what's worse, her attempt to seduce Dr. Isaacs the night before failed miserably. He talked her down and gave her a mood stabilizer pill. It mellowed her and made her drowsy.

She pulled the SIG .45 from under her pillow and shoved it in her bra. "I'm tired of being screwed," she said to herself.

After the morning class and breakfast, she called on her clique to find out where Leila and the doctor were. As luck -- or whatever -- would have it, they were together. It angered her that the same chick that jacked her up managed to get her doctor's attention, but she'd handle that in a minute.

She made a beeline for the cafeteria. Mandisa stepped out of Carmen's counseling room into Patrice's path. Without a second thought, Patrice pulled the .45 on Mandisa. Carmen and Mandisa hollered. In her usual fashion, Patrice mowed Mandisa, who was taller and thicker than she was, right into the double doors. She almost wanted to laugh as Mandisa crashed onto the cafeteria floor. But that's not what really made her day. Her two targets stood right in front of her: Doctor Isaacs in front, Leila not far behind. Diana stood off to one side, giving her a pleading look. She felt eyes behind her a looked over her shoulder at a younger husky girl, one who wanted to get in her clique, but was turned down. The girl slowly shook her head at Patrice. "Shut up, Sabryna," she growled.

"Patrice..." Doctor Isaacs entreated. He held his hands up in surrender. "Put the gun down. Talk to me. What happened?"

She thought about it: Deon getting in trouble, despite her effort to control the situation, her kids learning the truth about their fathers because she trusted her big-mouth useless sister, her having to be here and take the numbing pills he wrote up for her all because dumb-ass Deon wasted the money instead of at least using it to pay the rent, forcing her to come here, Leila jacking her up in the bathroom, Doctor Isaacs turning her down last night... "Everything," she says with a heavy laugh.

He risks a few steps closer, looking back at Leila.

She stared Leila down, aching to put a hole in her head.

"Patrice," he called again. "Gimme the gun. Please. What are you even doing with it?"

"Keeping you in check, obviously." She stepped back and aimed the gun at his head.

"Who pissed you off?" he asked.

"Every scrub in here." She rubbed her nose with an arm. "I hate this place and everyone in it."

"No one's keeping you here, Patrice, you know that," Isaac said in a gentle voice.

"I have no place else to go!"

"Alright, alright. Just...take it easy. Just...let me have the gun. We can talk to about this."

She pressed the gun against his sweaty forehead. "I'm tired of talkin'! You don't even listen to me!"

He clasped her gun hand and put it to his chest. "Then do something, Patrice," he says softly. "Never aim a gun unless you know for sure you're gonna fire. Never hesitate with a gun."

Was he serious? Is that a challenge?

"Coward," Leila said.

The rest seemed to unfold in horrific slow motion. He looked back at Leila, as did Diana, and so did she, in burning outrage. The stupid bitch didn't even realize Patrice was having second thoughts and might've put the gun down. Just to spite her, she pulled the trigger.

In that moment, the loud crack of the gun brought her back to her senses. She watched in horror as Isaacs and Leila flew backwards, both with holes in their chests. She dropped the gun and covered her mouth as two pools of blood appeared on the floor, spreading rapidly.

"Leila! Leilaaaaaaaa!" Isaac's scream made Patrice shake. She broke into hysterical crying as she watched him scrape his way to Leila, calling to her, begging her to stay alive.

Before she could say anything, Patrice heard an army of heavy footsteps, and she was suddenly tackled from behind. Two heavy men, uniformed Broward County Sheriff officers, nailed her on the floor, and one cuffed her. "No!" She screamed with all her might, sobbing. "Noooooo! Get off me!" She began to scramble under them. They stood her up and took her towards the front exit. "Nooooo!" she sobbed. "Pleeeease!"

Her haunting cry was instantly muted when the front doors slid shut.

THE AFTERMATH

9

I haven't gotten this much sleep in all my life. I wake up to dreary walls, a long curtain, and an annoying beeping sound. The blinds are shut, making the dim fluorescent light overhead the only light in the room. I suddenly feel painfully lonely. And very weak.

The nurse comes in and greets me with a surprised smile. Dude looks like a retired bouncer. "There she is! Welcome back. How are you feeling?"

I barely tell him I'm fine, and he tells me I've been in and out of consciousness for two weeks.

That's a long time. And I have no hope in hell of paying for it.

He sees my concern and tries to be nice, smiles a lot and makes several weak jokes. I just force a half-smile out of respect for his effort.

"What about my baby?"

His face falls. "Um, I really hate to tell you this, but uh, unfortunately we couldn't save her."

"What?! What you mean you couldn't save her?"

"You lost too much blood, Leila," he says, sincerely heartbroken. "You were barely stable by the time you made it to the ER. She, uh, she died while the doctors were operating on you."

The room suddenly starts to spin and the sound in my ears closes off as if someone just poured a bunch of water in them.

"Leila?" I barely hear him say.

I let the feeling envelop me. My head rolls back against the pillow and my eyes shut.

By the time I wake up again, it's much later in the day -- 6:27, according to the big boring analog clock on the wall. Much to my surprise, the blinds are finally open and my curtain is drawn aside. My vision finally focuses and I realize why.

Diana is standing by my bed. I remember the horrible news I got earlier and look away.

"How are you feeling?" she asks in her usual shrink style.

"Like I should be dead." My half-gone voice makes me sound like a 20-year smoker.

"Well, thank God you're not. And it's good to see you're finally awake again."

"What difference does it make, really?"

"Leila."

Her gentle, motherly tone forces me to look at her again. For the first time, I don't feel suspicious of her.

"I'm sorry for what happened to you. I know this has all been...quite a trial for you. But the good news is the world could have one less person, but it doesn't."

"Yes it does."

She takes a deep breath. "You're right," she says in a lower voice. "It does. I'm sorry for your loss."

"How you know about that already? I just found out today."

"Because I've been checking on you a couple days a week. The nurses updated me on everything."

I look straight ahead of me. What else could this woman possibly have to tell me? I didn't even know my child's gender while she was inside me. She had to die for me to find out.

"And you still think God loves me." I look back at her. I have to see how she'll explain this one.

She takes a deep breath and moistens her lips, stares at me for a few seconds. "I know He does."

"Explain that to me," I growl. "Knowin' what you know 'bout me already, how the hell does a loving god let me go through all this and then snatch the one good thing away from me. My baby woulda been loved! I wouldn't do her like my parents did me! I would be there for her!"

She takes another deep breath and looks me in the eye. Her momma voice is still on. "Would you?"

"What?!"

"Sweetheart, you need help in your own life, right? You're at the women's home to get help, right?"

"What that gotta do with nothin'?"

"God never gives us more than we can handle, Leila."

"You tryin' to say--"

"Let me finish. You asked me a question, remember? Do you want the answer?"

I scowl hard, but I nod.

"He sees and knows everything," she continues. "I can't tell you what He knows about your daughter and why He took her so soon, I don't know. We may never understand it."

She leans in.

"But *your* life is important to Him. He's got something amazing planned for you, so He saved your life. But He sees that you need help. You're strong-willed, you're smart, you're proactive, but you need help. He set your daughter free before you could meet her, but in a way, He set you free, too."

"What? That's so in--"

"It's not insensitive, let me finish," she says. "He knows you're in a difficult place in your life, and bringing a child into that would be twice as hard."

"Food, clothes, shelter, and love. What's so hard about that?"

She leans in even closer. "Knowing what we know about you already, it would be more than you could take, Leila. You're currently at a women's facility and looking for a job. The only clothes you have are what you wore the night you went in and the home's uniforms. You would literally exhaust yourself to provide food, clothes, and shelter for her, even if that meant doing some pretty desperate things you wouldn't be proud of, but you wouldn't be able to give her what she needs most."

"You tryin' to say I'm a unfit mother? What the hell you know?"

"You can never give what you don't have, Leila. Who in your life has truly loved you?"

That shuts me up.

I think back to Alice the hypocrite, but she doesn't count. Christine came pretty close, but even she doesn't count. The only male who showed me anything near love was Kalvin, but he's my little brother, so his love came from his dependence on me. And he's locked up, so he can't come see me. He doesn't even know I was pregnant.

Wow. This is absolutely awful. Nobody loves me.

Like, seriously. Nobody. Loves me.

Sorrow overpowers me before I can stop it, and I cry. Within seconds, I'm bawling. Every failure, every terrible moment in my life flashes before my eyes. The last image I see is Patrice with that cannon in her hand, and the flooding sadness burns into a ball of anger in my chest, and I scream.

I hate Patrice. I hate God. And I hate Diana for telling me no one loves me.

All that's left for me now is to die.

To hell with this place.

A wide-eyed nurse runs in, terrified that something happened to me, but Diana holds a hand up. "She's okay, she just -- it's my fault."

"Ma'am?"

"I, um...I said something...pretty terrible," Diana continues. I look over at her and realize her face is wet.

"Let's leave her," she says with a sniffle. "She needs her rest."

The nurse glances at the white board on the wall to find out who my assigned nurse is. "I'll go grab David, okay?"

I shook my head. "I just want to be alone."

The two of them glance at each other, then at me, and leave.

Diana returns the next morning. Unfortunately. I'm seriously starting to wonder if this chick got a jones for me or something. She comes in with pursed lips and folded arms. I guess she took yesterday pretty hard.

"Good morning."

I nod.

"I, um...I'm not staying long. I just wanted to apologize for yesterday. I was trying to explain -- to answer your question--"

I shake my head. "Don't worry about it. I shouldn't have asked you."

"Um...you should be outta here in four weeks depending on the doctors' assessment after they check up on you. You can stay with me if you want to."

"No thank you. I'll just go back to the home."

"Even after what happened?"

"Patrice still over there?"

"No."

"They full?"

"Not that I know of."

"Then yeah. I'm goin' back."

She slowly nods, as if disappointed, and her eyes wander. "Alright, well...I guess I'll see you."

As I watch her leave, something occurs to me: she was my one visitor this whole time, even when I was unconscious. Something in me tells me to thank her, but I can't bring myself to. My chance to make nice gets locked out of the room as the door closes behind her.

10

Time almost stops when I walk into the Godhand Women's Home. Every eye is on me, and wide as ever. Mandisa looks me up and down as she heads out the door, not to size me up, but in disbelief that I survived.

Since I was gone for six weeks, I have to go through the entire sign-in process all over again. New room, new set of uniforms, new counselor.

I enter the new room and immediately notice something's off. Something I took for granted in my previous room.

There's no Bible in here.

I had assumed every room had one, since all the main areas had one: the cafeteria, the counseling rooms, the waiting room, the activity area, even the snack room where the vending machines are.

After taking a quick shower, I threw on a fresh uniform and headed to the activity area. The room looks slightly different now. The tables have been rearranged and it looks like there are more academic workbooks on them now. Fewer games.

The more obvious change wasn't even a thing, but a person. My little shadow friend isn't in here, and she used to practically live here. She loved playing the games, even if she was playing alone.

I head for the now fully stocked bookshelf. I don't know why I'm so fixated on finding a Bible, but I spot a spare one and grab it. Unless the policy changed while I was gone, I should be able to take this to the room without asking anybody, as long as I bring it back by the end of the day.

Sabryna, seated at a table with her white pot partner, sees me and does a double take. "The pastor lives. Bible and all."

"Welcome back to the land of the living," the partner says.

I give them a nod as I walk off.

* * * *

During my job search run, I decide to take a much-needed detour to the library to search the address for the Broward County Women's Correctional Facility. Once I get the address, I head out and catch the next bus.

The facility is even more oppressing than the County Jail. The women in here can rightly be called bitches. They look and act like dogs. They're all tatted up, butched up, scarred up, muscled up, or beat up.

I follow the guard through the double-lock corridors to the visiting room and find myself praying for self-control. I'm only in this hellhole for one reason, and I better not blow it, or this'll end up being my new home.

The guard on the other side ushers in the inmate, who is the polar opposite of the psycho I met before. Patrice is visibly thinner, and even a little lighter in skin tone, which means she hasn't seen the light of day the entire time she's been in here. There are no visible scars though, so she's not doing too bad.

She sees me and her eyes bug out.

Good.

I pick up the receiver on my end, forcing her to follow suit. My jaw locks so tight my teeth start to grind.

"I'm only here to deliver a message," I barely say through curled lips. "Congratulations."

She gives me a confused look.

"You successfully aborted my pregnancy."

The confused look melts into horror.

"Now my daughter's innocent blood is on your hands for the rest of your rotten life."

I slam the receiver down and get up to leave. Her face crumples in regret as she tries not to cry, but the tears still come. She mouths the words "I'm sorry" over and over again until we're out of each other's view.

Mission complete.

11

Two weeks of chillin' in the activity area opened my eyes to why my little shadow friend used to live in here. It's the perfect place to snoop. I'm in here under as many pretexts as I can come up with now: to brush up on my chess, to borrow the Bible, to browse one of the new college-level workbooks, or to play one of the other games.

I finally started paying attention to the details of the space, too. It's wide but slightly stuffy, thanks to the constant air conditioning. The slim metal chairs have stiff red cushions that are just waiting to burst open and the metallic tables are painted a drab gray.

Mind you, these colors are set against sea green walls with white accents. A resident must've come up with this decor. She knew she wouldn't be here long, so she decided to torture everybody else with the color scheme.

Tackiness aside, I'm in here often. I even managed to catch up on everything I missed while I was gone. My shadow friend apparently moved on up -- she scored a job that pays well enough that she was able to get her own place. Lucky girl.

I can't lie, I'm jealous.

Anyway, I heard Mandisa started getting hooked on the sedative the home's psychiatrist gave her, so she quit taking it. The withdrawal symptoms put her in the ER for a day, but she's decent now.

Turns out Sabryna's booed up with her pot partner now. Her name is Zoe. I didn't know she rolled like that, but whatever. I guess that's bound to happen when you're in a place like this.

Not that I plan to switch sides. Damn that. Women are too disgusting for me. Too unstable. Too dishonest. Too damned evil.

I even found out Diana didn't leave at the end of her monthly visitation like she was supposed to. I'm guessing she lingered to visit Doctor Isaacs and me. As for him, he flatlined twice during surgery, but he managed to pull through.

My heart fell when I heard that. I couldn't focus for the rest of that day.

Today I'm seated at a table with a Physics workbook when Sabryna and her boo Zoe come in and start chatting. I always sit at a table in the corner of the room with my back to the rest of the area, so they don't realize I'm here. I take my phone out and check the time first to appear harmless, then I let the screen go off and prop it up against the small stack of books, sneaking it far enough to the side that I can see them in the screen's reflection. I go back to browsing through the book with my ears wide open.

They crack jokes on Diana at first, then on the newbies, and then the conversation finally comes around to me. "What about your girl Leila?" Zoe says. "She's technically a newbie all over again."

From my phone's reflection, Sabryna's back is to me. She shrugs. "She ain't my girl. I still dare her to try somethin'. She walkin' 'round like she own the place."

"And you don't?" Zoe fires back with a soft laugh.

"Difference is I actually own it. She just act she do."

"No point in provin' a point now, though. She just cheated death, for God's sake."

Sabryna's quiet for a good minute. "She was lucky."

"How? She got shot in the chest. And lost her baby."

Sabryna goes quiet again. Her voice is much lower when she finally speaks, almost remorseful. "I know. That's screwed up." She takes a deep breath. "But she survived, and that's what I mean by lucky. Most people who get shot in the lung with a .45 die."

Zoe shrugs. "Who knows, maybe losing the baby's a blessin' in disguise or somethin'."

"What?" Sabryna sounds irritated. "What you mean blessin' in disguise?"

"Well, a child's a pretty big responsibility, you know that. You got a little one--"

"Hell yeah, I know that."

"So...she doesn't have to worry about that now. And it ain't her fault the baby's dead, so she's in the clear."

"Oh, you a red-bagger, huh?"

I can't see Zoe's facial expression from the phone, but she leans forward on the table, staring Sabryna in the face.

"Don't you judge me," she says in a much lower voice, her twang even thicker than it already is. "You have no idea what I went through. I wanted to keep it."

"It?"

"I wasn't far enough along for them to determine the gender yet. My mom..." She sniffles. "My mom was ashamed of me, and of the child, so she paid for the operation under the table. And I wasn't showin' yet, so nobody would know the difference."

"What about the dude?"

"What about him? He's gay. He was just a donor for me and me fiancée Jessica, he didn't care."

"Oh...she was ashamed of that."

"Yeah. Not exactly the traditional American family. She said the child didn't deserve the terrible life we would put it through. Snooty bitch. She was just mad 'cause her picture-perfect traditional Christian marriage didn't work, so she was *sure* mine wouldn't. Can't wait for her to freakin' die."

Sabryna let that comment breathe for a while. I don't blame her.

"What happened to Jessica?"

"What you think? She found out about the abortion and swore me off. I tried to explain what happened, but she wouldn't hear any of it. I'm dead to her."

The girls go silent for several minutes. Curious to know why, I glance at my phone's reflection again.

And they're looking back at me.

12

I keep my face in the book as if I'd been reading the whole time. Sabryna and Zoe flank me. Sabryna pulls the book out of my hands and looks at it for herself. "What's the force of an object?"

Oh. She can actually read the thing. She earns points for that already.

"The energy applied to an object that makes it move. You get it by multiplying the object's mass by its acceleration."

She claps the book shut, seeming satisfied that I didn't lie. "You picked a hell of a time to study. What you studyin' for, anyway, huh? You ain't gonna use none of it."

I stay as calm as I can and put my phone in my pocket.

"I asked you a question, *pastor*."

I finally look her in the eye and just stare. Whether she "owns" this place or not, I have no time for her low self-esteem games. I've got nothing to lose now, so I don't give a damn about anybody or anything.

She sizes me up. "You gotta be stupid to come back here after what happened to you. You coulda gone anywhere."

"So could you."

"I ain't get shot."

"Maybe you shoulda."

The smug look on her face disappears, and the hard face I'm used to, the one I always saw back at the church shelter, comes back. "But I didn't. You the half-dead gimp now. Nothin' but worthless, useless, damaged shit. What you gonna do about it?"

My nostrils flare as my jaw tenses. I really didn't need to hear this bull right now.

"I thought you had more important things to do, Sabryna."

The three of us look toward the door for the familiar voice. Diana's leaning in the doorway with her usual folded arms and smirk.

Sabryna loudly drops the book on the table and walks toward her, stopping inches from her face. "You don't own me, fake saint."

Diana's calm smirk stays. "I don't have to."

Sabryna leaves the room. Zoe gives me a lingering look, as though she wanted to tell me something, but she leaves too, barely acknowledging Diana with a nod.

Turns out it's that time of the month again -- for her visit, I mean. For some reason, she tells me the course schedule for the seven days she'll be here, but I don't have the energy to be mean, so I just sit through it. She already knows I'll attend the classes.

"Where's your other half?" I ask when she's done.

She blinks a couple times at me.

"The Doc, man. Where's he at?"

"Oh. Um, Doctor Isaacs isn't with me for this visit."

"What? Why?"

"He's taking care of some personal issues right now." She shoots me a curious look. "He got shot too, you know."

"Of course I know. I had to remind him of that when he was worryin' 'bout me."

"You'll get your chess buddy back next month, don't worry."

I look at her. The comment sounded forced, like she's disappointed about that. Or maybe displeased. It's hard to tell.

"So, you still looking for jobs?"

"Every day. But I catch the bus now."

"That's good. Should increase your chances."

"Not so far, it hasn't, and I started as soon as I got back here."

"Well, you have my card, plus I'm here now. It's up to you to let me help you."

I suddenly thought back to what she told me in the hospital, which made my mind recall the nasty tripe Sabryna just told me, too.

Unloved. Worthless. Useless. Damaged.

"You've done more than enough," I reply, almost under my breath. "Thanks."

The heartbreak suddenly sags her face, as if her invisible mask of confidence fell and was desperately hanging on by her chin. "I really blew it, didn't I?"

"No. You said what needed to be said. Truth is always the best medicine, but nobody want it ‘cause it's freakin' bitter. Anyway, you need to get over yourself. *I* asked *you* the question." I rise to leave. "See you in class tomorrow."

A wave of relief washes over her, and she smiles again. "Yeah."

I check my phone's clock again, realizing I wasn't paying attention the last time I checked it. 3:16 p.m.

I'm an hour early for my job search run, but I'll need the extra time. I'm making another detour today.

I've got a doctor to hunt down.

13

First stop: the library. These days the old workplace is a little less oppressing. The dirty looks stopped a while ago. I wonder if any of the girls heard what happened.

Anyway, I sit at an Internet terminal and do a search for Doctor Isaacs. The search is fruitless at first since I don't know his first name, but I try the U.K. angle. Thankfully the search narrows a little, then I search deeper by adding Charlotte to the mix.

Then I find him. Doctor Kendall Isaacs.

I follow a link to his profile in the Manta.com directory, which not only lists his phone number and main office address, but the latest news updates related to him. The top link immediately catches my eye: "Doomed Psychiatrist Suffers Fourth Patient Failure."

I open the link in a separate tab and get floored. According to the article, Doc's latest client, a man from Boynton Beach with paranoid schizophrenia, committed suicide. The reporter then ran through Doc's history: his very first "failure", a teen with severe depression, committed suicide as well. The second fail was a sex offender released on parole. He couldn't handle the pressure of being shut out on every side in society, and despite Doc's counseling, he stopped trying. He got himself a gun on the black market, hunted down the sexual assault victim who pressed charges against him in the first place, and killed the man.

The victim was a priest. The case was a hot mess. They pretty much threw Doc's client under the prison.

Fail number three was a product of abuse, like me; but unlike me, she couldn't bounce back at all. Even after Doc's counseling, she started taking drugs. It started with weed, which led to heroine, and she's been hooked and homeless ever since.

Ironically, none of this counts Patrice. She's technically a fail, too.

I suddenly remember our agreement -- I was supposed to earn this info by beating him in chess. What a way for me to find out.

I shake off the guilt as I step outside and call the number from his profile. I get his voicemail, but at least he was nice enough to set up his voicemail message using his name so I could know for sure I dialed the right number.

I go back inside and return to the computer to find out where he lives. Within minutes I find his home address: 301 Cascading Palm Court, Lauderdale Lakes, Florida. I find it on Google Maps, map out a route, and find the buses I need to take to get there. Once I get everything together, I log out and leave.

* * * *

To my surprise, Doc lives in an apartment complex. I figured he'd be in a mansion with ten bedrooms or something bougie like that. Although for what it's worth, this is as close as it comes for an apartment complex: the black gates are tall and fancy with beams that narrow to sharp points at the top to ward off thieves, and the entrance ground is laid out in rich red brick, flanked on both sides by small fountains. Large brick complex name signs are also on both sides, with large gold-ish lettering against a black rectangular background: Whispering Pines.

Florida's full of cheesy complex and subdivision names like that: Sunrise Park, The Oasis, Emerald Palms, Northwest Gardens. I'm dying to see a complex whose name tells the truth, like Morning Sirens or Waking Bass or Thieves Cove or something.

I stop at the guard shack and tell the overweight man who I'm here to see. He asks for my driver's license, so I comply. The oily guard, whose sunburnt face was sloppy with sweat from the hot afternoon, hands me my license. The poor little card feels three degrees hotter.

I ask him where the apartment is.

"Look for Building 15."

I wait to see if he would say anything else, but he's done. "Thanks."

I walk for nearly a half-hour looking for Building 15. This apartment complex is a lot bigger and wider than any I've ever been in before. It's almost set up like a condo subdivision, with its own streets and street names. I turn left onto Osprey Circle and the building numbers jump to the thirties. I stop with a heavy stomp and grunt loudly at the sky. It is way too hot for this foolishness. I've already sweated out all of my deodorant and my mouth is growing dry. Why am I doing this to myself?

I head back in the direction I came from and turn left onto next block, Palm Lane. As I check the building numbers I finally notice what's weird about this place. It's quiet. Too quiet. No music playing out of anyone's apartment or car window, no chattering teens or young adults anywhere, even the basketball and tennis courts are empty. It's nearly 5 p.m. Some people should be home from work, and some kids should be running around, they're home from school already. The random green trees and the sun are my only company, and not a lick of wind to relive this afternoon heat and humidity.

I find Building 15 at the end of the block on the right side of the parking lot, which actually faced the intersecting street, which I realized was Cascading Palm Court. A breezeway cuts through the center of the building with a staircase on each side to access the apartments. I take the staircase on the left to the third floor. His door is the first one on the left side. I ring the doorbell on the wall to right of the doorframe with my heart in my mouth.

14

A few minutes pass, and I knock like 5-O, as Diana would. I hear a muffled holler, so I knock again, but a little more softly. "Go away!" I finally hear.

"You owe me a game, damnit!"

Silence.

After another minute or so I reach for the doorbell, ready to ring it off the wall, but the door finally cracks open, tattling the total darkness inside. I hesitantly step in and the musty smell of morning breath, old sweat, old McDonald's food, and spilled alcohol immediately punches my nose. The place is stuffy, more humid than outside. Clothes are thrown across the couch, the fast food trash litters the floor, and empty liquor bottles and cans are fighting for space on the coffee table. The blinds and curtains are drawn.

Doc emerges from the hallway shirtless, nearly scaring me to the ceiling, and walks around me to the couch, carrying a scented trail of body wash and shampoo as he lets himself fall into it. I can barely see this stranger in the dimness of the room. He let his hair go untrimmed, and it's a mangled wet mess, some of it covering his face. He perches an elbow on a knee to rub his forehead, and I realize he's not wearing shorts -- those are white boxers.

I feel so violated.

"How the hell did you find me?" His groggy words crash into each other.

"What are you drinking?"

His tone sinks, taking on a growly depth I've never heard before. "I asked you a question, Leila."

"You act like you someplace remote or somethin'. Anybody with a Internet connection can find you. Ain't no privacy left in this world, man."

He runs his fingers through the matted mess on his head.

"And how can you be cooped up in darkness? No windows open, no AC, no nothing."

"I don't recall letting my mother in, and I sure don't need you to replace her." He looks over at me, his face nothing but a shadow.

I really don't need his stank attitude right now. Not after the hassle I went to find him. And I tell him as much.

I see his shoulders bounce in the sliver of sunlight sneaking in from a curtain corner. "Nobody asked you to look for me. If you're looking for sympathy, you're not gonna find it here."

"You stank son of a bitch."

"Old news, Leila," he snaps back, grabbing a bottle from the table and drinking the few drops left in it. "And she's dead now, so be nice."

"You brought her up, not me."

A slow laugh bubbles out of him. Without looking at me, he lifts his bottle he's holding and points in my direction. "That's why I always liked you, Leila. You're sharp. You never miss a beat."

"Which is why I hunted you down."

"What do you want from me?" he asks after a pause.

"I wanna know what happened. Diana showed up and you didn't. I wanna know how you holdin' up."

He spreads his arms out. "Now you see it. I'm alive. I have a place to live."

"What drove you to drink?"

He pauses and looks at me. "Nothing new. I've been at this for quite a while--"

"I ain't stupid, Doc, I knew that from the moment I met you. But you never OD. You way over the edge now."

He puts the empty bottle on the table with a hard tap. "I said I'm alive now, and that you're not replacing my mother, so feel free to drop it now. Or see yourself out."

Fury spreads across my body in an explosion of heat. Before I know it, I walk to the table and knock everything off it with one swing. Glass clatters and cans bang loudly as they crash against each other on the carpet. I sit down on the table facing him, our faces only inches from each other. "No."

15

He stares at me in silent outrage, his jaw shut tight and nostrils flaring. Now that I'm closer, I see his hazel eyes are afire even in this darkness, just as they were the day we got shot. Part of me suddenly craves for more light so I can see them more clearly, and right away I wonder what's wrong with me.

Why do I feel this way around this dude? And why am I not afraid that he might beat me up? He's definitely angry enough to do it.

He moves in even closer to make me uncomfortable, but I don't move. "And what are you gonna do about it?" he snarls through clenched teeth. "Hm? You can't even save yourself, but you're gonna try to save me?"

"Don't flatter yourself, Corporate Boy," I fire back, immediately kicking myself for letting the nickname slip. He winces. "I ain't here to save nobody. I'm here to hold your feet to the fire. Diana's at work and you're not. Those girls need you. Do your damn job."

Another slow laugh erupts. "No they don't. If you knew anything about me, you'd know that."

"Well, I know it all now, since you chose to disappear. I wanted to hear it outta your mouth after I beat your ass in chess, but that ain't happen."

For once, the sly smile I'm used to finally appears, and my heart jumps. I never realized how much I enjoyed seeing it.

"So what do you think you know?"

"That you took five hard L's to the head. Two suicides, a murderer, a homeless drug addict, and now a convicted felon."

The smile disappears again as he looks away, slowly nodding. "You did your homework."

"Not on purpose. I was looking for your contact info and saw an article."

"And with a track record like that, you want me to do my job."

"You think those girls know or give a damn about that? Patrice was nuts. Most of them are just lost like me."

He looks at me again. "You're not lost, Leila. Not truly, anyway. You allow yourself to wallow with those girls. You could be anywhere else if you really want to."

"I choose to be here." My voice was way softer than I intended, and I suddenly find myself alternating between looking at his eyes and his lips.

He leans in close again, and my nostrils finally flare. Not in anger, but in a desperate effort to breathe and stay calm. His tone softens to match mine. "You could've just called if that's all it was."

"I did. And left a voicemail. Thanks for not paying attention."

"I saw the call, but I don't answer unknown numbers. I just haven't checked my messages yet."

"Tell me something. How many successes have you had?"

"More than five, I can tell you that," he replied with more clarity.

"That alone should get you outta this dungeon," I reply. "You know your own skills and limits. You can't win 'em all."

"That's *my* line."

I catch him looking at my lips too, which doesn't help.

"Be honest with me, Leila. Are you really here to give me a pep talk, or are you just here because you missed me?"

Bastard. Did he really have to go there?

"Both," I confess after a long, uncomfortable pause.

"I missed you too," he whispers. He reaches for my face, careful to only graze my cheek with his fingertips. It feels like four flaming rods are running down my skin. A hidden heat from deep within me spreads across my body. I'm forced to take another deep breath.

"I didn't know what happened to you after we got to the hospital," he continues. "I was afraid you were dead."

The doorbell suddenly buzzes like scratching marbles, startling both of us. He glances at me and gets up. He stands at the door with his head low. "Who is it?"

"It's me, Ken," I hear Diana say softly.

Doc looks over at me again before opening the door. Diana comes in and looks around in curious disgust, just as I did, and her eyes stop on me. "Oh, hey, Leila. What are you doing here?"

"Vandalizing my apartment," he groggily replies, nodding at the mess of cans and bottles I'd tossed on the carpet. Diana's eyebrows jump for a second, but she quickly redirects her attention to him. Judging by her sudden frown it finally dawns on her that this man really is walking around wearing only his undies with no intention of covering up.

She proceeds to talk some sense into him too, but with much more suave and style, using her ten-dollar words and that soft concerned look she always gives me. His previously rigid body language finally loosens a little bit, but not entirely, since she's standing.

Almost as if on cue, she moves next to him on the couch, and what happens next twists my stomach. Her voice lowers and softens, much like mine did earlier. She runs a hand through his hair, and his eyes close as he savors her touch. "Ken, don't do this to yourself. Those girls are depending on you. You're their only source of hope, and they already have to wait four long weeks for you. They love you."

Her words made my chest burn. They were both right. That's exactly the reason I wasted my time and energy coming here. I missed the fool. I waited these four weeks and looked forward to seeing him, just like his clients at the home. Even after all the bull I've been through with the men in my life, I still managed to foolishly attach myself to him. Somehow I thought he cared or wanted me before, but he was just doing his job. I'm not special to him. I'm just another resident. And Diana apparently already owns him.

"You okay?" Diana's words break my concentration.

I lift my head to her. I didn't realize I'm frowning. I look at Doc, whose face looks apologetic. "I'm fine." I glance at the near-non-existent gap between them on the couch and notice she's holding his left hand. My adrenaline suddenly surges and I have to take another deep breath to calm down. Why does that bother me so much?

I look away. "Never mind, I lied. I'm not okay."

Diana stands up and moves toward me. "What's wrong?"

"Nothing you can help me with," I reply in a cold tone as I head for the door. "Never mind the game, Doc. Glad you're alive."

I walk out without looking back.

16

I get back to the home in time for the evening class, which was a lecture titled "Why Hope?" The staff set up the cafeteria's projector and long white screen and played a DVD. With a series of deep quotes from dead philosophers, writers, and professors, and some relatable real-life stories, the speaker basically made a case for why believing in Jesus was the best decision anyone can make, and why Jesus is the only real source of hope in the world. This guy uses a lot of big words, but I have to admit his lecture was good. It made me think.

I had jotted down some of the quotes he read in my little notebook and was reviewing them when a shadow appeared over my book. I look up into Sabryna's face with surprise. "You get lost somewhere? You ain't watch the video, did you?"

She doesn't play along. Her face stays stiff. "I watched it." She straddles the bench, sitting just inches from me. Our knees almost touch. "What you think about it?"

"It was aight," I say without lifting my eyes from the book. "What *you* think 'bout it, Bible thumper?"

"You don't forgive, huh, pastor?"

"Stop callin' me that, I ain't no pastor. I don't know why you even started using that name on me."

"You forgot 'bout that little debate between you and Mandisa already?"

"I ain't say nothin' Christian."

"But you were preachin'."

"I thought you hated that."

Sabryna looks away, her lids low. This is the first time she's ever looked troubled. Why is she showing me this side of her all of a sudden? She was ready to fight me earlier. Called me all kinds of names.

I play it cool though, still eyeing my notes. "Can I help you with somethin'?"

"You believe any of that?" she asks after a long pause.

"What difference does it make?"

She rolls her eyes. "I'm just askin', damn. Do you ever answer a question straight up? You one of them bitches that always gotta get the last word on everything."

I think on that for a second. It never occurred to me before that I did that. I guess it's a habit of mine. "I believe God, Jesus, and the devil are real. I believe Heaven and Hell are real. But that's about it."

She reads my face for a few seconds. "Why? How you came to believe that?"

"Because I was raised to believe it," I reply hesitantly, studying her face in turn, wondering where this is coming from. "My grandma's Christian, and I grew up with her."

"You hate God too, huh?"

My mouth shuts tight on me. I think back to the hospital and suddenly remember the fact that my belly's now childless. My eyes start to fill with water, and I desperately blink it away. I look down at my notebook and just shake my head repeatedly.

I'm not sure what she saw in my reaction, but she decides to give me a quick-and-dirty summary of her life, constantly looking away. I have to stop myself from smiling or showing any sign that I already know what she's saying. When she's done she shakes her head, reflecting on it all. "Then I watched you get shot. And heard you lost the baby," she said. "You should be dead."

"Wish I was."

She doesn't entertain my comment. "Every time I see you now, I think back to my daughter Simone...I shoulda taken her with me. I feel like such a asshole. I'm not a deadbeat mom. I don't wanna be."

I look in her face, and for the first time, I see the real Sabryna. This is just a young girl who's lost, confused, lonely, and filled with regret, like me. She blames herself for everything that's wrong in her life, and she's mad because of it. That anger just happens to spill over unto everyone she sees and everything she does. I'm not exactly making much of an effort to control mine either, to be honest. Her dark brown eyes are heavy as they finally meet mine again.

"What would you do if you could see her again?" I ask.

"Please, that won't happen."

"I asked you a question," I said sternly, shoving her words back at her. That old angry Sabryna flickers in her eyes, but she stays calm.

"I...I don't even know what I would do. I wouldn't know what to say. She probably mad as hell at me."

"For now."

She gives me a confused look.

"She a kid, Sabryna. All kids really want is love. You and I know that the hard way. She'll be mad as long as she don't see you, but once she does, and she sees you love her, she'll forgive you."

I get up to leave, since we're the only two in the room. The staff will want to lock up soon.

"Have you?" she asks.

"What?"

"Forgave your momma."

"No."

" 'Cause you ain't seen her?"

"It goes deeper than that with her," I say after a long moment. "You?"

She shakes her head. Neither of us makes eye contact while we speak. "She ain't do me wrong directly. She just...She never told me 'bout my little half sister. I don't appreciate that."

"What you goin' to do, then?"

"What you said, I guess," she says with a shrug. "I'll probably forgive her once I finally meet the little girl in person. Daddy's another story."

I turn to face her now. This part I never heard about. "Where he at?"

"Up in New York, according to her. He supposed to be some big Wall Street baller. Got some other woman pregnant while he was with Momma, livin' a double life and all that. He stayed up there to live with her when Momma had me and moved down here. Bastard. To this day, I still wanna cut his nuts off."

There's the venomous Sabryna I know. "I'm sorry to hear that," I offer.

"Where yours at?"

"Dead."

She turns to look at me.

"My brother killed him for beatin' on me. He in jail for it right now."

She rubs her face with a heavy sigh. "I guess we all screwed up in here."

"That's a understatement," I say on my way out the door.

UPRISING

17

The next evening, my job search run takes longer than usual. So long, in fact, that I stop in a Burger King to grab dinner -- or something like that. I order a Whopper Junior and the smallest fries and drink from the value menu to keep the cost down. The gum-smacking Latina behind the counter rings the meal up to $4.28, including the ridiculous and unfair takeout tax. I pull out my last five-dollar bill and hand it to her. She puts the money away and calls for the next customer. No receipt, no nothing. "You forgot my receipt and change, miss."

She gives me an annoyed look and finishes ringing up the white man standing next to me. She hands him his receipt and calls the next customer forward. She prints up a receipt and hands it to me while the customer stares at the menu, still not sure what to order.

"The meal's $4.28 and I gave you five bucks," I say. "Where's my change?"

"I'm out." She opens the register and shows me. She really has no coins in the drawer.

"You ain't got no coworker or manager to give you change? What about the person workin' the window?"

"The manager's workin' the window," she replies, popping her neck a little. "We're the only two here and the drive-thru's more crowded than in here." She gestures to the line behind me.

The cook in the back puts a takeout bag in the front case. She looks in it and brings it to me. "Thank you," I say with a sigh and left. With a line this long, there was no point fussing over seventy-two cents. I could certainly use that change to grab a nice treat from the home's vending machine, but whatever. At least I have the meal.

I start heading back to the home, forcing myself to channel the disappointment over the lost change into energy to walk faster. I had two miles to hoof before the nearest bus stop, so I close the gap as quickly as possible, barely aware of my surroundings.

I reach the stoplight across the street from the bus stop, and a shaky voice brings me out of my haze. I look over at the off-white building behind me, which doubled as a restaurant on one side and a residential space on the other, and sure enough an old silver-bearded black man with only a handful of teeth in his mouth is singing "Alpha and Omega": "We give yoooou aaaaaaaaall...the...glooooorryyyyyyyy, we worship you our Lord, you are worthy tooo beee praised." He was all in it too -- arms raised to the sky and everything.

Something in me stirs. This man is worse off than me. He's on a street corner; no roof of his own, no bed to lie in, and he's praising God like he's living the greatest life ever. He looks at me when he finally stops singing and wipes the tears from his eyes with a tattered, dirty windbreaker sleeve. "Can you spare me a dollar, ma'am?"

I sigh, unable to mask the sadness in my face. I barely have any money left, definitely not enough to help him buy anything he would need, and I'm mad hungry. I want this meal, especially considering the seventy-two cents I had to sacrifice to get it. "How can you sing a song like that, considering where you are?"

He smiles and looks out at the street. "I'm alive, ain't I? God obviously ain't done with me yet. Plus I'm still in my right mind, no Alzheimer's, no dementia, none of that. I'm just broke and homeless, which can change at any minute. I don't know when, but as long as I have life I have a chance, and that's enough for me to sing."

I pay closer attention to the now filthy dark blue ball cap on his head. There's a big gray ship in the middle of the face, and embroidered yellow letters curve around the top and bottom of the ship that read: USS BONHOMME RICHARD, LHD 6. "You a vet?"

"Yes, ma'am. Thirty-five years." He taps the brim.

"And you homeless? How that happened?"

His weary black eyes shift back to me. "What happened don't matter now. Past can't change. Future's out of reach. All we can control is now. So. Can you spare a dollar? I just want to buy some water or something to munch on."

I look down at my bag and realize my hunger isn't as serious as it was before. I couldn't *not* help this dude. I walk up to him and hand him the bag. "I ain't got enough money, but you can have that. I just bought it. You can have the drink too if you don't mind drinkin' after a stranger."

Another smile spreads across his face. "God bless you, sista, thank you. You can keep the drink. Not because I mind drinkin' after a stranger, but because you'll need it since you travelin' on foot." He nods toward the street. There's the bus, if you waitin' for it."

I look behind me, and the bus is sitting at the red light. It would make a U-turn and pull up to the stop any second now. "Enjoy that," I say, pointing at the food as I walk away.

The last I see of him before breaking into a sprint is a slow, proper, meaningful salute. I salute him back, even as I run.

I board the bus and stand in the aisle, despite the several seats available. I think back to my encounter with the veteran and realize this is my first time ever in life doing something good for someone else. I can't explain what this is I feel, but it's good. Whatever it is, it's good. I want more of it. And though I hate to admit it, I want what that vet has.

I'm tired of being aimless, confused, and angry.

18

The next week is nothing but a hunt to feel that high again, and I do as much as I can to get it. I show up early for the classes, helping the speakers get ready by setting up the podium and any electronic stuff they need in case they're playing a DVD or music. If the cafeteria staff chooses to use the individual chairs instead of the long folding benches, I help put them out. During the classes that involve in-class practice, like math and finance, I help the other girls with their work once I figure the concept out for myself and finish mine.

Of course it's a pain-and-a-half with Sabryna and Mandisa, since they're not used to that kind of thing. They curse at me the first few classes, but I help them anyway. Some of the other girls are equally mean, mostly out of insecurity -- they think I think I'm better than them and choose to rub it in their faces by helping them, which is a stupid assumption, but whatever. They can think what they want. I want my high from helping people, and they're going to help me get it.

Besides, I heard something crazy in one of the Christian lectures: we're supposed to love our enemies, and do good to them that hate us. I couldn't believe my ears when I heard that. Why in the world should we waste our time and energy on people who will spit on our efforts? But after helping in the first two or three classes, I saw why it's so important. It's uplifting, and even the ones that don't want my help eventually warm up to me. And there's an added benefit in my case: since I help set up and clean up, the cafeteria staff now sets some snacks aside for me to enjoy at the end of the night classes. Good stuff, too: fresh fruit salad, little fruit cups, a couple snack bars, cracker sandwiches, and even some boxed juice.

Want to know something crazy? Instead of sneaking off and stuffing my face in my room, I sneak the snacks to my room then shove some in my pockets to take with me on my job search runs. Every homeless person I see gets something from my pocket. One gets a juice and a pack of cracker sandwiches, another a snack bar, another a smuggled cafeteria dessert, like a cake slice or cookie or brownie.

Of course, I've learned the hard way that some of these people aren't actually needy. Some have the nerve to tell me, "Oh, can I just hold some money instead?" Those people get a stern choice: take the food or get nothing. I don't have money anyway, but even if I did and they tell me that foolishness, my kindness disappears. I have no desire to help people who take me for a bank.

In the end, they shut up and take the food.

In general, I don't chat much with the homeless, though. I just pull a Santa on them. I spot them and just hand them the food. Only when they thank me do I respond, either with a nod or a small smile. Alice the hypocrite didn't really teach me how to interact with strangers, so I close up when I'm around someone I don't know.

In week two of my good-girl campaign, I sit in on a Christian lecture that's even harder than the love-your-enemies lecture: forgiveness. Ironically, the two principles actually tie together. When somebody does me wrong, I'm supposed to pardon them. Not excuse the wrong they did and let them walk all over me, but not hold a grudge against them for the rest of my life. The crazy old woman on the DVD explains that forgiveness isn't meant to benefit the person who wronged me, it's meant to benefit *me*.

As I watch the video I feel someone's stare on me, and I realize it's Sabryna studying me from across the bench. She gives the projection screen a disbelieving glance. "I grew up on this chick," she mumbles. "My uncle watches her all the time. If you hear one of her messages, you done heard 'em all."

"So what you doin' in here?"

She gives the screen a sad look this time. "Good question."

She thankfully ends the conversation there.

That night, after cleaning up and collecting my smuggled snacks, I go back to my room and get ready for bed. I lie on the hard bed staring up at the boring white ceiling, and finally come to the edge of myself. "God, I'm tired of being angry and alone and helpless. I don't know why you took my daughter from me or why You let so many terrible things happen to me, but I'm tired of being mad at You for that, too. I've had a screwed up life, and I'm screwed up because of it. I don't think it's possible to forgive anybody or love my enemies, but if it is possible, only You can make it happen. I want what that old vet has, peace or joy or whatever. Please help me."

19

The visiting room feels somehow colder than it was the last time I was here. And I'm forced to wait much longer, by nearly fifteen minutes. I timed it.

The guard brings Patrice in. She looks even skinnier than before, and completely emotionless. By some miracle, she's still scar-less too. She simply sits and stares at me, barely even blinking. I finally reach for the phone receiver, gripping it tight to steady my trembling hand as I put it to my ear. My guts are already on fire and my mouth is dry. I can't believe what I'm about to do, but it needs to be done. She picks her receiver up without taking her eyes off me.

"I um..." I can't seem to look her in the eye. I lick my dry lips. "I um...I came..." Feeling pathetic, I take a deep breath and force the damn thing out. "I came to say I'm sorry." I pause to check her reaction, and the closest thing I could make out was a deep breath. "Sorry for what I said about you. I was real mad. Mad at you, mad at God, mad at everything. I said what I said to make you feel bad, and it worked. I was satisfied."

Her eyes barely narrow for a split second, but she catches herself, staying silent.

"I was wrong for that. I just um...wanted you to know I forgive you for the shooting, for what it's worth." I look around the room. "I'm sure it's hell in here."

Still no reaction.

"I don't know if you'll ever forgive me for what I said, but the most I can do is ask. That's up to you."

I stare at her for a few seconds. When I realize she has no intention of moving, I put my receiver back on its cradle. For some reason she keeps hers at her ear.

I give her a confused look, which she answers by holding up an index finger. She lays her receiver on the table in front of her instead and signals to the guard as if she's texting. The guard gives her an unbelieving look, but gives her his phone. She quickly works the touch screen with her left thumb.

I think back to the day she shot us and remember how shaky her hand was. No wonder she could barely manage the gun. She was using the wrong hand. A chill suddenly shoots up my spine: if she shot us in such fatal spots with her weak hand, imagine if she shot us with her good one. Me and Doc would be past tense.

She holds the phone close to the glass: I CAN'T SPEAK.

I put my receiver to my ear. She puts hers back at her ear. "What happened?"

She thumbs the screen again, and the two words she holds up forces me backwards a little: TONGUE'S GONE.

"They cut it out?"

The miserable sadness I saw in her face last time reappears as she nods.

I close my eyes and rub my face. "Oh my God," I groan. "That's horrible."

She shakes her head with a soft smile. She thumbs one last message and holds it up: ROM 8:28.

I jot it down and nod, despite not having a clue what she just showed me.

She nods back and finally puts her receiver back on its cradle. I follow suit. She hands the guard his phone, and he gives her an impressed look, as if he expected her to steal it.

She looks back at me as the guard leads her out, and her eyes tell me some sad silent message like "I'm sorry" or "help me" or "I wish I was free again."

For the first time, I actually pity her.

* * * *

I get an interesting surprise the next morning. I'm in the activity area after class practicing chess, barely able to concentrate. I can't believe Patrice lost her tongue. I'm not sure which is worse, losing an important part of your own body or losing an unborn child. She can't speak, and probably can't eat either, which would explain why she's so much skinnier. And then there's Doc with his five fails. I wonder if he even knows about Patrice's situation.

First thing this morning, I double-checked the code she gave me before I left the prison last night. It was a scripture reference, Romans 8:28: "And we know that all things work together for good to them that love God, to them who are the called according to his purpose." No offense to God, but He has a sick sense of what's "good."

Shaking off the mental noise, I grab a knight and take a bishop, landing the knight diagonally next to the opponent's pawn.

"Tsk. You just wasted that knight." The female voice coming from behind me sounded familiar, but I couldn't place it. I know the tone, but don't recognize the clean, proper American English accent. She talks like Doc. I look over my shoulder and my eyes nearly fall out.

My shadow friend is back, looking clean as ever. Her hair is back to its natural black color, and her skin glows. Her slender frame almost looks ready to fly away with the breezy bright multi-color sundress, which dances nicely at the back. The baby bump is gone, too.

"Did you...?"

She looks down at her stomach. "Oh no, I took the baby to term. It's a boy. He's so beautiful."

"Who are you and what have you done with my friend? I don't recognize you at all."

She laughs. "I’m still right here, and I came back to give you some good news. Sorry I couldn't visit you at the hospital. I left the home shortly after you went in. I got a job."

My eyebrows jump, but deep inside, I'm jealous as hell. Why is she so lucky? "That's dope. Congrats."

She sits in the chair across from me and leans in close so the other girls in the room don't hear her. "I got a staff job at Florida Community College. But that's not the good news. I came to tell you I scored you a paid internship in their Engineering and Computer Science department."

I blink at her for several seconds in complete disbelief.

"Did you hear me?"

"Yeah, I just -- wow. Wha-- how did you do that?"

She winks. "Pulled a few strings."

"When do I start?"

"You interview on Friday at seven A.M. You already got the job, but they'll want to meet you and tell what you need to know before you start next week."

The interview's in three days. How is this happening? "Oh my God," I whisper, covering my mouth to control my emotions. "Thank you."

She takes my free hand and smiles. "I'll be back tomorrow. You'll need some clothes."

"O-okay."

Some of the other girls mean-mug her as she leaves. She smiles back, probably laughing at them on the inside.

20

Florida Community College's downtown Ft. Lauderdale campus is like a whole other world for me. I've been on the beach-bound Las Olas Boulevard many times during my trips to the prison to visit Kalvin or to catch a bus from the terminal, but this was slightly different. For one, it was a shorty among the skycrapers on the boulevard. The building right next to it stands six stories tall, basically daring the little building to try something crazy. The campus has the same inlaid multicolored brick pavement that most of the downtown buildings have, the same kind Doc's apartment complex uses. It's played out, but I can see why it's so popular. It looks clean and stands out nicely from the boring tannish concrete. One side of the grayish building has the school's name and logo in reflective letters and several wiry benches with their backs to the trees they sit under. Palms are lined up along one side like soldiers I've seen in the movies waiting for orders. This whole area is full of trees of different species, really. Not that I know any of them.

My little shadow friend, Esther, leads me to another entrance of the campus across the street. I finally asked her what her name was on the way here. It was mad embarrassing, considering how long we've known each other and what she's done for me here, but thankfully she was cool about it.

Anyway, this entrance looks even cooler. The wall above the name has black wiry metal artwork shaped into unique images with rectangular borders.

The double-doors slide open and a gust of cold A/C air hits us as we walk in. The artsy walls attack my eyes with color. Each is a different bright shade: deep orange, yellow, red, beige, sea green. She leads me to the front desk and gets me registered for a temporary pass. "You'll get the real one next week," she says with a smile. She leads me past crowded classrooms with thin, odd-shaped tables and desks. Students of all colors type away on their laptops as their teachers talk in front of projector screens and scribble on white boards.

It's all new and scary to me, but I can't front, I wish I was sitting in one of these rooms with a laptop of my own.

"We're almost there," Esther says with an apologetic look. "I know I've had you walkin' all over this place. Your feet okay in those shoes? Do they hurt?"

I look down at the strappy red sandals she lent me and shrug. The heels give me a three-inch boost. "Nah, I'm aight."

She looks me up and down. "That outfit actually looks really good on you. I might let you keep it."

I do look kind of fly in this dress and dress-sandal combo. The dress is bordered with navy blue short sleeves and a matching collar, and the body is a white background filled with small squares of various colors: red, olive green, gold, navy blue. It stops just above my knees too, so I get to show off my diesel legs, which is worth it considering how long it took for me to shave them.

"Here we are."

Esther leads me into the Engineering Program office lobby and motions to a couch. My heart comes up to my mouth as I sit down, beating at the speed of light. She goes to the desk and tells the receptionist I'm here for my seven o'clock appointment. The woman at the desk looks at me, checks her computer, then gives Esther a nod. After a few minutes, the door to the left of the desk opens and a tall, husky black man in his forties with a nine-months-pregnant paunch waves for me to come in.

The interview's over in fifteen minutes. I step out rubbing my forehead. Esther jumps up from the couch with a very worried look. "What happened?"

"He asked some pretty personal questions, and as much I ain't want to go into all that, I told him the truth about me," I confess. "He might not gimme the job now."

Her worried look disappears. "Don't say that. You'll be alright." She walks into his office without even knocking on the closed door first. She's out within seconds. "Like I said, you'll be alright. Let's go."

21

I started my internship that next week, just as Esther said I would. The part-time internship pays minimum wage, which at this point is seven dollars and seventy-five cents an hour. That's a hundred and fifty-five dollars for a twenty-hour workweek. It's a boring desk job pushing papers, but it's a job. It's a start. And I go as hard in that office as I did back at the library. I'm packin' six hundred and twenty dollars by month's end, and with the food stamps, that money doesn't even get touched. Esther visits me at the home once a week to take me shopping for work clothes and was nice enough to give me the dress and shoes I borrowed for the interview.

I never really pay any attention to how I look, but with this job and the dope clothes Esther helps me buy now, I'm forced to, which is mad uncomfortable. I honestly don't like looking at myself in the mirror. At least my hair finally outgrew the dye; it's just a bland brownish black now, which I guess looks a little better against my dark brown skin.

Looks aside, the job has me feeling much better overall. I feel like I actually have purpose now, like I actually matter. Even if I don't matter to anybody else, I matter more to me. Even my swagger's different. I used to walk hard, like a dude. Now my walk is a little straighter, more feminine, and I look ahead of me more often now instead of counting cracks in the pavement or floor, trying to avoid eye contact with people.

The only setback to the job is I'm not at the home as often to help set up before the morning classes, and I'm missing some good ones according to Diana's schedule, especially one I really need now: Setting Up a Checking and Savings Account. Oh well. I'll just ask Esther about it when she comes back next week. Or maybe even Sabryna, if she shows up to listen.

Speaking of her...

* * * *

This 'hood fits the name with a vengeance. Dead and dry or un-mowed lawns with weeds reaching for the sky, old or beat up cars parked on the grass or in the driveway, houses looking faded as hell, crying for a paint job; even the streets themselves look unwanted. They could use a fresh coat of tar.

It's 3:13 p.m. when I knock on a double-painted green door. I glance at the driveway while I wait. It's laid out in brick, which is completely painted over in an ugly, pasty, bright red. And the candy Dodge Magnum parked on top of it is even worse. I thought candy cars died with the last decade. Anyway, this one is full blown "hood": it was about two feet off the ground with big tires and big chrome rims. No less than twenty-fours.

I hear a muffled holler through the door and straighten up, taking a step back. The door clicks about four different times before it opens. Guess they've been robbed a few times. A young pregnant girl stands in the doorway in faded blue coochie cutters and a short-sleeved white v-neck shirt with no bra, holding the door close to her body so I wouldn't see too much inside. "Yes?"

I'm guessing she's Indian. She looks it. Long wavy black hair, petite and skinny, skin as dark as mine. Her lips are gray from smoking. Dad's lips were dark like that too, and he was a freakin' smokestack. It makes her ugly. "Um, I'm lookin' for Keyshawn Patel, he here?"

She rolls her eyes. "You his next one?" Her accent sounds Trinidadian or Guyanese.

I pop my neck for a second, but miraculously catch myself. "No, ma'am. I'm here about his daughter."

"Pssh. Which one? He has three, including one from me."

TMI, miss. "Can I come in and talk to him, please?"

She eyes me from head to toe and sighs. "At your own risk. He's leaving soon to DJ a party." She pushes the door further open.

"Thanks."

I step in and immediately cough. The house is a smoggy haze, and every window in sight is shut. Ugh. The weed's stink was already making me sick. And very worried. If the job orders a piss test tomorrow, I'm screwed. I shake the nasty feeling off.

"And who is this beautiful stranger in my house?" another Indian or Trini accent, but much stronger. And much deeper.

I turn around and look up. Keyshawn looks...kinda black and kinda not, like he's half and half. His short hair's wavy like the girl's, and he's dark-skinned. Clean shaven, I guess to look young. He's probably six-two or four, his wifebeater hugging his muscles. I suddenly remember Bryce and I'm all too eager to get the hell out of here.

"Oh. Hey, I'm Leila." I hold my hand out and he gently shakes it. "I'm here to ask you 'bout one of your daughters."

He chuckles. "Which one?"

"Simone."

The smile's instantly gone, and by some miracle the chattering TV has a silent moment between commercials, making his and the girl's sudden silence even more awkward. "What about her?" he finally asks.

"I been in touch with her momma."

His eyebrows dip. He looks like he's not sure whether to be angry, sad, or happy. He moves in close. "Damn her mother. She left us. She left her."

"I don't blame you. But she wanna start over--"

"Start over?" he asks in outrage.

"She wanna be in her life now."

"Simone's almost two now, does she even know that?"

I take a step back, sensing his rising rage. Unlike Doc's anger, I recognize this. This dude is one second away from throwing hands or throwing an object. I see the girl retreat to the wall from the corner of my eye. She's used to this.

"You ain't never had no second chance before?" I finally ask.

"She doesn't deserve one."

"Neither do you."

He looks ready to punch me, balled fist at his side and all.

"Or me. Or her." I glance at the girl. "But that kid deserve to see her momma again, especially if momma's tryin' to get right with her. You can't really deny that."

He walks off down the narrow hallway behind him. "Bitch is lucky. Almost called DCF on her for that bullshit. She would never see Simone no matter how much she wanted to."

Little Simone steps out of the dark bedroom holding her father's index finger, and I get a nasty chill. She's only a deep silhouette thanks to the sunlight from the rooms behind her, and her huge uncombed Afro casts an even bigger shadow on her face and shoulders. The heavy haze makes her look out of place, like a baby Angela Davis messed with somebody's time machine, accidentally fell in it, and just landed in front of me. He tells her who I am and why I'm here and she just stares at me.

"Mommy?"

My heart falls to my feet.

"No no, she *knows* Mommy," he says.

"You want to see Mommy?" I ask her. He gives me a dirty look.

She shyly nods.

"You can see her. I know where she is."

She lights up with excitement, and pulls on her dad's hand. "Mommy! Mommy!"

Keyshawn makes an annoyed sigh. "I'm about to leave, and I really don't trust you with my child. We only have the one car."

"So drop us off and be on your way," I reply with a shrug. "You'll be with her in the car, and when you drop us off, she'll go straight to her mother."

He goes back to the room and emerges a few seconds later wearing a button-up shirt over the white tank top, jingling the car keys in his hand. He nods towards the door.

* * * *

Simone grips my hand and sucks her free thumb as we walk into the home. This poor little girl looks numb. She told her dad goodbye, but there were no tears or fear. She didn't cling. I got the chance to study her face on the way and realized she's very beautiful, a perfect mix of both parents. She has her mother's brown skin, almond eyes, and jaw, her father's nose and mouth, and the kinky-wavy mix of both in her hair.

After checking her in as a visitor and asking the receptionist to contact Sabryna, I take Simone to the activity area. All eyes are on us, but I don't bother explaining myself. They'll figure things out in a minute. I wave my hand at the tables for her to see. "Wanna play?"

She nods, pointing to a table with a Hungry Hungry Hippo game sitting on it. I lead her to the table and set the game up for her. She doesn't say anything and just starts playing.

"Hey," I say nicely. "What are you supposed to say?"

For the first time I see some emotion. Her brows wrinkle up, warning of tears.

"Oh, don't cry. You're not in trouble. Just say 'thank you'."

She relaxes. "Thank you."

I watch her play for a few minutes, smiling at her cute little face as deep dimples appear and disappear from her cheeks, another gift from her mother, and suddenly realize my daughter would probably look similar if she was the same age, but darker. She would've had Bryce's dimples and the same kind of Afro, since his hair is wavy. Her eyes would probably be almond brown like Simone's too, since his eyes are that color. Mine are dark brown.

Her eyes wander to her left and she does a double take. I follow her gaze and see Sabryna frozen in the entryway, with her boo Zoe a few feet behind her. It's absolutely amazing: Simone and Sabryna haven't seen each other in over a year;

Simone isn't even old enough to remember what her mother looks like, but she somehow knows that she and this woman are connected.

I pick her up and carry her on my hip so she could look her mother in the eye. Sabryna studies her face in silent disbelief.

"Here you are, Simone," I say. "This is Mommy."

The numb haze lifts again and she lights up. "Mommy!" She reaches her arms out to her.

Sabryna can barely contain her tears. "Hey, baby girl," she whispers, taking her from me. She gives me a quick questioning look, which I answer with a wink and smirk.

As I return to the table and clean up the game, I smile wider to myself, silently thanking God for this brand new high I'm feeling. Sabryna's reaction was priceless.

This blows my encounter with the homeless veteran out of the water.

22

"You ain't 'bout this life, yo. How the hell you tellin' me how to live?"

I pass a counseling room on the way to my room in time to hear the resident bark after her counselor. I think nothing of it...until I hear the counselor's response.

"You'd be surprised." Her voice was low. Angry. Threatening. "I've been dragged through the dirt with the best of them, sweetheart, believe me."

I look at the door in disbelief. Diana? When?

I quickly walk off before I hear anything more or get busted for snooping. I didn't even realize it was time for her monthly visit again. That was quick.

Class is in another two hours, so I freshen up to take Simone back to her home. I go to the activity area and find Sabryna and Simone enjoying each other's company with some strange dark-skinned man. This one wasn't the father -- he looks straight up black, not mixed with anything. Simone waves at me with a bright smile. Sabryna gives me a tender look, as if she wants to thank me, but is too shy or proud to say it. I shift my eyes to the man, and she calls me over.

"This the one," she tells him.

He chuckles as he shakes my hand. "Hi, I'm Gus, Sabryna's uncle."

"Leila." I wasn't sure what else to say to him, so I look back at Sabryna. "I came to take her back home since I brought her here--"

Simone's face falls.

"You don't wanna go home?" I ask her.

She shakes her head, clinging to her mother's arm.

" 'Course not," Sabryna says softly, hugging her. "I called Uncle Gus to spend some time with her to soften the blow." She and Gus exchange looks. "Daddy's waitin' in his car outside. Uncle Gus can walk her out with you."

I look at Gus, then back at her. "Um..."

"Oh, Keyshawn and Uncle Gus know each other, they're cool," she explains. "Uncle Gus babysits her all the time."

He gives me a reassuring nod.

She squats to be level with Simone. "Don't be afraid, baby girl. You, Daddy, and Uncle Gus know where I am now, so we'll see each other soon, okay?"

"Okay." She hugs Sabryna, smiling from ear to ear.

"Sabryna told me what you did," Gus tells me. "Thanks for bringing them back together."

I nod as I take Simone's hand, and Gus and I walk her out to the parking lot. The two of them look back at Sabryna as they leave.

Once I'm back inside, grief suddenly rushes in hard and before I can fight them, the tears rain down. I can't even walk. I have to go into a nearby bathroom and lock the stall.

What happened? This was a high for me earlier. I did a great thing. Why am I bawling like this?

...Because my daughter should be here. And she's not.

Part of me wants to call Apostle Thompson and tell him everything, but I know he won't care. He'll probably breathe a sigh of relief. Asshole. I know I'm supposed to forgive, but heaven help him if I ever see him again. I'll take a page out of Sabryna's book and cut it *all* off. I'll make him *useless*, so he can never rape another desperate little girl again. And then he had the nerve to tell me to abort my child? That's a double-crime. God should fry his ass.

I finally calm down and step out of the stall. As God in His sick sense of humor would have it, Diana's at the counter washing her hands. I didn't even know anybody else was in here when I came in. "Leila! I didn't realize that was you. What's wrong?"

My mind flashes back to Doc's apartment, and my nostrils flare all over again. "Nothin' you can help me with." I yank the door open.

"Hey, wait. Doctor Isaacs is back this month--"

"That's nice."

The door shuts.

I could give a shit less if he's back. He's her puppy. To hell with her *and* him. My life's looking up now, and I can't get out of this place fast enough. Let me go set this evening class up. I only hope she ain't the instructor.

If she is, I'm gone.

* * * *

Class starts at seven on the dot and sure enough Diana walks in with the Doc in tow. They both look at me as they walk across the room to find a seat, but I just mean mug 'em like the rest of the girls do. Doc gives me a confused look as they cross the room.

Thankfully, Diana didn't teach. It was another financial class on how to set up special savings plans, like a six-month emergency fund, or a Christmas savings pool so we don't go into debt shopping for people. That's pretty smart, actually.

I hang around until everyone leaves as usual. As I help clean up, I see Diana lean over and whisper something in Doc's ear. He gazes at me for a minute before he leaves. Those hazel eyes were bright as usual, but they did nothing for me now.

Diana watches me work. Her usual caring look is completely gone. That chick she counseled must've rubbed her the wrong way. By the time I finish, Diana's waiting by the door with her arms folded and that stony look.

"Move, please."

"No. Not unless you're coming to my office."

"You're off the clock for the night."

"Exactly."

I stare at her for a second. She sounds mad suspect right now. "What do you want?"

"I'll explain that when we get to my office."

"And if I refuse?"

"Your loss. If you want to walk around mad and confused, that's on you."

With that, she walks out.

23

The office almost looks like one of those poetry lounges in the movies. There are small lit candles all over the place, no lights on. The spare spaces on the shelves are loaded with snacks. Diana opens a drawer and pulls out two big Starbucks cups, placing one in front of me, then leans all the way back in her chair.

This looks like some real lesbo stuff. If she tries anything, I swear things will turn out real bad. For her.

"I don't drink coffee."

"It's tea. Shut up and drink it." Her dark eyes seemed that much darker and evil in the dim dancing candle flames. This is a totally different creature I'm dealing with. Even the diggin'-in-your-mind look is gone. No smile, no soft tone, no nothing.

I slowly sit in the chair, studying her face as I grab the cup and sip. I'm surprised by a nice berry-ish taste. "What's this?"

"Raspberry white tea."

"It's nice. Kinda relaxin'."

"Exactly."

I look at her again. She just stares at me from above her cup's rim. "What you drinkin'?"

"Chai latte."

"What?"

"It's tea too," she explains. "With milk." She puts her cup on the desk, leans back in her chair again, and folds her hands in her lap. "Enjoy that. Grab whatever you want from the shelves."

"How you get all this?"

"You're not the only one who smuggles snacks."

"What you help them with?"

"Keeping all of you in line, which isn't easy."

"How? You only here one week outta the whole month."

"And I make it count. I bring the girls up to my level when I'm here, and hold them accountable when I'm not."

"How?"

"By showing them my true colors. Which you haven't seen yet." She finishes her latte. "Which is why you're here."

I stay silent, still wondering what the hell I've gotten myself into.

"Number one, I don't know what you think Doctor Isaacs and I have going on, and at this point, I really don't care. We're not together, so get over yourself."

"But you were in the past."

"No," a male voice cut in from behind me. I look over my shoulder in surprise and embarrassment as Doc walks from his hiding place next to the door to the wall next to me. "She adopted me."

What? She's his mother?

She answers my look by sitting up and leaning in on the desk. "God led me to do for him what this home does for you. Provide food, clothes, shelter, and sometimes money."

I glance at him, then at her. "He was homeless?"

"More like clueless. He came here from Wales an arrogant brat, which you know America has no patience for, especially in non-citizens, no matter what color you are. He was shut out on every side, so he did what you know he does best."

I look at him again in time to see him lower his eyes.

"And that's how I found him. Stumbling drunk on a curbside. I lifted him into my truck kicking and screaming, took him home, stripped him down, and ran a cold shower on him. He hadn't washed in probably a week. For that first month, he wasn't allowed to touch a bottle, and I kept him away from the bars. He wasn't even allowed to leave the house without me -- it was the only way to keep him accountable.

"I prayed over him and rubbed him with oil every single day. Sometimes I'd pray and fast for a whole week at a time. I shared the Gospel with him, and he received Christ. That's when things turned around. He started going to school and got back on track with his career."

"Where and when was this?"

"Back in New York, end of the nineties."

"Why? He coulda been anybody. He coulda killed you."

He gives me a disgusted look.

"I didn't choose him, Leila. I'd prayed for someone to minister to that very morning, and God led me to Doc twelve hours later."

"So you just a robot? You just do what He says? You don't think for yourself?"

"Of course I think things through, but when God tells me to do something, I know it'll work out. I don't always benefit, but someone does. You think this counseling thing is easy? Hearing other people's stories doesn't make me feel better about myself, Leila."

My heart drops at the memory of barking those words at her when we first met.

"It breaks my heart. It breaks God's heart. He sent me to help all of you to the best of my ability. Everything else is up to him. And for the record, my story isn't any better than yours. But you never think about that, any of you. You girls see me where I am now and judge me for that. You have no idea the hell I've lived to get to this point."

I give her an unbelieving look.

The stony look returns. "How much is your life worth, Leila?"

I shrug. "Probably nothin'."

"Anybody ever tell you you were an accident?"

I hear the sadness in her voice and my attitude drops. "I never *heard* it, but I always thought I was."

Water rushes into her eyes as she clenches her jaw. "I heard that almost every day of my life. *At home*."

DIANA'S STORY

"I wish I had that three hundred dollars!"

Diana was hearing this for the umpteenth time. Her mother always hollered it at her when she was mad, and it always made her cry. "Is that all my life's worth?" she wanted to ask. Three hundred dollars is all it would've taken for her mother to abort her in the womb, but she couldn't afford it at the time. Diana was the result of a one-night stand. Her mother didn't even really know the man, and he wasn't in Diana's life. Though it wasn't Diana's fault, her mother made it so.

"I didn’t ask to be here!" Diana screamed back instead.

She got her usual slap in return.

"I didn’t ask to get pregnant!"

Diana stood trembling and sobbing as her mother walked off. She ran to her room and slammed the door. She knew a violent beating was coming. Paddle, cord, shoe, whatever. It would all hurt.

But things only got worse for her.

Taking One for the Team

Nadine Robeson hardly ever took her daughter anywhere, but she made an exception for Diana's thirteenth birthday. She dressed her up in makeup and brand new, pretty clothes.

"Where are we going?" Diana shyly asked.

Nadine kept her eyes on the road. Her voice was cold. "Don't ask me anything."

Diana lowered her head.

Nadine pulled into a motel parking lot and put her old green Ford Taurus station wagon in park. "You're gonna become a woman tonight. All that wishy-washy girly stuff's goin' away. Stay calm and don't be nervous, you hear me?" She guided Diana's glance to a tall man leaning against an old black Honda Civic. He had the same light skin and curly hair her baby brother Manny did. He had on a black Adidas tracksuit and white shell tops. Diana couldn't place it, but there was something weird about him.

Nadine, with her two-year-old son in hand, sensed her hesitation and shoved her in front of him. "This is Diana. Diana, this is Pedro."

"Hey, Diana." His deep voice didn't fit his teenage-looking body and baby face. "You're probably wondering why you're here, right?" He walked to her and put his arm around her. "You're here because I need your help."

"You're helping the family, Diana," Nadine added.

"Yeah, see my wife's having a hard time with kids, so your mom said you'd be good at that."

"What?" Poor Diana was lost. "What are you talking about?"

In minutes, Pedro led the brand new teen up to his room and stole her virginity in the roughest way, to the point that she completely blacked out. When she came to, she ran into the bathroom and cried softly to herself.

These little trips happened for two years with increasing frequency, from once a month, to twice monthly, to once a week, and she blacked out and cried each time. All of that while still enduring Nadine's daily physical, verbal, and emotional abuse.

She knew nothing of her mother's manic depression, and didn't realize she was falling into depression herself. Like her mother, Diana was starting to keep the blinds in her room shut. She didn't want to do anything for fear her mother would randomly beat her, and she didn't want to go anywhere for fear of seeing Pedro, who she'd come to learn was her little brother's father. How was this saving their family? All he did was tear her up inside.

Blown Up

In the middle of her fifteenth year, Pedro finally "saved the family." She was pregnant. As a pregnant minor, she had to see a pediatrician. She looked around the sterile doctor's office with dread. It was bad enough for a family member to touch her or see her whole body, let alone a stranger. Doctor Elizondo, a Latino like her stepdad, automatically gave her the creeps just based on that fact. Much to her surprise, he was neutral -- not overly caring, but not overbearing.

"Who's the child's father?"

Diana locked up, scared of the outside chance that he might beat her if she told him the truth.

He saw her fear and altered his approach. "Have you ever been raped before, Diana?"

She immediately broke down. All she could do was nod.

The doctor spoke to her gently. "Diana, let me help you. Who is the father of the child? Who raped you?"

"My stepdad." She rubs her eyes with an arm. "Pedro Mercer."

She felt a wave of relief as she watched police handcuff Pedro and shove him into the back of a police cruiser. Doctor Elizondo called CPS right there in his office as soon as she had named Pedro. He then called a female nurse in to examine her, who was gentle with her, continually promising her she would be okay.

However, while Pedro was no longer in her life, CPS took her and her little brother Manny from Nadine as well. She fell into a painful cycle of foster homes, most of whom wanted her gone as soon as they realized she was pregnant. They tolerated her for one month -- long enough to collect their check -- and let her go. Abuse followed her everywhere she went, whether in excess like her mother did, or in complete neglect. Poor living conditions in some homes didn't help things. She was made to starve in some homes, while in others she had to starve because there wasn't enough to go around and the parents were only willing to sacrifice for their biological children and not her.

At her last foster home, Diana was taken with nightmarish pains. One terrifying night, she released a soul-chilling scream. The mother, who was actually a caring woman, rushed her to the hospital. The doctors examined her and diagnosed Diana as having a tubal pregnancy. Her tubes had ruptured, which caused the unbearable pain; and because of the rupture, she had a miscarriage. She stayed in the hospital for several months after surgery, crying every single day, wishing she would die. Her womb was broken. She would never be able to have children. She felt empty. Destroyed. Useless. "Why?" she kept sobbing to herself. "God, why would you do this to me?"

By month four, she was numb, but sober enough to notice she always had one faithful visitor: her foster mother.

New Hope

During Diana's four-and-a-half-months in the hospital, foster mother Ruth Dennis formally adopted her ailing child. She watched the girl sway between pain and unconsciousness, and often knelt at her hospital bedside, praying to Jesus for her deliverance. Sometimes Diana would hear bits and pieces of the prayers in her half-asleep state. When the hospital brought solid food for Diana, she would gently wake her and feed her as if she were still a baby. Diana would silently cry and look at her as she fed her. It was the closest she could come to telling Ruth "thank you."

Diana was happy to learn Ruth adopted her, so the terrible foster cycle was over, but she didn't adjust to her new life easily. Despite Ruth bringing Diana to church and Bible study, praying over her every single night and exposing Diana to wholesome media like contemporary Christian music, Christian movies, and even Christian Hip Hop, Diana still had nightmares and sometimes even night terrors, keeping her mother on edge with random screams and convulsions.

It also took Diana a little while to get used to the overall peace in Ruth's home. Every time she made a mistake or accidentally broke something, she would give Ruth a fearful look, but all Ruth ever did was scold her, and only used her hands to comfort her.

One night during her senior year of high school, Diana and Ruth were eating dinner at the table. This was Ruth's norm, to teach Diana a) all food is to be had at the table, and no other place in the house, and b) that dinner at the table is a great way to discuss each other's day, answer questions, and bond closer overall. Ruth would always tell her that family dinners at the table were a "dying custom," so she kept it alive.

"How was school today?"

Diana shrugged. "Okay, I guess."

"How are your friends? What's their names? Renee, Jasmine, and Jermaine?"

She shrugged again, picking at a chicken chunk with her fork. "Jermaine's not my friend anymore."

"Why not, what happened?"

"He wanted more, and I freaked out."

"He wanted to date you?"

She nods.

"Oh, sweetheart, you shouldn't drop him like that, though. All you had to do was tell him you weren't interested."

"I tried that," she quickly said, still staring at her plate. "He just stopped talking to me after that."

Ruth sighed. This was the one thing she hadn't taught her yet -- how to deal with boys without falling apart. "I'm sorry to hear that."

Another shrug. "Happens all the time. A lot of my friendships with guys are short like that."

Ruth dropped the subject. "What else happened today?"

"Barely passed my math test."

"But you passed, yes?"

She nods with lowered eyes.

"Hey. That's good. Only kick yourself if you fail, and even then only kick yourself for a few seconds and move on. Comprende?"

"Why do you always say that? That's Spanish, isn't it?"

"Yes," Ruth replied, wondering where that came from. "What's wrong with it?"

She shook her head and sulked at her food. "Nothing."

"You know Spanish culture isn't bad, right?

She slowly nodded, but didn't look her mother in the eye.

"Diana, look at me," Ruth gently said.

She obeyed.

"Why does my Spanish bother you? I use it to help you learn the language."

Diana shifted uncomfortably in her chair, hugging her arms. "I know, and I try to memorize it 'cause you want me to. I just...I don't want to speak it. I don't...like to hear it."

This hurt Ruth to her core, but she tried her best to remain calm. There had to be a reason for this, and she would get to its root if it was the last thing she did. "But why? Why does it bother you so much?"

Diana's low eyes began to shift all over the place. "Because..." An image of Pedro humping on top of her flashed in her mind. She held herself more tightly. The humping flashback continued, and she could hear the Spanish curses fly from his mouth in a roar as he came inside her. By now her face had crumpled and her eyes were filled with water. "I hate it," she said, her voice low at first from the tears. Then it flew from her in a scream. "I hate it!"

Ruth was taken aback. Diana's trauma symptoms had died down this year, so seeing this immediately put her on edge. She was on the verge of tears herself. "It's okay, sweetie, it's okay. Calm down. Just forget I asked, okay?"

Diana wiped her tears in vain. "I'm sorry," she whined.

Ruth went to her side of the table and held her. "You don't have to apologize, sweetie, it's alright. It's alright."

Ruth wasn't a night owl, but after she prayed over her daughter and said goodnight, she went online and researched Diana's medical history, and came across Dr. Elizondo, the pediatrician who saw her two years ago. She then researched his number and called him. She checked the time as the phone rang. 10:49 p.m. She should be in her own bed at this point. Elizondo answered. "May I ask who's speaking?"

"Hi, Doctor Elizondo, this is Ruth Dennis, Diana Robeson's adoptive mother. She was one of your patients during her pregnancy."

"Um...okay. How did you get my number?"

"Doctor, please. I need your help. The girl is severely traumatized. She can't stand the sound of Spanish words. Why? Who was the unborn child's father?"

"Diana Robeson..." he tried to remember her, but couldn't. "Can you describe her for me?"

"She was a minor when she saw you, probably fifteen. Black girl. Tubal pregnancy."

"Oh, her. Yes, I remember now. The child's father was her stepfather Pedro Mercer. I'd called CPS on the spot, the police arrested him. You didn't see it in the news?"

It didn't even occur to Ruth to try that. "No. So he's Latino."

"Yes, ma'am. I hate to admit I'm embarrassed by that."

Ruth's heart was broken. "Me too. Did she have any siblings?"

"Yes, a younger brother Emmanuel. He was two at the time."

Of all the names... "Thank you, Doctor. Sorry for the late call."

Ruth waited a month. This time she had the conversation with Diana in her arms on the couch. An older, robust man was on TV preaching on forgiveness. Diana grew to love watching him. She said his words were comforting even when he was discussing a difficult subject. "Listen, Diana. I want to talk to you about something important, okay?"

Diana gave her a worried look. "Am I in trouble?"

"No, sweetheart. But there's something we've both been running from that we're gonna have to face now. You'll be graduating from high school next June, and you want to step out into the world on the right foot. Right?"

Diana nodded.

"I understand now why Spanish bothers you so much."

Diana sat up straight and looked at her.

"But that's technically prejudice, you know that, right?"

Diana lowered her eyes and nodded.

"You deal with plenty of that every day, right? People who don't like you just because of what you look like?"

"Or because I have boobs."

Ruth laughed a little. "That's called sexism, which is another type of prejudice."

"Based on gender."

"Yes."

Diana hugged her arms. "I guess I'm guilty of that too."

"I'm glad you can admit it. At least you know you're doing it, which means you can choose to stop it."

Diana looked at her again.

"Many people do it and don't even realize it."

"But is that really so bad, Mom? I mean, people are gonna do what they do anyway. My feelings against them aren't gonna stop them. And my feelings being hurt *by* them doesn't stop them either."

Ruth moved closer. "Shedding the prejudice isn't for them, sweetie. It's for you."

Diana thought on that. She'd never heard it in that way before.

"You know God looks at the heart."

Diana nodded.

"So, if that's what's more important to Him, and we're all His creation, how do you think it looks to Him when we exclude, dislike, or disrespect a whole group of people based on what *one person* did to us?"

Diana started sulking. She knew the answer, but she didn't want to talk about it. "Like we're insulting Him."

"Yes. And we don't insult the people we love, right?"

"Not on purpose."

"That's just it, sweetie." Ruth caressed Diana's hair. "Prejudice is deliberate. It's something we choose to do."

"I thought you said I wasn't in trouble."

"You're not. What I said was I want to teach you a life lesson."

Diana went quiet, listening to the pastor, who was reading Ephesians 4:32 aloud: "And be ye kind one to another, tenderhearted, forgiving one another, even as God for Christ's sake hath forgiven you."

"You see? That's what God wants us to do, sweetheart. I understand the cause for your aversion to Spanish culture, but I want to help you understand that your issue is with one person, not all of us."

Diana looked at her in shock. "What do you mean all of us?"

Ruth took a deep breath, ready for an outburst. "I'm half-Latino myself, Diana." Diana's eyes nearly fall out of her head. Ruth quickly spoke again before she could react. "The things you say and do against the culture hurts my feelings. Especially against Latino men. I'm Latino on my father's side."

Diana felt the room spin. She could barely breathe. Why was God doing this to her again? What kind of sick sense of humor did He have? "Why didn't you tell me?"

"I'm telling you now. And what would you have done if I told you before? I'm no different than I was before I told you. I still love you, and I still want what's best for you. I will love you until the day I die. That's my duty to you as a parent. I'm responsible for your life and well being."

Diana didn't bother to hide her emotions. She covered her face and let the tears flow. "He only talked Spanish around me," she said. "He was always mad at me when I didn't understand what he was saying. He hated speaking English, he hated America, he hated black people. He always talked bad about my mother and me, always cursed at me in Spanish. Especially when he--" The flashbacks began again, and she began to cry more intensely. "Mom told me I was saving the family by being with him, but he told me he was doing what he did with me to get back at her." She started to sob uncontrollably. Ruth held her tight and hushed her.

"I know, sweetie. Hearing the language brings the memory back, I understand that. That's why I stopped."

"You did?"

"Of course. You said you hated it."

"I'm so sorry, Mom. I swear. I didn't mean to disrespect you."

"It's okay, you didn't know. And I didn't know."

"How did you find out, then?"

"I spoke to the pediatrician who saw you while you were pregnant. You came to me long after that, so I knew nothing about what happened."

"I hate him," she said.

Ruth let out a disappointed sigh. "That's a lesson for another time, but at least you narrowed it down. Don't hold what he did against all of us, okay? Not all Latinos are rapists or monsters, just like not all black people are criminals and not all Middle Eastern people are terrorists."

Diana nodded on her mother's bosom.

"People like him come in any color. Criminals, rapists, terrorists, drug addicts, can be anybody. Their race doesn't define their evil. They either choose to be evil, were taught to be evil, or something within them is unbalanced and causes them to act out in that way."

"Okay."

Diana spent the rest of her senior year researching colleges and scholarships, based on Ruth's recommendation. She got into Weill Cornell Medical College majoring in Psychiatry and worked her way up to a Ph.D. in Psychology. It was during her college years that she came to know the Lord herself. Once she began her relationship with God, she finally understood in the truest way what Ruth taught her, especially the hard lesson of forgiveness.

The Long Road Home

During her tenure at New York-Presbyterian Hospital, Diana got the urge to find her baby brother. She searched online and found him living in Charlotte, North Carolina. Emmanuel Ambrosius, he was now called. Like her, he'd taken the legal name of his adoptive family. She reached out to him, and they reunited in a Google Hangout. He came on the screen and she was immediately taken aback -- he had grown to resemble his father. Same lanky build, same baby face, same curly hair.

He was equally amazed. "Wow, sis. You look just like Mom."

"And you look just like your dad."

"Pssht. I don't even wanna talk about that dude, man. How you doin'?"

"I'm pretty good. How are you? How *old* are you?"

"Nineteen."

"Are you serious?"

He laughed. "Yeah. It's been a minute, ain't it?"

"A hot minute."

"So where you at?"

"New York. I'm a psychiatrist with New York-Presbyterian Hospital."

"Look at you! Congrats. That's good. I know you paid."

She wasn't sure what to make of that. "Working my way up. Um, have you heard from mom?"

The question sucked the brightness out of his face. "I live with her."

Diana jolted forward. "She's in Charlotte? How'd she end up there?"

He hissed his teeth. "She lost the house and the car, man. I'm in mechanic school and I get this phone call outta the blue from some Florida doctor asking for the nearest next of kin. Of course, I'm Honest Abe, so I tell 'em it's me, 'cause I ain't know where you were."

Diana chuckles to herself. He just revealed something about himself without realizing it.

"So they ask me to go get her and gimme the address. She was in a shelter, sis. Not even a group home or nothin'. A shelter."

Diana rubbed her face.

"This woman done got bone cancer. The doctor I spoke to down there said it was stress-related--"

"Caused by her depression."

"Yeah, yeah. He said something along those lines. But she ain't want no doctors around, she ain't wanna be diagnosed with nothin'. She kept making a fuss, so they wanted her gone."

"So they called you."

"Mhm."

"How is she?"

"How you think? She worse now with the pain in her bones. Always wishing she could die and all that. It's depressin', man. I was depressed when we lived with her, but once I was adopted, I grew outta that."

"So did I."

"It sucks to be back in it, sis. It takes so much outta me. She just cries all damn day. She don't wanna eat nothin'. I keep tellin' her she gotta eat."

"All that'll do is extend her life, Emmanuel, you know that. She wants to die, so she knows the quickest way to do it is starve."

Emmanuel's face twisted as he ran his hand through his hair. He sniffed to fight the tears. "I just want this to be over, sis. Either she needs to be healed, or she just needs to go on home. I know that's mean and selfish, but damn. It ain't fair. I didn't ask her to be miserable. I don't deserve to be miserable. I can't even be in a relationship right now, this woman takes up all my time and attention. She's like having a damn kid! An ungrateful one at that!"

Diana let him calm down before she spoke again. "Do you have any help? Any in-home support for her or anything like that?"

"Nah. It's just me. I had to drop outta school to take care of her. I do odd jobs here and there to keep the roof over my head."

That was all Diana needed to hear. "You won't be alone anymore. I'm coming."

* * * *

For three dark years, she and Emmanuel nursed their mother. Instead of being happy to see Diana, Nadine seemed to slip into an even deeper depression. She resumed her cursing and abuse as if they were never separated. Diana endured it, insisting her brother re-enroll in his mechanic school so he could finish his degree. Unlike in her childhood, Diana was able to filter out the abuse and ignore the hurtful words, reminding herself of the scriptures: Ephesians, chapter five, and the fifth commandment: "honor thy mother and thy father, that thy days may be long on the earth." She dutifully fed her mother, bathed her, and cleaned her when she soiled her clothes. Nadine complained, wondering if Diana was even trained for this, but Diana simply smiled to herself, remembering what Jesus warned his disciples: *when you're young, you get up, get dressed, and go where you will. When you get old, someone else will take your hand and take you where you don't want to go*. Jesus was speaking to Peter in a different context, but it applied nicely here.

Now Nadine was living that warning. This woman who refused to dream, refused to improve her situation, refused to believe there was any hope, was helpless. Diana used her psychiatric advantage and officially diagnosed Nadine with clinical depression. She prescribed antidepressants for her, but Nadine would pretend to swallow them and flush them down the toilet, or swallow them and vomit them up later, so Diana let the prescription expire. She tried many times to share the Gospel with Nadine, but Nadine always refused her. "You're wasting your time," she would say. "There is no God." And she would always follow up with yearning for her own parents.

In her final year of life, she'd lost her ability to speak. She went from cursing her daughter out to simply staring at her with a very sad face. Diana wasn't sure whether she was finally thanking her, kicking herself for her condition, wincing in pain, or continuing her wish for death. After Diana would pray over her, the tears would fall.

When Nadine died, her only audience was her two children. They carried her into Emmanuel's backyard and buried her. Diana gave him a tight hug. "You're free again, Manny. I'm glad you went back to school, now you can start your career. And have a relationship."

He laughed. "Yeah. What about you, what are you gonna do?"

"Start a private practice or be a consultant, or be an adjunct professor. I have options."

"You stayin' here in Charlotte?"

"For now. We'll see what happens from there."

Meeting Her Reflection

After finally putting her mother to rest, Diana followed through with all three options: she launched her private practice, and became a consultant and adjunct professor to market the practice. She was renting an apartment and saving up for a house, but the funds were tight in the beginning.

A year after launching the practice, she got an unexpected call. The gentleman sounded familiar, but she didn't bother to guess. "How can I help you?"

"Do you remember me?"

"Um, you have to give your name, at least."

"It's Ken. Ken Isaacs."

"Ken? Good Lord, I didn't recognize you at all! Your accent's gone. You sound perfectly American."

"Yeah," he laughed. "Years of practice."

He thanked her for saving his life back in New York. He'd been evicted from his very expensive Manhattan apartment and was drowning his sorrows -- an old habit from back in Wales. She'd taken him in, got him off the liquor cold turkey, helped him through the withdrawal, and got him to focus on his initial reason for coming to the U.S. in the first place. She helped him get into Weill Cornell Medical College through her connections there, and even helped him land a residency with New York-Presbyterian Hospital.

"How are things going?" she asked.

"Great. Needed a change of scenery, though. NYC can make you really hard."

"Seriously. That city has no mercy. I guess that's why they say if you can make it there, you can make it anywhere."

"Same story in London. Anyway, just wanted to offer you a more spacious abode than your current sardine can."

Diana was suddenly creeped out. "You're in Charlotte?"

"Yep. I live in a three-bedroom house about fifteen minutes from downtown."

Though hesitant at first, she lived with him and brought him on board her private practice. He even developed an interest in her social work. She gave him one client so he could learn the ropes and decide for himself if he wanted to pursue social work further. Sure enough, he developed the same passion she had. When she decided to move back home to Florida, he followed her. They lived in separate locations, but they still worked together in the practice.

In 2008, Isaacs landed a consulting contract with Godhand Women's Home. For the first two years, he visited on an as-needed basis. He brought Diana with him on a visit in December 2010 and noticed the girls responded much better to her than they did him. He asked her to accompany him on his future visits. "Sure, I'll be glad to," she said. "But we've gotta increase the frequency."

"What do you mean?"

"They call you in, what, twice a year? On average?"

"Something like that," he said with a shrug.

Diana shook her head. "Those girls need us more than we care to admit. We've gotta help more often. Once a month, at least."

"Can't hurt to try it. We'll have to draft a new contract, though."

"Let's do that."

That next year, she saw a girl so rough around the edges and so angry, she was immediately reminded of herself. Diana realized the girl hated everyone equally, including herself. And she hadn't even spoken to her yet.

By day three of their visitation that month, Isaacs brought Diana the girl's file. "This one's a doozy, be careful."

Diana opened the file. "Leila Sudders. Pretty girl, not counting the frown."

"You talk to her tomorrow morning."

Diana made a vow to herself right then. Leila must be rescued. She would do whatever it took to lift her up. She couldn't imagine what Leila's life would be like without help, and she didn't want her to have the same dark, lonely end her mother had. "Good," she said to him, clapping the folder shut. "Bring it on."

THE WHOLE TRUTH

24

Diana's eyes are soaking wet, and her gaze is so intense I have to look away. Doc looks equally disturbed. I guess she never told him the personal stuff, either. She really did go through her own hell, but no one could ever tell. "Do you see the difference, Leila? God offered me a hand, I accepted His help, and He lifted me out."

"What happened to your brother?"

She sighs with low eyes. "I recently found him on Facebook, but he's behind bars now. Just like yours."

"What for?"

"I don't know. He won't tell me."

"You seen him?"

"Yeah. He's in the same prison with your brother Kalvin."

"So you just...forgave your family? Forgave your momma, your stepdad? After what he did to you? You'll never be able to have a kid of your own."

"Once I stopped feeling sorry for myself, it was much easier to do. Mom's death made it much easier to forgive her. As for my stepdad, I know now that he's mentally disturbed. He needs help, just like some of the young women in here. He's part of the reason I do what I do."

I think back to the greasy bastard that raped me and start crying. "How? How could you forgive him? He used you even longer than the Apostle did me. *And* you lost your baby just like I did!" I shake my head repeatedly, rubbing my forehead. "I don't think I can ever forgive him."

"You can." Her tender tone is back. "If you want to. And you wanna know something? You wanna know how to break free from this place? Give your heart to Jesus first, then forgive everyone who's ever wronged you, just as He forgives all the wrong you've ever done. You'll experience a freedom like nothing you've ever known before. One that no one can ever take away."

"I did," I barely say.

They both look at me in slow amazement. "You did? When?" she asks.

"Last month," I reply with a sniffle.

"That's awesome," she whispers. She can barely contain her excitement.

"And I um, I forgave Patrice...or something like that. But not him. I can't...I can't."

"If you don't, then you'll be no different from Nadine. She never forgave my father and never took responsibility for her own choices. Don't make her mistake, Leila. Please."

She comes around to me and holds me. Like Christie did. Like Doc did. Maybe they really do count as people who love me. "I may not be able to have kids by birth," she says, "but I have plenty of beautiful daughters."

"Thank you. And I'm sorry. About everything."

She kisses my head. "I forgave you a long time ago, sweetheart."

* * * *

The next day after I return from work, I spot Esther at the front desk talking to someone I thought I would never see again, and I'm suddenly in a rage. Midnight blue three-piece suit with a white button-up, five gold rings between both hands, gold chain, diamond cufflinks, and expensive sunglasses with gold trim.

Apostle Randall Thompson.

My legs draw me toward them, and I grip my phone tightly in my pocket, ready to beat him in the head with it. My eyes are wide and wild. I fantasize of three different ways I can kill this man as I walk, getting more pissed by the second as I watch the two of them laugh. Of all the people this nasty bastard could chase after, he wants my friend? My *one* friend who's just starting to do well for herself? Filthy thief. As if his sick sorry ass don't have enough already. I think of Diana's stepdad and get even more pissed. "He's mentally disturbed," she'd said. "He needs help." What about pigs like this? Pigs that have followers and money and are too proud to admit their weaknesses? Can we kill them since they can't control themselves? Please?

"Ayo, pastor." Sabryna's low-voiced call stops me in my tracks. I look at her over my shoulder, not bothering to hide my fury. She's not fazed. She just nods in the direction of the activity area. I look at the two once more and I realize he's looking right at me. My angry face gets even uglier.

Remember this face, you slimy shit. It'll be the last one you ever see.

Sabryna leads me to the activity area, which is empty for once, and puts an arm around me. "What's wrong with you?" I ask her. "Since when you start touchin' me?"

"Shut up and calm down," she fires back in a sharp whisper. "I'm savin' your ass."

"From what?"

"You think I don't know what you was 'bout to do? Listen, if you tried that, them sheriffs will take you down so fast, you won't even know what hit you. I done seen it."

"With who?"

"Two crazy bitches got into it while you were gone, yo. White bitches fightin' over meds they were sellin' to some of the other girls. The blonde knocked the brunette out, and two dudes took blondie down. Quick."

"You lyin'."

"What you think they did to Patrice when she shot you? Them dudes showed up out of nowhere, cuffed her, and drug her ass outta here."

Really? I wish I could've seen that. I don't mean that in a spiteful way, but it would've been interesting to see.

"Wait 'til you leave the premises. Then take your revenge on your own terms. He should be outta here by, like, three-thirty."

I check my phone. He's got ten minutes.

"Go do somethin', yo," she says in an annoyed tone as she turns to leave. "Go play chess or somethin'."

"Wait. Why you helpin' me?"

"After what you did for me and my daughter, you gotta ask?"

"...Thanks."

A short while into my practice chess game, I check my phone. 3:37 p.m. Is he still here? We do go by CP time, usually.

"Bishop takes pawn."

I turn to see Esther walking up to my table with a warm smile, as if all is well. "You've gotten pretty good," I tell her. "You can play blind now."

She sits in the chair across from me looking at the board. "I've had lots of practice. Folks at work play, too. Your turn, by the way."

I move her bishop according to what she announced, then take the bishop with a nearby rook.

"Blitz chess, huh?" She takes my rook with a knight.

"Not really." I move my bishop to just behind her last pawn. Out of her knight and queen's range, and protected from the pawn. "Though I gotta say I'm pissed off."

"Why?"

"You know who that man is?" I can't wait to air this man's dirty laundry. She'll be one less victim.

"Yes," she replies softly. It almost looks like she's laughing on the inside. "He's my dad."

25

"What?!" I nearly throw up in my mouth. Is this woman serious? Lord, she better be joking.

Esther smiles and leans in close, taking my pawn with one of hers. "Calm down. The walls have ears now." She nods toward the main doors, so I obediently look behind me. More girls have come in, including Mandisa, who's at a table with Zoe.

"Anyway, yes," she quietly continues. "He's my dad."

"How can you stand him? I know him. He's done some pretty shitty things to me."

She looks me in the eye and takes a long silent breath. "I know."

Anger completely kills my shock. I feel like somebody just pulled the rug out from under me. "What you mean you know? He told you?"

"...Yeah."

"So this was all a setup? He told you, so you came to find me and be my friend? You his spy?"

Her face turns desperate. "No, Leila, no. I didn't find out until I after met you." She sighs. "Listen. You asked me before who I was and what I did with your friend. The truth is *this* is me." She gestures to herself. "I come from a wealthy family and I'm well-educated--"

"That's the first thing I noticed when you came back. You talked different."

She nods. "But I was...a spoiled *brat*, even into my twenties. I disrespected my dad, my mom...do you know about her?"

"Yes," I mumble, glancing at the board.

"Even while she was in the hospital, I was acting a fool. So dad put me here to teach me some humility, see what life is like on the other side of the tracks. I had to check in with him every two weeks by phone. By *the home's* phone, at that. Did you notice I never had a cell phone?"

I shake my head.

"The baby's hers, by the way. She was having problems conceiving and really wanted another kid, so she asked me to be her surrogate."

My jaw drops.

"Anyway, after I met you and we became friends, I told Dad about you during one of my check-in calls, and that's when he told me what happened."

She suddenly taps the board with freshly manicured fingernail, reminding me that it's my turn. I look at the board, frozen in my current sitting position. I lost my desire to play. Her knight is one move away from taking my last rook, and her bishop is lined up to take my queen. I hate losing either piece, but oh well. I take her last bishop. To my surprise, she doesn't kill the rook. She instead moves her pawn forward. "A mercy play?" I ask.

She shakes her head and smirks. "It's on you again."

I check the whole board now: we both cleaned up pretty good. She had seven of my eight pawns, six of which were already killed before she sat down, a rook, and a knight. I had seven of her eight pawns as well, a knight, and a bishop. I move my last pawn forward. It's just out of her queen's range, far beyond the knight's reach, and safe from her nearest rook. For now.

"Safe play." She moves her pawn forward. "I'm sorry for what my dad did to you. I know how you feel."

I give her a dirty look. "Don't do that. You don't know how I feel."

"Actually, yes I do. He did the same thing to me growing up."

Shock hits me again. "No wonder you were a brat. You did all that to get back at him."

"No, I was a brat because he spoiled me to keep me quiet, and I got used to having my way. To this day, my mother doesn't know. Besides him and me, you're the only other person who knows."

"So what you told your counselor here? What you told Diana?"

"Dad gave me a script to use. Wild kid, high school dropout, got too drunk at a house party and got pregnant from the one-night stand. I used a different name."

This monster is unbelievable. "What name?"

"Janae Joseph."

"That sounds cooler anyway."

She chuckles. "But Esther Thompson sounds more professional. My real name gets me hired faster because it *doesn't* sound 'black'."

"Psssh. That's messed up."

"But true. Trust me, my family deals with it all the time."

I move my queen in position to diagonally kill her rook on the other end in case she lines it up to take my pawn. She moves her pawn forward, blocking my queen's path to the rook, so I take it instead.

"Someone's hasty," she says, smiling.

"So you already knew how to play, then," I continue.

"Only a little," she confesses. "You taught me the rest, and as I said before, I practice with a couple coworkers on lunch break." She lines her rook up with my pawn.

I hear the harsh scraping of a chair against the floor behind me. Zoe had jumped out of her chair at the sight of a very angry Sabryna. Mandisa stands up too, ready for the worst.

26

I jump out of my chair and rush over, managing to stop Sabryna before she could harm Mandisa. I back her up a few feet and get right in her ear. "You saved my ass before, and I'm grateful, but now I'm savin' yours." I shake my head at her. "Don't do this. They probably ain't got nothin' goin' on between 'em. You know you ain't Zoe's only friend, come on now."

"Back off, Leila," she replies through clenched teeth. "You don't even know the half. They been creepin' since you got back."

"Then leave her," I beg in a sharp whisper. "She ain't worth getting arrested or kicked out. I don't even know why y'all booed up in the first place. You heard her story. She's gay, you're not. Stop wastin' your time."

That strikes a chord. She gives the two women a blank look, looks at me, and walks out. I walk past them and catch a thankful look from Mandisa. I simply eye her, wondering what happened to her aversion to physical contact. Zoe's still shook as she sits down.

I get back to my table and Esther's all quiet smiles. She's a lot like Diana in that way. I check the board and move my knight towards her side. Her rook finally kills my pawn, which is suicidal, because it lands right in my queen's path. I take it.

"You see, it's things like that..." she discreetly points towards Zoe and Mandisa's table, "It's little things like that that kept me by your side. Because despite what Dad did to you and how bitter you were when you got here, you never disrespected me. I'd been here probably a whole month before you came, but you were my first and only friend. The others didn't give me the time of day, and some bullied me." She nods at Zoe. "Like her."

Part of me suddenly wishes I hadn't stopped Sabryna, but whatever. It's water under the bridge now. Zoe will get what's coming to her.

"Anyway, I said all that to say I'm here to help you now."

"You already do."

"No, no. I'm here to pour into your life, Leila. You remember that business startup class we took? That person that loans you a lot of money to start a new business?"

"An angel investor."

She smiles again. "That's me, plus a little bit more. I'm investing in you."

I'm speechless for several seconds. "How would I pay you back?"

"By trusting me. And letting me guide you. You can start by being my neighbor."

"You have your own place?"

"Of course I do, silly. I own a duplex and live in one of the units. I'm renting you the unit next to me, so you'll have it all to yourself. Two bedrooms, one bathroom, decent kitchen. Four hundred a month for now, including utilities. It'll go up once you get a full-time job."

My bubble immediately bursts at the thought of seeing her father again. She catches the look and lifts my face. "Forgive him, Leila. He's already paid the price for what he did. Besides, your holding the grudge doesn't affect him. It only slows *you* down." She lets my chin go and sits back. "And quite frankly, I ain't got time for that."

We both giggle.

"Thank you. When should I pack?"

"When do you want to be free from this place?"

That catches me off guard. I never really wanted to be here in the first place, but I'd gotten so caught up in everything that I'd lost the urge to escape.

She moves her other rook all the way down to my corner of the board, three squares from my unprotected king. "Check."

"Well played."

"What's your answer?"

"Still thinking," I reply, frowning at the board.

"Not the game. I mean you leaving."

"Oh. Today, I guess."

"Why not now? I know you don't have much to pack, and we can always play this at home."

We. Home. Those are words I never thought I'd hear. Not this soon, anyway. Talk about checkmate.

"What price did your dad pay?"

"The church found out what he did to you through a witness."

"What witness? Nobody saw what he did."

"No, but someone learned you were pregnant and looking for him and put two-and-two together."

Sean. Bryce's horny friend.

"Once the rumor began to spread, other girls from the church shelter came out too."

"Wow. No offense, but your dad's sick."

"I know. And so does the church. The board fired him, obviously. It was a nasty mess with the media and everything, but he's in therapy now, and on probation, which is no joke. These days he only dresses like that out of habit."

"How does he live money-wise?"

"Well, they own a lot of real estate, so the income is still steady."

Oh, that's right. The church owns that whole parking lot.

"This is his too." She points her index finger upward and rotates it.

Seriously? I've stayed in two of his buildings? I just swallow my disgust move the conversation on. "Y'all still on TV?"

"We were. Once everything came out, Mom and Dad left the church, and the church stopped the programming."

I pack up the game. "Let's get outta here. I wanna go home."

She grins. "That's what I'm talkin' about."

Esther helps me clear out my few belongings and smuggled snacks from the room and we carry them out to her car. I go to the front desk to check out of the place, and return all my uniforms: the clean ones in a folded stack, the dirty ones in a bag.

They ask me for my email address. I tell them I didn't have one, so they request a mailing address. Apparently all the lectures we completed actually count as educational credits, so they want to send me my transcript, either a digital copy by email or hard copy by mail. Esther gives them the duplex address and I'm set. Officially free.

We're headed for the car when I see Doc heading for his. I let Esther know I'll be right back and go to him. He looks surprised to see me. "Hey! Leila. How are things?"

"Much better."

He nods, but his eyes are soft, sad. "That's good, that's good. Sorry we never got that game in."

"Don't matter now. Found out your dirt anyway."

"To my shame," he sighs. "Anyway, uh...I saw you turning your uniforms in. You checkin' out?"

"Did."

His eyes light up for a second. "That's good. I'm glad to hear that."

He's not, but I know why.

We're silent for a good minute, and I look around the parking lot for witnesses in that time. So far it looks clear.

"You tell Diana goodbye?"

I shake my head.

"Why not? She'll wanna--"

" 'Cause I'll see her again."

He's about to ask another question, but I lift a silencing finger to his lips, pull him in close by his collar, and kiss him. Slow and deep. I pull away and playfully push him back a little. He stumbles against his car, breathless and confused. I give him a sly smile and walk away without looking back, not caring whether I'd ever see him again.

I just needed to get that out of my system.

EPILOGUE

A lot can happen in six months. And I should know, I've seen the changes. I found out Diana's visitation schedule for the women's home and visit when she does.

Sabryna gradually softened with every visit from her daughter. Keyshawn even shows up now. They're not patched up, but at least they're not trying to kill each other anymore. She still doesn't have a job, though, and she's been in there almost a year now. I feel sorry for her.

I step in this afternoon and give Diana a hug as she greets me at the door. "The cafeteria folks miss you when you leave, you know that right?"

I laugh. "Once a month ain't enough, huh?"

"Not at all."

"What's tonight's topic?"

"A refresher on STDs."

"Fun. I sat through, like, three of those when I was here."

She gives me a long smile. "Feels good to say that, doesn't it?"

I smile back in reply.

"I'm so proud of you."

"Well, don't be too proud yet, you've got three more years to go."

"You got into Florida Community College?"

"Yeah. Engineering major."

"Great!" She high-fives me.

We set up for the class and I see Mandisa walk in. For the first time since I've met her, the house arrest anklet is gone. That's good...but interesting. She swore she would disappear as soon as it was taken off. "Congrats," I tell her. She looks over at me in surprise, but offers a disappointed nod.

"What's her story?" I quietly ask Diana.

"Her whole story?"

"No, no, I mean...now. She's off house arrest, so what's up? Why she still here?"

Diana makes a heavy sigh. "I hate to say this, but even non-profit homes like this can institutionalize some people."

"Like prison?"

She nods. "Some people get so used to the place that they can no longer function without it. They don't know how to live outside of it."

"Wow."

"You can't really blame 'em. As long as you're here and making an effort to look for work, you get food stamps, a roof over your head, clothes on your back, and three meals a day. It's a lot easier to make a life for yourself from in here than it is to try out there."

"Yeah. It helps to have help, though, even after you leave."

"True. Anyway, her anger management requirement is complete. She's technically free to stay home with her family. She just comes to get away from her husband."

"Still beatin' on her, huh?"

"And still cheating, which I guess is why she's here for this particular class."

A blast from the past suddenly walks in, someone I barely recognize now. She's light-skinned and obese, tatted up on both arms; her red weave is sloppy and ready to fall out of her head. But there's no mistaking that face, the high cheekbones that would jump up to laugh at people, the big indecent lips that I'm sure men have taken advantage of by now, the narrow nose, which is now crooked, and those big pillow breasts.

"Who's that?" I ask Diana to be sure.

"Tawana Miles," Diana replies with a grave tone. "Our newest resident."

So that really is her. And judging by Diana's demeanor, Tawana hasn't changed at all. Still the stank troublemaker she always was. Interesting irony, though -- she came from a well-to-do family, too. How'd she end up here?

"Hit me up when class 'bout to end," I tell Diana.

"You're leaving already?"

I check my phone's clock. "There's somethin' I gotta do, and it's time-sensitive. I'll be back."

* * * *

Visiting hours end at nine, and it's already 8:30. I park and quickly drop the quarters in the meter. The Broward County Women's Correctional Facility is pretty familiar to me now, and the double-locking corridors that used to help me feel safe before just seem inconvenient now -- they slow me up.

I finally meet up with Patrice in their open activity area at 8:43 and, with a guard standing over us to make sure we're not exchanging forbidden items, hand her small tubes of body wash, shampoo, and toothpaste. She's thankful as usual.

I started visiting her during Diana's week as well and I always bring some small thing she can use each time I visit, so I've gotten to know her better. It wasn't easy, but at this point, I'm over being mad at her.

I hand her my phone so she can type what she wants to say using the text message function. During our quick convo, I find out she and her family are doing much better. They'd left her to herself the first three months or so, but they visit more often now. Her young baby daddy's in prison too for illegal gun trafficking and illegal drug possession.

Ouch.

With a gentle smile, she texts, "THANKS FOR EVERYTHING. IT KEEPS ME GOING."

I smile back. "You're loved, that's all that matters."

She nods and texts, "I RECEIVE IT THROUGH YOU."

I shrug modestly. She's technically right. Only God would drive me to do this. "Take care, okay? You be good."

"THAT'S MY LINE. :P IT'S A LOT EASIER TO BE GOOD IN HERE THAN OUT THERE."

"True dat."

We both giggle as she returns my phone.

Technically, that's my brother's line. It's what he always says to me when we exchange goodbyes. Thankfully he's still holding his own. I asked Esther if it would be possible to get him a lawyer who can shorten his sentence, but she said that's technically double jeopardy since it has to do with the same case and same charges, so it won't happen.

I get in my car and think on Tawana in amazement, then I'm immediately reminded of my mom. I still have no clue where that woman is, and she hasn't called me since before I graduated high school. I sure wasn't about to call her myself.

* * * *

I get back to the women's home with no text message from Diana. I guess class is running long tonight. I arm the car's alarm and put the keys in my purse when a gentle hand grazes my left arm, and trails all the way down to my naked ring finger. I freeze at the sight of the dark skin.

"Nice ride," he says, nodding to my black Hyundai Genesis.

I look up into the handsome dimpled face, not sure whether to cry or run screaming into the home for help.

"Where's your ring?"

-END-

Hey. You there. You're awesome.

You're awesome because you're beautiful (that kind of goes without saying, right?), but you're also awesome for taking the time to read *Faded Diamonds*. We really appreciate it.

Now that you've read the book, your mind is grinding with thoughts and questions about the story; all of which are pretty precious -- not only to you, but to us as well.

Please don't let them go to waste. Go to Amazon.com and Goodreads and search "Faded Diamonds" (include the quotes). Click the *Faded Diamonds* link and leave a review. We (and the rest of the world) would be honored to know your thoughts on the story. The more specific you are, the more powerful your review will be.

By the way, you can keep the conversation going with us on the web:

- **Website**: http://fadeddiamondsbook.wordpress.com
- **Facebook**: https://facebook.com/fadeddiamondsbook
- **Twitter**: @FadedDmnds
- **Email**: fadeddiamondsbook@gmail.com

We look forward to growing and sharing with you.

About the Authors

Camille Burke is an MSW social worker that has experience as a clinician, medical social worker, medical case manager, counselor, and outpatient therapist. She is also an entrepreneur with a business mind and social work heart that have motivated her to start CFB Solutions, a social service agency.

She is very involved in the community and often spends her time doing outreach for the homeless, providing them social services. She has been writing fiction and non-fiction stories since the age of seven, as that has always been her passion.

Camille won several poetry contests as a young girl; and she was so inspired in high school by William Shakespeare's "Romeo and Juliet," she wrote a poem commencing their love. Her poem was so impressive that her English teacher, Mrs. Baker, publicly displayed it for the sophomore class to read.

She obtained her B.A. degree from Nova Southeastern University with a major in psychology and her Masters degree in social work (MSW) from Barry University. She also has experience as an adjunct professor teaching sociology at a local community college.

She has a passion for serving clients both young and old with combined areas of expertise in social services and community building. Her dedication to this field allows her to help people enrich their lives and make positive life changing decisions.

Faded Diamonds is Camille's first of many books to come.

Stacey Pacouloute (pack-oo-loot) is from Miami, Florida. She's the fifth of six children to Haitian immigrant parents. Stacey received her masters of social work (MSW) from Barry university in Miami in 2008. She has worked with children, mothers, the elderly, and clients experiencing mental health and substance use issues. Stacey owns Pacouloute Services, Inc., a full social services company. *Faded Diamonds* is Stacey's first book and she hopes to inspire others to uncover the diamond in them.

Mellissa Thomas is a Christian Jamaica-born writer who grew up in the U.S. from the age of six, and served in Uncle Sam's Navy for five years (her first place of employment). After the Navy, she barely took a breather before diving head first into a Film Bachelors degree at Full

Sail University in Winter Park, FL, using the Montgomery G.I. Bill, then went straight into Full Sail's Entertainment Business Master of Science program thereafter.

After interning and working full-time at the school for two years, she quit and dove into entrepreneurship cold turkey. She's currently available for hire, writing web content, blogs, and marketing copy (print and digital). She also writes poetry and screenplays, and ghostwrites books. You can find out more at http://mellissathomas.com.

Prior to *Faded Diamonds*, she published three other books: *From a Babe: A Weekly Devotional*, *From a Babe: A Weekly Devotional Small Group Bible Study Workbook*, and the first of her 5-ebook suspense series, *Abstracted: Episode 1 of the Tenderfoot Series*.

Mellissa's P.S.: If you love the cover, thank Kim Alaniz for the awesome diamonds photo and show her some Flickr love: http://www.flickr.com/photos/kimberlyeternal.

www.ingramcontent.com/pod-product-compliance
Lightning Source LLC
LaVergne TN
LVHW010638110826
845149LV00014B/2872